D1552969

THE DEVIL BY HIS HORNS

AMERICAN LEGENDS COLLECTION,
BOOK 7

THE DEVIL BY HIS HORNS

MICHAEL ZIMMER

FIVE STAR
A part of Gale, a Cengage Company

LIBRARY OF CONGRESS CATALOGING-IN-PUBLICATION DATA

Names: Zimmer, Michael, 1955– author.
Title: The devil by his horns / Michael Zimmer.
Description: First edition. | Waterville, Maine : Five Star, [2022] | Series: American legends collection ; book 7
Identifiers: LCCN 2021039514 | ISBN 9781432890445 (hardcover)
Subjects: LCGFT: Novels.
Classification: LCC PS3576.I467 D48 2022 | DDC 813/.6—dc23
LC record available at https://lccn.loc.gov/2021039514

First Edition. First Printing: March 2022
Find us on Facebook—https://www.facebook.com/FiveStarCengage
Visit our website—http://www.gale.cengage.com/fivestar
Contact Five Star Publishing at FiveStar@cengage.com

Printed in Mexico
Print Number: 01   Print Year: 2022

For Jim Crownover
A good friend, a good man, and a great writer

A WORD ABOUT THE AMERICAN LEGENDS COLLECTION

During the Great Depression of the 1930s, nearly one quarter of the American workforce was unemployed. Facing the possibility of economic and government collapse, President Franklin Roosevelt initiated the New Deal program, a desperate bid to get the country back on its feet.

The largest of these programs was the Works Progress Administration (WPA), which focused primarily on manual labor with the construction of bridges, highways, schools, and parks across the country. But the WPA also included a provision for the nation's unemployed artists, called the Federal Art Project, and within its umbrella, the Federal Writers' Project (FWP). At its peak, the FWP put to work approximately 6,500 men and women.

During the FWP's earliest years, the focus was on a series of state guidebooks, but in the late 1930s, the project created what has been called a "hidden legacy" of America's past—more than 10,000 life stories gleaned from men and women across the nation.

Although these life histories, a part of the Folklore Project within the FWP, were meant to be published in a series of anthologies, that goal was effectively halted by the United States' entry into World War II. Most of these histories are currently located within the Library of Congress in Washington, D.C.

As the Federal Writers' Project was an arm of the larger Arts

Project, so too was the Folklore Project a subsidiary of the FWP. An even lesser-known branch of the Folklore Project was the American Legends Collection (ALC), created in 1936, and managed from 1936 to 1941 by a small staff from the University of Indiana. The ALC was officially closed in early 1942, another casualty of the war effort.

While the Folklore Project's goal was to capture everyday life in America, the ALC's purpose was the acquisition of as many "incidental" histories from our nation's past as possible. Unfortunately, the bulk of the American Legends Collection was lost due to workforce shortages caused by the war.

The only remaining interviews known to exist from the ALC are those located within the A.C. Thorpe Papers at the Bryerton Library in Indiana. These are carbons only, as the original transcripts were turned in to the offices of the FWP in November 1941.

Andrew Charles Thorpe was unique among those scribes put into employment by the FWP-ALC in that he recorded his interviews with an Edison Dictaphone. These disks, a precursor to the LP records of a later generation, were found sealed in a vault shortly after Thorpe's death in 2006. Of the 80-some interviews discovered therein, most were conducted between the years 1936 and 1939. They offer an unparalleled view of both a time (1864 to 1916) and place (Florida to Nevada, Montana to Texas) within the United States' singular history.

The editor of this volume is grateful to the current executor of the A.C. Thorpe Estate for his assistance in reviewing these papers, and to the descendants of Mr. Thorpe for their co-operation in allowing these transcripts to be brought into public view.

An explanation should be made at this point that, although minor additions to the text were made to enhance its read-ability, no facts were altered. Any mistakes or misrepresentations resulting from these changes are solely the responsibility of the editor.

Leon Michaels
June 2, 2020

SESSION ONE
ELIJAH (LIGE)
TWO-BUCK INTERVIEW
PAULS VALLEY, OKLAHOMA
23 JULY 1937
BEGIN TRANSCRIPT

I was born in the afternoon on June 25th, 1876. If that date sounds familiar, it might be because some six hundred miles away, more or less and as the owl flies, a man named George Armstrong Custer had just stomped down on a hornet's nest of wild Indians. They say Custer didn't live to see the sun set that day, but I did—a dusky half-breed with jet black hair and a fine set of lungs, or so I've been told.

I'm not as famous as General Custer and I never will be, but for a brief period there in the early 1890s, right here in Chickasaw country of what is today the state of Oklahoma, my brother Jason Two-Buck was just about as famous as the man the Sioux called Yellow Hair.

By the time I showed up, folks were already calling him Kid Jace, like he was some kind of notorious outlaw or politician, but he was neither of those. Nor was he a gunfighter, like the newspapers tried to make him out to be. I'd say that of all the members of the Kid's gang, only Bob Hatcher and Pit Middleton had any kind of reputation as man-killers, but neither of them were even with us at the end.

Before we get too far along, let me say that I know it isn't my story you came here to record, and that's all right. It's Jace's story and always will be. The problem for me is that there have been so many tales told about him over the years that the truth has kind of gotten trampled by the myth. History writers will read old newspaper articles and police reports and think they've got a tight rein on what happened. I say that if those historians were using their deduction skills for hunting, they'd starve mighty quick, because their aim is generally way off target. The reason I know that is the same reason you're here today with your Dictaphone. I was there when it all went to hell for Jace—for all of us, really. I *know* what happened, and I say it's time the truth was finally told about Jason Two-Buck, the Two-Buck gang, and its ride into infamy.

Jace—that's what we called him, all except for Mama—already had a reputation by the time I stumbled into the story. It was undeserved, but stuck like a cocklebur and tinted everything he did after his release from the federal penitentiary in Leavenworth. I knew what folks were saying about him. We all did, Mama and my sisters and my younger brother Noah. Hell, every time we went into Davis to get supplies we'd hear another version of some past wrong Jace was supposed to have committed. His biggest crime at the time, they said—and some still believe it—was that he stole a racehorse from Kermit Watson that he used in his ride with the Dalton boys when they robbed the Katy Flyer outside of Adair, up in Cherokee country. But if you do a little digging, you'll see Jace was still in Leavenworth when that robbery occurred. I've got strong doubts he had anything to do with Watson's missing racehorse, either, although I'll admit I never asked him about it.

Even though my family's troubles with Kermit Watson began long before I came along, I never had any personal interaction with the man until the year I turned sixteen, back in 1893. That was the year he showed up at our place in the Arbuckle Mountains of the Chickasaw Nation, down in what is now south-central Oklahoma. I didn't know he was even around, but I guess Mama must have spotted his coming, had likely been watching for him for longer than I'd ever know. I still remember the timbre of her voice when she summoned me to the house that day. Scared but determined, she was, and my name echoed off the surrounding timber.

"Elijah," she yelled, then, *"Elijah James,"* real sharp-like.

The shrillness of her voice immediately caught my attention, as did her use of my full name, which generally meant: *Now!*

I'd been down by the barn with Noah, popping bots out of the hides of our Guernsey cows—the botflies were especially bad that year, and it was a constant chore to keep our stock free of the damn things—when Mama hollered. Noah gave me a wide-eyed look of alarm, probably wondering what I'd done to cause her such agitation. I didn't hazard a guess, but took off in a long-legged lope, already approaching my full-grown height of five-eleven, although still gangly and with a clumsiness I wouldn't sprout out of for another couple of years. I met Rachel halfway between the corrals and the house, hurrying in the opposite direction.

"What's wrong?" I asked as we swiftly passed one another along the barn path, but she just shook her head and continued on. Rachel was my older sister; at eighteen, she was between me and Jace, who was twenty-four that year.

I found Mama at the front door, shading her eyes northward. Our house sat on a little three-acre shelf of flat ground about halfway up the north slope of Two-Buck Mountain. It was a twin-storied affair made of logs, with a summer kitchen in back and the barn, corrals, chicken coop, and other assorted outbuildings scattered downslope from there. The view in any direction was fairly limited during the summer months when the trees were leafed out, but by late October they were starting to drift groundward, and you could see a good long ways through the denuded branches.

I skidded to a halt in front of the stoop, my pulse racing more from concern than my uphill sprint from the milk shed. Mama knew I was there, but she didn't say anything as she continued to stare into the valley below, where Lick Creek made its slow meander eastward toward the Washita River. Following her line of sight, I spotted a dozen or so men crossing the open meadow that bordered the nearside of the creek. Although they were too far away for me to identify, Mama seemed to know who they were. I could tell by the firm set of her jaw that she understood why they'd come, as well.

"Elijah," she said, soft but terse, keeping her gaze on the approaching horsemen.

"Yes, ma'am."

"I sent Rachel to fetch Minko. I want you to put a kit together and go find your brother."

I started to say I'd just left Noah at the barn, then realized she meant Jace, and my throat went all cottony. I glanced again to where the horsemen were nearing the foot of Two-Buck Mountain. "Who are they, Mama?"

"It's Kermit Watson. He's come to arrest Jason."

Now, Kermit Watson was no more a lawman than that bot-infested cow me and Noah had been wrestling with. He hadn't a stitch of authority to arrest anyone. What he did have, though, were several wheelbarrows full of money and five hundred acres of good cropland along the Washita River, west of the Chickasaw capitol at Tishomingo. He also owned a couple of mercantile stores, including the one just down the road from the store in Davis where Mama did most of her bartering, and the First Bank of Erda—Erda being a trifling little burg between his farm and Tishomingo. He was also a major shareholder in the Chickasaw Express Company, which ran stagecoach lines throughout that part of the Nations. Kermit Watson was a rich man, no doubt about that, and it's an unfortunate fact that rich men can pretty much be their own government in a lawless country, which we often were in those early days.

Staring into the valley, I spotted a two-horse hitch coming

out of the trees close to the ford. It surged up to level ground and started across the Lick Creek Bottoms at a swift trot, as if hurrying to catch up with Watson's *ad hoc* posse. I couldn't make out what they were pulling, but thought it must be some kind of twin-wheeled cart, maybe to carry supplies—or to haul Jace away to wherever it was Watson intended to take him.

"You know where he is?" Mama asked, meaning Jace.

"Yes, ma'am."

"Tell me."

"Somewhere close to Billy Goodwin's trading post."

It was as much question as answer, but she nodded affirmatively.

"Go on and pack your things," she told me. Then, after a brief glance at my callus-soled bare feet, she added, "Take your boots and your heavy coat, too." She looked at me, and I saw a rare apprehension in her eyes. "When you find Jason, I want you to stay with him, you hear?"

"Why do—" I started, but she cut me off.

"Don't argue, Elijah. You tell Jason that Kermit Watson has come for him, and that he's to stay out of sight until I send word it's safe."

"Yes, ma'am."

"Tell him I said for you to stay with him, too, at least until we see which way the wind is going to blow around here."

I nodded and told her I would, and she motioned to the door.

"Get your kit packed. Hurry now."

Well, I did as instructed, and it didn't take long, having only three changes of clothes, and one of those my Sunday meeting and funeral suit, which I elected to leave behind. The clothes I did wear were already riding up my ankles and wrists and starting to bind in the crotch; I'd really pushed the bud that year, and had about outgrown everything except my impertinence, although my time on the owlhoot soon trimmed that back to proper size. [*Editor's Note:* "Owlhoot trail" was a vague term sometimes used to describe the life of outlaws—men and women who often rode at night, under cover of darkness, to avoid detection.]

I crammed everything I thought I'd need into a pair of old saddlebags with CSA stamped on the flaps and was back downstairs in probably five minutes. I found Mama stowing food and a few small cooking utensils into a burlap sack. There was a bedroll on the table, the blankets the heavy wool ones we used in winter, and a rifle scabbard with Papa's Marlin sheathed inside of it. I paused at the sight of that—the Marlin instead of my own over-and-under rifle and shotgun—then solemnly went outside to where Rachel was holding Minko on a short lead. [*Editor's Note: Minko,* in the Chickasaw language, means "King" or "Chief."] The pinto was carrying Papa's old Texas saddle, and he had his head up with his nostrils distended as he sucked in the cool autumn air. I reckon he could sense something was up, as you could just about slice the tension in the air around us by then.

Mama came out of the house right behind me with the bedroll and sack of food in her arms, the Marlin tucked under an elbow. "Take this," she said, tipping the scabbard my way.

I carried the rifle around to Minko's off-side and fastened the scabbard butt-forward under the fender, while Mama laid my saddlebags across the rear skirt and threaded the saddle strings up through the leather bridge to snug it down. She added the bedroll on top of that, while Rachel hooked the grub sack to the horn. By the time I had the scabbard adjusted and the stirrups lengthened, that horse was rigged out and ready to ride.

Glancing down the slope behind me, I saw Watson and his men already feathering through the timber near the foot of Two-Buck Mountain, spread out and cautious. They weren't more than twenty minutes away, the cart not far behind.

"Use the back trail," Mama ordered crisply, and I nodded that I would.

Biting her lower lip, Rachel handed me the reins. Minko was tugging at the bit, eager to go. He was a pretty little paint gelding Mama had purchased from a Louisiana horse trader a few years earlier. He was a four year old, and in the cool autumn air he was as full of sass and vinegar as any colt. I figured he'd take off like a startled blue jay the second I gave him his head.

As I climbed into the saddle, Mama reached into the pocket of her apron and brought out a coin that she handed to me. I recognized it right off as the two-and-a-half-dollar gold piece Papa had shot out of the air at some kind of rifle frolic—which is what the old-timers used to call a shooting match—not long after he and Mama were married. It was kind of domed in the middle where Papa's bullet had struck it dead center. He'd used the Marlin booted under my leg to do his shooting, as accurate a rifle as any I've ever shot.

"When you find Billy Goodwin, tell him who you are, then show him this," Mama said. "He'll recognize it and know I sent you."

That arched my brows in curiosity. Goodwin was a well-known trader in the western part of the Chickasaw Nation, and something of a rascal to hear a lot of folks talk, but I'd no idea he was familiar with anyone in my family other than Jace. I kept my questions buttoned, though, figuring I could ask them later when things weren't so chaotic. Standing in the stirrups, I slipped the coin down into the right-hand pocket of my trousers, then settled back and adjusted the reins along Minko's neck.

Patting my knee, Mama said, "You be careful, Elijah. Watson's liable to have men watching the back trail. Don't let them catch you."

"No, ma'am, I won't," I promised, and as she stepped back I

would have sworn her lips trembled a little, as if she might actually shed a tear or a whimper. I think the look on her face at that moment scared me even more than Watson's posse.

"Hurry, now," she hissed, and I nodded and pulled Minko around and touched his sides with my heels. The last I saw of Mama and Rachel, they were standing side by side staring downslope to where Kermit Watson's men were making their way through the timber in a ragged line. Like skirmishers going into battle, I'd later realize.

Behind the house was a 200-foot-wide piece of flat ground with a well-worn path running down its center. To either side lay an extensive garden of summer vegetables, enough to sustain us through the winter, as well as bring in some extra cash after the harvest when we took what we didn't need down the mountain to the trading post at Davis. We grew sweet corn, green beans, squash of all kinds, rhubarb, cabbage, turnips, onions, and more types of herbs than I'd care to count. We even grew tomatoes, which isn't all that unusual today, but was kind of a rarity back in the fall of 1893.

I've mentioned, haven't I, that this all took place in the autumn of 1893? If I haven't, I should have, and maybe I ought to explain a few more things that might help you understand what happened that year.

Papa's name was Edward Two-Buck. He was a full-blooded Chickasaw from down along Sandy Creek, where his family had a farm. Mama was a white woman, a niece, I think, of old John Carr, the Methodist minister who'd founded the Bloomfield Girls Academy near where Kemp is now. Papa and Mama met at the academy long after old man Carr had moved on to another position in Texas. [*Editor's Note:* John Harpole Carr (1812–1876) was superintendent at the Bloomfield Academy from 1852 until his reassignment by the Methodist Church to Texas in 1867.]

Papa'd hired on at Bloomfield one summer to put up hay for the school's livestock, and Mama taught machine sewing and needlework, the latter a class she despised as useless to a girl's future. They'd married after courting for less than six months, but stayed at the academy until Jason was born the following year. After that they moved up into the Arbuckle Mountains to stake a claim of their own. Although I didn't know it at the time, Kermit Watson had had an acquaintanceship with both of my parents from back then, the animosity between them having its roots in the soil along Sandy Creek. But I won't get into all that just yet.

Anyway, at the far end of that path through our garden, behind a whitewashed single-seater tucked inside a clump of tall lilacs, was what we called the "back trail," which led to the top of Two-Buck Mountain. I don't know what that timbered ridge was called before my parents settled there in the late 1860s—it might not have had a name at all—but it was known as Two-Buck by the time I came along in '76.

It was a several-hundred-foot climb from the garden to the top of the mountain, where the trail teed in two directions along its crest, one running east, the other to the west. But there was a third option too, and that's the one I took, forging a path down the mountain's south slope through a dense forest of briars and post oak, the low-hanging branches like steel claws clutching at my flesh and clothing. It was a tough descent and Minko didn't like it one bit, but I figured if Watson had men lurking up there, they wouldn't expect me to cut due south, nor try to follow me through that mangling hell of timber.

It took us the better part of two hours to fight our way through to clear ground again. By then the day was waning, the sun already hunkered down behind the heavily forested ridges to the west, although it was still light when I heard a curiously muffled thunder. I lifted my head to study the sky but it was deep blue, the clouds floating along up there as wispy as snagged cotton bolls. Shrugging it off as an oddity, I kept on with my southerly course, just in case I'd miscalculated the determination of Watson's counterfeit posse. Twice more as the light softened into dusk I thought I heard the faint rumble of thunder, but the sky remained clear on into full dark.

I made a cold camp that night and continued first thing the next morning, pushing deeper into the Arbuckles than I'd ever ventured before. By noon I was making my way across the mountain range's rocky crown, with spectacular views in every direction and a buffeting wind quartering out of the northwest. I tried to avoid the slabs of granite protruding from the soil as much as possible, but often had no choice but to cross over the top, either that or backtrack to find another way; in every case I went forward, Minko's shoes clacking a steady beat as he picked his way carefully back to firmer footing.

It was late afternoon before I cleared the mountains and reined west toward Billy Goodwin's trading post on Cow Creek, over near the old Chisholm Trail. The country here was a gently rolling prairie, with scattered forests of oak and pecan. There were a few farms and small ranches that I shied away from, keeping to the brush as much as possible. I camped that second night along a little brook, picketing my horse close and lighting no fire to give away my location, and was back in my saddle again at first light.

Although travel was easier here than it had been in the mountains, it was still nearly nightfall before I spied the fresh-laid tracks of the Rock Island railroad. Taking a gamble, I followed the rails south to where they eventually crossed Cow Creek. It was here, with the light fading and the first stars popping out in the east, that I spotted a low-roofed building on a bend of the creek maybe a hundred yards east of the tracks. There were hitching rails out front and corrals in back, and down near the deep banks of the stream were a couple of canvas tents pitched next to small farm wagons. The smell of supper cooking over a single campfire between the wagons immediately set my stomach to rumbling.

I say I was on Cow Creek, but I wasn't sure of it then, or if I even had the right place, until I got up close enough to see the sign tacked above the broad veranda spanning the front of the building. It read *Goodwin's Store* in simple lettering, with smaller print and little silhouette drawings for those who couldn't read surrounding the larger type that advertised things like coffee pots, footwear, canned goods, and such. Dismounting, I looped Minko's reins around one of the rails and climbed the steps to the veranda. A single wooden door was propped open to the evening breeze, the light from inside creating a warm, amber glow. Before reaching it, I caught a glimpse of my reflection in one of the windows flanking the entrance and came to an uncertain standstill. For a second I just stared, taken aback by the rawboned kid I saw in the glass. The view included bibless overalls riding above the ankles, a homespun shirt under a tattered wool vest, blue kerchief knotted around the neck to wipe away sweat, and a wide-brimmed hat with lots of sag, confirming the poor quality of its felt. The portrait as a whole was that of a lost and vaguely intimidated farm boy on his first visit to a strange land—a true-enough rendition, I suppose, but as displeasing as it was embarrassing, and I vowed right then to change it.

Goodwin's Store seemed larger on the inside than it had appeared coming up from Cow Creek. It was an old-fashioned trading post dealing mostly in furs, hides and horns, tallow, honey, and probably some garden truck in season. There was a counter across the back of the room where a broad-shouldered man with salt-and-pepper hair leaned sleepily. Despite his lidded eyes and slack posture, I could tell he was watching me closely as I came over.

"I'm looking for Billy Goodwin?" I stated loudly, still several feet shy of the counter.

The guy neither stirred nor replied, but continued to stare at me like I was some kind of bug crawled in out of the dark. Looking back on the incident now, I can't say that I blame him. If I hadn't been so tired, I might have started out more amicably, offering at least a howdy or a comment on the weather. Sheepishly, I dug the domed coin from my pocket and placed it on the counter between us.

"My name is Elijah Two-Buck," I began again. "If you're Billy Goodwin, my mama said I was to tell you that, and to show you this coin."

Well, that got a response, and a damned quick one, too. He straightened and scowled down at the coin like it might sting or bite, then raised his gaze to study me more closely. "You kind of look like your daddy," he allowed after a long moment. "Skinnier, but you likely got that from your ma."

"You know my folks?"

"Did, back when. I was sorry to hear about your daddy. He was a good man."

My gut tightened at his words. People say Papa had been killed trying to escape from some Chickasaw Lighthorse who were taking him to Tishomingo for questioning in regard to a dead whiskey peddler found along Lick Creek, a couple of miles downstream from our place. Mama insisted that was a lie, and as proof she would point out how both of those lawmen had disappeared just a few days later. [*Editor's Note:* The Lighthorse were the native police forces of the individual Nations, assigned to enforce Indian laws within each district (Chickasaw, Choctaw, Cherokee, Creek, and Seminole, primarily); traditionally, they had no authority over nonmembers of their tribe, but would cooperate with federal authorities out of Fort Smith, Arkansas, when the need arose.]

Mama said even though she knew who was behind Papa's death, she wouldn't voice an accusation without proof. The problem was, without the testimony of those two Lighthorsemen, proof was going to be harder to find than cash money in a drunkard's pocket. I knew she suspected Kermit Watson, though; I think we all did. Hell, I still do.

But Goodwin's expression said his words were sincere, and I forced my bristles to lie back down. Even so, I couldn't stop myself from blurting, "He wasn't trying to get away from those Lighthorsemen. He was murdered."

"I suspect he was," Billy agreed, and placed both hands flat on the counter. "What brings you here, Elijah?"

"I'm looking for Jace."

Billy's eyes narrowed. "Any special reason?"

"I got a message for him from Mama."

I was keeping my reply deliberately vague, and Billy knew it. After a moment's silence, he said, "What do they call you? Elijah, Eli, or Lige?"

"Lige, mostly." I saw no reason to mention those times Mama hailed me with Elijah James.

"When was the last time you saw your brother, Lige?"

"Early March, I think, but it wasn't for long. He showed up one afternoon and took supper with us, but he was gone before first light the next morning."

Billy's brows wiggled in either sympathy or some secret knowledge he wasn't ready to part with yet—another puzzle I didn't know what to make of.

"Mama said you'd know where to find him."

"I likely do." He looked past me to where Minko stood in the light spilling out through the door and windows. "Is that your horse?"

Well, he was Mama's horse, truth be told, but it looked like I was going to be responsible for him until I got back home, and no telling when that might be, so I said, "Yes, sir."

"Your rifle, too?"

I nodded concurrence.

"Don't leave it on your saddle after this." He looked at me. "Is that your daddy's Marlin, the one he shot this coin with?" He tapped the gold piece with a finger. When I told him it was, he said, "There're folks who'll steal it in these parts, or try to rob you if they see you're unarmed, so keep it close, and keep it loaded."

"Yes, sir."

"You got ammunition for it?"

"Half a box."

"Ten rounds?"

"Plus what's in the magazine."

Billy twisted partway around to take a couple of boxes of cartridges down from a shelf behind him. "It's a .40-60, right?"

"Yes, sir, but I don't have enough money for that."

I'd left home with about four bucks and some change in my pocket that I'd earned cutting firewood for folks in Davis, but that was going to have to last me awhile, and I was already running low on food.

"You can pay me later," Billy said. "What else do you need?"

"I just need to find Jace. How far away is he?"

"A couple of hours." His gaze shifted to my waist. "You carrying a knife?"

"I've got my Barlow," I replied defensively. Barlows had a poor reputation in that neck of the woods, but I'd never been left wanting by mine, whether it was to skin a rabbit or carve a spoon out of a piece of hickory.

Billy walked down the rear of the counter. When he came back he was toting a sheathed belt knife that he slipped from its scabbard placed in front of me. It was a Green River with a six-inch blade, about as good as a knife got unless you had a blacksmith make you something special.

"This is better," he said, which irritated me even if it was true.

"You're taking a mighty big shine to someone you don't know," I pointed out.

"I'm not doing this for you, Lige. I'm doing it for your folks, who I respect the hell out of." He put the knife back in its sheath and slid it across the counter. "Pocket that coin," he told me, nodding to the gold piece, "and hang that knife on your belt. Have you eaten anything lately?"

I picked up Mama's coin and tucked it away, then grudgingly accepted the Green River. "I had a slice of bacon this morning," I replied as I began threading the sheath onto my belt. I didn't add that I'd consumed the bacon raw because I hadn't wanted to risk a fire. "How do I find Jace?" I asked.

"You need to stay clear of that bunch tonight."

"What bunch?"

"Kid Jace's gang. Your brother might not—" He stopped talking at my reaction.

"*Kid* Jace?"

Billy smiled. "I believe you have some enlightenment coming your way, Lige. Yeah, they're calling him Kid Jace nowadays. They say he's leading a band of cattle thieves and cutthroats that run through this part of the Nation, although I have my doubts anyone truly leads that crew."

I was frowning and shaking my head, but Billy remained stubbornly undeterred.

"You can head out there tomorrow and see for yourself," he said. "I'll have my woman fix you a bowl of stew tonight. Go ahead and put your horse in the corral behind the store. See that he gets a few ears of dried corn along with some hay. The water trough is full, but you can add to it in the morning if you're of a mind to help."

Considering two boxes of cartridges and a Green River knife, not to mention the stew I knew I was going to eat, I didn't see where I'd have much choice but to help out. In fact, the idea of paying my own way, even through labor, was appealing. It was something Mama and Papa both had taught me, taught all of us, as I recall, and it made me wonder if there was any truth to what Billy was saying about Jace being a thief and a hooligan. I'll tell you, it just about sunk my heart to think about it, and especially about how Mama would feel if word of his activities ever got back to her.

SESSION TWO

I'm still not sure how much I want to trust you, but I will say I appreciate you not interrupting my story so far. I reckon that Dictaphone isn't going to spin my words around too much, either. Not like those reporters did. No offense, but I've been led down a stony path more than once by folks claiming they wanted the truth, only to twist it to suit their own agenda later on.

I was telling you about how this all started for me, and how I ended up at Goodwin's Store there on Cow Creek, on the western fringe of the Chickasaw Nation. Billy was good to his word and fed me a big bowl of mutton stew, along with a chunk of bread and black coffee strong enough to lift a mule. It was the first warm meal I'd had since the grits and fatback Rachel had fixed us for breakfast my last day at home, and I wolfed it down with considerable enthusiasm.

Billy's wife's name was Elizabeth, and she smiled as she watched me eat. Like Billy, she was a Chickasaw, although I couldn't tell you if they'd been married in a recognizable church, by a justice of the peace, or in the old way, with the prospective groom showing up with a bolt of cloth that he'd gift to the mother of the intended bride. I'd learn later on from George Holly, who I haven't mentioned yet but soon will, that the Goodwins had a sizable brood of their own that included five boys, so I reckon she and Billy were familiar with teenage appetites.

Considering what would soon happen there and elsewhere around the Nation, I should probably mention that none of the Goodwins' children were still at home. The girls had married and moved off to raise families of their own, and the boys were scattered to the winds in one career or another. Those folks I mentioned in the tents down on Cow Creek were older Indians who'd lost their land allotment for one reason or another—mostly to scoundrels and con men, according to Billy. They'd moved close to Goodwin's Store for protection from the outlaw element that haunted that country in those days, trading chores around the place or meat hunted in the hills to the south for what they needed. Billy said they'd move on with the first hard frost and spend the winter with their children, but that they'd be back again in the spring.

"They don't want to be a burden to their families, but tent living is too hard on them when the snow flies," Billy told me. "Not that their kids would mind having them nearby all year, but it gives the old folks some independence to live here and make their own way for a few months."

He went on to explain that they weren't capable of doing much heavy lifting, though, which is why the next morning, after a hearty breakfast of ham, eggs, and fried potatoes, I decided to stay on and help replenish Goodwin's woodshed. Billy already had a sizable pile of uncut timber hauled in from some distant bottomland. All that needed to be done was to cut it down to size. It was hard work on a bucksaw, but nothing I wasn't used to, and I was still feeling as fine as frog's hair by the time I stacked the last piece of stove-length firewood inside the shed late that afternoon. Billy offered me another meal and the suggestion that I spend the night, but I declined.

"I have to find Jace," I reminded him. I'd been feeling edgy all afternoon about the delay, and knew I wouldn't have the patience to spend another night at the Goodwins.

Billy nodded that he understood, although I don't think he approved of my leaving so close to dusk. Studying the western horizon a moment and gauging the sun's position above it, he allowed I could probably make Jace's camp before nightfall if I didn't get lost. Squatting in the dirt and wood chips next to the shed, he smoothed out a spot with his palm and drew a map in the dust as he explained how to locate the site.

"It's on Cottonwood Creek, two drainages over and southeast of here," he concluded. "Just head in that direction until you come to the second creek and follow it south." He stood, his knees popping like broken twigs, his expression sober. "Make sure you stop when someone pokes a gun in your face, Lige."

"Who's gonna poke a gun in my face?"

"I've never seen it myself, but I've heard there are some brush shelters and maybe a dugout or two," Billy continued, ignoring my query. "There won't be any store, though, so if you get hungry, come back here and I'll see you get fed."

I didn't push him to answer my question. Instead I thanked him for his kindness and went to fetch my horse. The sun was no more than a couple of hands above the horizon by the time I pointed Minko toward the morning side of things; it was already sinking from view by the time I reached the second creek and reined south to follow its off-side bank. By the time another hour passed I was starting to worry that I'd overshot my mark. The shadows were growing thick and the light had turned soft as a duckling's gray down when I finally spied a grove of hackberry trees on the far side of the creek; a single column of smoke rose above it.

Recalling Billy's warning to approach the site with caution, I hauled up about a hundred yards away to contemplate how best to do that. It was a brief halt. I hadn't been there more than a few seconds when a voice from the scrub along the creek barked, "Shuck that rifle, mister, and anything else you might be carrying."

My breath snagged in my throat as I jerked around. It came to me that I probably ought to say something, maybe explain who I was and why I was there before whoever was down in the creek pulled a trigger, but it was like the words had gotten all jumbled up inside and wouldn't budge.

The voice from the creek hardened. "Damnit, boy, are you deef? Toss that long gun. The pistol, too, if you got one."

I saw him then, hunched down behind a patch of prickly pear growing along the bank's lip. He had a rifle trained on me, its bore looking big enough to stick my thumb in to the knuckle. Having something solid to focus on sort of unfroze my vocal cords, although it still sounded kind of squeaky when I spoke. "I'm . . . I'm Elijah Two-Buck, Jason Two-Buck's brother."

The guy behind the cactus didn't seem impressed. "Yeah, and I'm Buffalo Bill. Throw that goddamned rifle down, or I'm gonna buffalo you outta your saddle."

"It's my papa's rifle," I explained—foolishly, I suppose, considering the guy had a small cannon pointed at my belly. "He's dead," I went on, as if that might make a difference, "but my mama wouldn't want me dropping his rifle in the dirt. Not from the back of a horse." Then I added, "Neither would Jace."

After a moment's hesitation, the guy raised up a few inches for a better view of who he was dealing with, which also allowed me a closer examination of him. He was older than I was, although not by much, a white man judging by his appearance, with a scraggly beard and mustache and ragged clothing.

"What'd you say your name was?"

"Two-Buck," I replied. "I'm Jason Two-Buck's brother."

He came all the way up at that, but with uncertainty written across his face in bold lettering. "I ain't supposed to let no one pass without I know 'em," he said hesitantly.

"I'm Elijah Two-Buck. Now you know me, right?"

"I don't see that I do, but I suppose we ought to go find out for sure."

He motioned toward the trees with the muzzle of his rifle—one of those big Winchesters, I noticed—and I nodded and lifted Minko's reins. I didn't mention the Marlin in its scabbard under my right leg, and Scraggly didn't either, so I was glad to avoid that squabble. When we got closer to the grove he gave a shrill whip-o'-will's call, and I saw quick movement among the hackberry's slim trunks.

"Hold up," Scraggly ordered. "We'll wait here."

I drew rein, and within a minute or so a trio of men emerged from the trees to surround me. One of them, tall and dark-skinned with a mustache as big as a mule's uncurried forelock and a missing left eye—you could look right down into the pit of the thing—came over and yanked the Marlin from its scabbard. This time I didn't protest.

"Who is this," the pit-eyed man demanded of Scraggly.

"He says he's Kid's brother."

The other two, Indians in jeans and work shirts and wide-brimmed hats, their pistols drawn, moved in for a closer look. One of them said, "He does kind'a look like Jace."

"There's one sure, quick-fire way to find out," the pit-eye growled, and jerked his head toward the hackberry grove. "In there, and don't give us no trouble or one of these boys," he jutted his chin toward his companions, "will drop you from your saddle like a rock down a well. Savvy?"

I nodded that I did and the four of us—Scraggly silently returning to his prickly pear hideout—headed for the trees. It was a fairly scrawny grove as far as hackberries go, but thick enough I still had to duck low to keep from having my hat swept off my head or catching a twig up one of my nostrils. I aimed Minko for the light of a campfire and found it in the middle of a small clearing. I paused at its edge, uncertain where to go until I heard a voice from the shadows exclaim, "Lige?"

Relief flooded through me as Jace stepped out from behind a tree trunk and holstered his revolver. I shouted a greeting and spilled from my saddle, but caught myself before rushing forward like a damn-fool kid. "Howdy, Jace," I called across the clearing, tamping down the happy in my words until I sounded as solemn as a minister.

Jace stepped into the clearing and I went to meet him. His eyes, I noticed, were darting like fireflies, and his expression was as taut as a fiddle string until I told him Mama and the others were well. After that he relaxed and smiled and, glancing at the pit-eye, said, "Give him back his rifle, Middleton."

Pit-eye hesitated, then grumbled something under his breath and thrust the Marlin toward me. Recalling Billy's warning to keep the rifle close, I hung onto it with my left hand rather than return it to its scabbard. Others were easing out of the trees by then, wary as coyotes. Their guns were drawn, but they gradually put them away when Jace said, "This is my little brother, Lige. I'll vouch for him."

Coming close, he clamped a hand over my shoulder and gave it a rough but welcoming shake. Then he led me to the fire where the light was better. He looked pretty good, ol' Jace did. He was still taller than I was, but not by much anymore, and broader through the shoulders. He was clean-shaven in a land where men, who could, normally sported some kind of facial hair, a beard or mustache or such. Something else I noticed was the quality of his clothing—nothing fancy, mind you, but range-tough and well-fitted, without any hint of binding or shrinkage like I was putting up with. Jace had always had a kind of panther-smooth way of walking, too, always quick and sure of speech and movement, without any hint of the gangling clumsiness that plagued my journey through adolescence. It was something I'd always envied about him, and in looking back, I think it was a big part of what had always made him a natural leader, of boys first, then of men.

There was meat spitted above the fire—beef, from its texture—and a blaze-blackened kettle alongside a two-gallon coffee pot, both perched on flat rocks next to the flames. My stomach immediately made itself known. Hearing its rumble brought a chuckle to Jace's lips.

"You hungry, little brother?"

"Some, I reckon."

Catching the eye of a short, stocky Indian standing at the edge of the light, Jace said, "Take his horse, Thumbs."

The Indian hesitated only a moment, then came over to take Minko's reins. When he did, I saw how he'd gotten his name. The guy had a third thumb growing out of the top of the one on his right hand that wiggled eerily in the firelight, like it wanted to help the other fingers but didn't quite know how. I stared transfixed until he turned away, then watched apprehensively as he led the pinto into the trees. Noticing my concern, Jace said, "Don't worry, Thumbs'll take good care of him."

Not wanting to raise a ruckus about it, I shrugged and dropped my gaze to the meat, its sizzles and pops as beckoning as a siren's lullaby. My mouth was watering like a spring rain, but Jace had apparently forgotten the low growls emanating from my gut.

"Damn if you ain't about the last person I expected to ride in here tonight," he said.

"Who were you expecting?" I asked, and he laughed.

"No one, that's why I'm surprised." Then his smile faded. "Just why are you here, little brother?"

I glanced around. The others had all moved in close, eyeing me with the keen expectancy of predators. Not sure how much Jace would want them to hear, I murmured, "Mama sent me."

"Go ahead and tell it," he said. "Ain't no secrets in this bunch."

Taking a deep breath, I told him what I'd seen—the riders slithering up the mountainside toward our cabin, and Mama's conviction that they were Kermit Watson's men, and that Kermit was with them. Jace's expression hardened as the story unfolded. When I finished, the one-eyed man called Middleton cursed harshly.

"Did anyone follow you?" Jace asked.

"No, I watched close crossing the Arbuckles, then spent all day today helping Billy Goodwin cut firewood. There was no one there except those old folks that work for him."

Jace was staring northwest, as if he could see past the light reflected off the trunks of the hackberry trees and across the dark prairie all the way to Goodwin's trading post. After a pause, he said, "George," and a black man I hadn't noticed before lifted his chin in question. "Take a jaunt toward Billy's, see if Lige was followed."

Nodding, the black man disappeared into the darkness. Several of the Indians followed him, but the pit-eyed man and the two Indians who had accompanied me into the trees remained. Middleton was glaring at Jace like he was the source of all the troubles in the world, but Jace didn't shy away from him.

"You got something to say, Pit?"

"Yeah, I got something to say. I say we've gotta peel outta here, now."

"Watson was spotted two days east of here. There's no reason to think he's any closer to us tonight."

Middleton tipped his head in my direction. "If this tenderfoot found us, you damn sure know Watson will."

"Lige found us because Billy Goodwin told him where to look," Jace replied—something of a guess on his part, although accurate enough as it turned out, "but if you want to cut your pin, go ahead."

"Not until I get my share of that cow money."

"Then you'd better pull in your horns, 'cause we ain't going anywhere tonight."

Middleton's jaw sawed back and forth for a few seconds, like he was trying to work a piece of gristle down to swallowable size. "All right," he finally allowed, as if it hurt to give in even that much. "But we're pulling out at first light, savvy?"

"No, you savvy. This is my job and those are my cows, and where those beeves are concerned, I give the orders."

"Well, just make sure you give the right ones," Middleton flung back, although without much oomph. Then he spun on his heels and stalked into the darkness. After a moment's hesitation, the two Indians followed.

Me, I think I must have stood there the whole time with my jaw sagged down against my chest. Hell, I doubt if there was anyone in that part of the country who hadn't heard of one-eyed Pit Middleton. From the tales they told about him, he was as about as rough-barked as they came—killed thirty men, they said—yet Jace had faced him down without even breaking a sweat. It made me remember something Billy had mentioned the night before: *You got some enlightenment coming your way, Elijah.*

I reckon I did.

Glancing around the camp, Jace's expression remained grim. Five minutes before it had been crowded with watchful, glittering eyes. Now there was just me and him. Then I noticed a third person hanging back in the shadows. At first I thought it was a boy—smooth-cheeked and broad-chested, with raven-colored hair and a dusky complexion—but a second glance told me it was a woman. She was wearing men's clothing, which was something of an anomaly even for that part of the country, where Eastern fashions and Victorian morals were generally in short supply.

"Don't go getting any notions about that one, little brother," Jace advised me. "She's a wildcat who will cut your throat if you so much as wink in her direction."

The woman had been staring back at me like I was something dragged into a clean kitchen on a hog drover's boots, but quickly shifted her gaze to Jace, who grinned at her obvious annoyance.

"Watch," he said, and winked broadly. The woman's lips thinned down to a straight, pale slash across her face, and she pivoted away in much the same manner as Middleton had, although I noticed she marched off in the opposite direction from him.

Laughing, Jace said, "Sit down, Lige, and tell me the news from home."

Well, that didn't take long. As a rule, "news" seldom occurred on top of Two-Buck Mountain, nor anywhere within hollering range of it that I was ever aware of. I told him how well the garden had done that year, and that most of the vegetables had already been put up, with just some apples from the small orchard needing to be taken into Davis and pressed into cider. I mentioned the botflies and how bad they'd been, and that our winter's supply of firewood was already cut and stored, and how Mama had worked a deal with old Sam Davis to trade some of our cider and a couple of ricks of firewood for one hog and half a beef, once the fall butchering was wrapped up.

After running dry on "new," I returned to the men I'd seen coming through the trees toward us, and how Mama had felt confident it had been Kermit Watson leading them. I admitted I hadn't personally seen him, but Jace agreed that was probably who it was.

"It's a matter of elimination," he said. "Who else could it be?"

Searching for something fresh to add, I described the two-wheeled cart I'd seen following Watson's men across Lick Creek Bottoms, which I'd neglected to mention earlier. That brought a scowl to Jace's face. He questioned me about it some, but wheeled vehicles hadn't been the focus of my attention at the time, and I couldn't add much more than I already had. You could see he was puzzled by it, though. It puzzled me, too, once I started thinking about it.

The conversation lagged after a bit, then finally petered out altogether. Jace stared into the fire, his thoughts roaming who knew where, while I gave in to my hunger and helped myself to whatever it was bubbling in that tin kettle. I recognized carrots and squash and wild onions, but there was something else in there that tasted neither good nor bad, although it did help fill the emptiness in my belly. So did a slab of beef cut from the spit above the flames with my new Green River. None of that grub was half as good as what Elizabeth Goodwin had fixed the night before, although I was smart enough not to complain. The fire died down after a while, but Jace stopped me from adding more wood.

"We'll let it go dark," he said. "Just in case."

I didn't have to ask what he meant. That whole bunch was as jumpy as fresh-fried frog legs in a hot greased skillet. I was starting to feel fairly skittish myself. I forgot to mention that Thumbs—Three Thumbs Boy, was his full name—had returned shortly after Middleton stomped off. He dumped my saddle and gear next to a ratty canvas tent, then disappeared back into the shadows. It was kind of spooky the way folks kept showing up and vanishing, and all of them acting like there were ha'nts lurking among the hackberry trees, but other than appearing mildly distracted, Jace seemed pretty much his normal self.

After finishing my meal I started to my feet with the intention of washing my utensils at the creek, but Jace waved me back and made a motion above his shoulder, and that gal who'd glared at me so balefully earlier swept forward to snatch the plate and spoon from my hands. I watched as she tromped off into the dark, then looked at Jace. To tell you the truth, it kind of bothered me the way she'd jumped at his wordless command, like she hadn't any say in the matter. I didn't know her story or what kind of hold Jace had on her, but I knew damn well she wasn't some beat-down darky to be summoned without comment or consideration.

I was still simmering over it when George—Black George Holly was his full name—returned riding a horse not too much darker than he was. George was shorter than I was, but more stoutly built. He was quite a bit older, too. The tightly kinked hair under the broad brim of his hat was the color of dirty wool, and deep creases angled down both cheeks.

"Anything?" Jace asked.

"Nary a sign," George replied, stepping down and letting his reins trail. His mount stood firm, which impressed me. Minko would have wandered off in a heartbeat looking for fresh graze or other horses to introduce himself to. Hunkering down nearby, George cautiously patted the side of the coffee pot to appraise its warmth. "I did stop a spell to watch Middleton and his boys try to steal our cattle," he added, and Jace's gaze sharpened instantly.

"Did you stop them?"

"Didn't need to." He motioned to a small tin mug sitting next to Jace. "Toss me that cup," he said, apparently deciding the coffee was still hot enough to be palatable.

"Why didn't you need to?" Jace demanded.

"Cause they ain't smart enough to find their asses with both hands tied behind 'em. Now hand me that cup, before I come over there."

"You'd get your skull busted if you tried it," Jace growled, but tossed the cup over the coals. George caught it in his right hand and flipped it around with a finger through the eye of the handle while reaching for the pot with his left, which was something else I thought was pretty damned impressive. "What about the beeves?" Jace persisted.

"They're mostly just chousing 'em." George filled his cup, then set the pot back near the coals and took a tentative sip. To his credit he didn't grimace at the taste; having had a cupful with my supper, it wouldn't have surprised me if he had.

"What do you mean?"

"I mean they're mostly just riding around in the dark like a bunch of lost Texans, throwing nooses at shadows."

"Who's doing the roping?"

"Ain't none of 'em roped anything yet. Pit Middleton is the one barking orders, although not loud enough for you to hear him, I noticed. I believe Farrell Crow and Strong Wolf are out there, too."

"Thumbs?"

"Didn't see him, although he ain't usually too far away from Crow."

Jace muttered something under his breath. I didn't catch all of it, but did hear, *"dumb sons 'a bitches."* Returning from the creek, the woman threw my utensils on top of my gear, then stalked away again before I could thank her. Although Jace stared irritably after her, I couldn't fault her behavior. I'd have felt the same, had I been treated that way.

Standing, Jace tugged his holster around to where it rested more comfortably on his hip. He stared into the darkness for a moment, then wagged his head and mumbled a curse. Looking at me, he said, "You can sleep in the tent if you're of a mind to."

"I'd not recommend it," Black George added mildly. "It's fine, comes a rain, but buggy most other times. Was I you, I'd pitch my bed under the stars tonight."

"I reckon Lige can make up his own mind where to sleep," Jace said.

"I reckon it's a pure-dee fact that he can," George agreed. "I was just throwing my two *pesos* into the kitty."

"Well, pull 'em out again, 'cause you ain't playing this hand." Jace paused as if waiting for some kind of rebuttal, but George's response was to take another sip of coffee and ignore him. After a bit, Jace said, "I'm turning in. Wake me before it gets light."

George cocked a brow above the rim of his cup. "Is that a fact?"

"All right, damnit, *will* you wake me before first light?"

George seemed to mull it over a minute, before allowing that he would. He acted like he didn't notice Jake's fierce scowl as he walked away, but I could tell he was aware of it. When Jace was gone, George laughed softly and finished his coffee in one deep swallow. This time he did make a face after lowering his cup. Then he looked at me with an amused glint in his dark brown eyes. "Well, what do you think of this fine outfit so far, Elijah Two-Buck?"

I shrugged. "It's kind of . . ." I started, and my words trailed off.

Nodding solemnly, George said, "Yep, I reckon that'd be my opinion, too."

Milly, and not that much gear after we got our blankets rolled. The sun had yet to make its appearance when we rode out of that little clearing. I looked back just once, noticing the trampled grass and gray ashes of the fire, and the sagging tent we'd left behind. There was no sign of the brush shelters or dugouts Billy had mentioned, although I doubt if their presence would have dressed the place up any. Then my gaze strayed to where Milly was bringing up the rear on her bay, and she shot me a look that would have rivaled my Green River for sharpness. I didn't stare or say anything, but just kind of let my eyes slide on past her like any fellow would do sneaking a peek at a pretty girl.

She was that, too, I'd noticed—as pretty as a peach in August. Short but full-figured, with long black hair that kind of gleamed like a crow's wing will do in the right light, although still damp from her having washed it that morning. There was no mistaking the Indian in her—high cheekbones and smoldering dark eyes and a dusky smoothness to her round cheeks—but I didn't think she was Chickasaw. Maybe from one of the tribes farther west, I speculated, like Kiowa or Arapaho.

Since we're talking about Indians, I probably ought to mention that even though me and Jace were considered redskins— Papa being a full-blooded Chickasaw—Mama hadn't a drop of red blood in her veins. We were both tall like our parents, and slim like Mama, but neither of us were as dark-skinned as either Papa or Milly. [*Editor's Note:* Although terms like "redskin" and "nigger" are considered derogatory today, they didn't have the same negative connotations during the 1930s, when these recordings were made; it was the editor's decision to leave them unaltered and true to their times.]

We rode north along Cottonwood Creek for nearly a quarter mile until Jace reined off into a little east-running side valley. It was there we found the cattle. Jace swore when he saw how badly they'd been scattered by Middleton and them, although with a finger to make sure the flame was extinguished, and tossed it into the middle of the sandy wash. I always admired a man who was cautious around a flame, having once witnessed the results of a wildfire that had caught a husband and wife on the road south of Davis. They'd both been charred crisp, and their mule had looked like something Satan might have ridden through hell.

Jace looked at me. "You do it, Lige. If she tries to follow me, use your rope and tie her to a damn tree."

Sharing George's view on the matter, I shook my head. It was bad enough driving another man's cattle to market. I wasn't going to start roping women.

"Son of a *bitch*," Jace grated. "Do I have to do everything in this outfit?"

"It's what they call the mantle of leadership," George replied blandly, after which a grin leisurely unfurled itself across his face. He was careful not to push it, though, and kept his eyes on the tip of his cigarette, held at chest level between the fingers of his right hand.

Jace spat out another curse and pulled his horse around. "She just better not follow me, that's all I got to say. I'm gonna hold both of you responsible if she does."

I didn't respond to that and neither did George, even if he did continue to sport that sly grin that seemed to burrow so easily under Jace's skin. Although Jace had said he was going to wait awhile before venturing into town, I guess his temper got the better of him because he immediately wheeled his horse and struck out at a gallop. George returned the cigarette to his lips, his eyes narrowing speculatively as he watched Jace grow gradually smaller against the horizon. I glanced to where Milly was sitting her horse atop a small rise above the draw. She was also watching Jace ride away, but thankfully made no effort to follow him. After a while George got down and loosened Coal's cinch.

46

Raising an eye to where I sat Minko nearby, he advised me to do the same.

"Milly'll keep an eye on them beeves," he added.

Deciding to trust George's judgment, I dismounted and slipped the bit from Minko's mouth. After fastening my picket rope to the pinto's halter, I walked over to where George was stretched out on the grass with his hat tipped forward over his eyes, one knee cocked up and the other ankle propped over the top of it. If you'd have added a fishing pole and some snoring, it would have looked like a Sunday afternoon picnic on Lick Creek.

"You was surprised these were Watson's cattle, weren't you, Elijah Two-Buck?" George said into the hollow cavity of his hat.

"Some," I admitted, plopping down next to him. "Mama always told folks Watson had no call to go after Jason the way he did. I reckon she was wrong." It saddened me to admit that. Not the part about Mama being so mistaken, but that Jace was as bad as folks claimed. I wouldn't have believed it if I hadn't seen it myself. George viewed it from a different angle, though.

"I wouldn't exactly say she was altogether wrong," he replied, keeping his hat over his face. "I wouldn't say Jace was, either. I think it just got to a place where your brother figured if folks were gonna call him a thief, then he might as well be compensated for it." He lifted his hat up high enough to look at me. "Jace didn't steal that racehorse like Kermit Watson claimed, but he sure as hell got blamed for it. Spent a good bit of time in Leavenworth for it, too."

"Three years," I acknowledged.

"Uh-huh. Three mighty long years. I've spent a night or two behind bars myself, and I'll tell you, time ain't the same inside a cell as it is on the outside, where you're free to go about as you please, even if it's just to take a stroll along a creek somewhere, or chuck a rock at a tree."

"No, I guess not." I'd never been locked up like Jace or George, but I once stood in the slatted corncrib back home thinking of Jace while I stared out at the world—the woods and pasture and the sky arched overhead like a blue canopy. It made me wonder what it would be like to be locked inside permanent, and not able to hunt or fish or ride a horse if the notion took me to do so.

"You know your brother had a good job and a steady gal when those Lighthorsemen came to arrest him, don't you?"

I nodded that I did. "He was carrying for a survey crew outside of Pauls Valley, where the AT and SF was going to build a line. They never did, though." [*Editor's Note:* Two-Buck is referring to the Atchison, Topeka and Santa Fe Railroad here; the term "carrying" probably refers to either a Jacob's staff or Gunter's chain—both were instruments carried in advance of the official surveyor, depending on the type of terrain being mapped.]

"They still might, someday." George paused as if to consider the possibility, then shrugged it away. "Thing is, the AT and SF was payin' Jace a dollar a day, and that's damn good money, no matter how you slice it. Think about that, Elijah Two-Buck, three years in Leavenworth at a dollar a day. Jace figured it out on paper and it came to near eleven hundred dollars. That's what he figures Kermit Watson owes him."

"Is that why he stole these shorthorns?"

"Uh-huh. He's got a buyer in Tucker who'll take 'em two or three at a time. The guy butchers 'em outside of town, then sells the meat to folks he knows, or ships it up the Rock Island to other communities along the line. He'll only buy what he can cut up and move out in a night or two, though. That's why we were waiting back down the creek. Jace and some of the boys have been taking these beeves into Tucker a couple of times a week for the last month."

"What about the others, Pit Middleton and Three Thumbs and . . . whoever they were?"

"Middleton and Quintin Haus, he's the one with the scrawny beard who stopped you outside of camp last night, helped us run these cows off Watson's range, over south of the Arbuckles. The others were just hang-arounds, eating Watson beef and some beans and oysters Jace would bring back after making a sale."

"Oysters? Is that what was in last night's stew?"

"That and something called shrimp, which are kind of like crawdads, but not as muddy tasting. Your brother buys 'em in Tucker. Said if the railroad wants to bring that kind of food into Indian Territory, the least us savage redskins can do is eat it." He chuckled. " 'Course, I ain't rightly a redskin, but Jace says as long as I'm not white, it's all right with him."

"What about Middleton? He's white. So is Haus."

"I suppose that part about not being white ain't what you'd call a hard and fast rule, far as Jace is concerned. I think he sees it as more of an idea, like if you ain't with the enemy, then you're okay with him, no matter what color your outside hide is. Of course, we ain't had to deal with any purple or green folks yet." He looked at me and grinned. "You see what I mean?"

I nodded that I did. What George was talking about was a certain *kind* of white-eye, although I'll admit I've never noticed that kind of white man ever wanting much to do with the likes of Kid Jace or Pit Middleton or chubby Indians with three thumbs.

"Those other two hanging onto Middleton's coattails are Farrell Crow and Strong Wolf," George went on. "Wolf is a Kiowa, by the by, and not from around here, but Farrell and Thumbs are both Chickasaws from good Canadian River families."

"What about her?" I asked, jutting my chin to where Milly

sat her bay horse atop that knoll like some kind of lightly bronzed statue.

"Her name is Milly Bolton. I've noticed you eyeing her."

"I'm not eyeing her," I replied, way too quick for my protest to be taken seriously.

Smiling, George said, "I must be mistaken. Well, I won't say no more on the matter." Then, after a pause, he added, "Unless you're curious."

"I reckon I have been wondering. She acts like she's mad at me."

"She doesn't trust you. She doesn't trust me, either, and I've known her as long as Jace has."

"But she trusts Jace?"

"More than most, but not all the way." He sat up and pushed his hat back on his head. After a moment's reflection, he said, "We come upon her some months ago, along the Blue River over in Choctaw country. That was shortly after Jace got back from visiting with you and your mama. We were just moseying along in no particular direction like we sometimes do, and come onto a camp with two men tending it, and this woman chained to a tree like a coonhound. They'd been there a few days by then and were wanting to move on, so they offered to sell us the gal. Now, I right off started wondering if we could pool enough money to buy her and set her free—that's just the way my head works—but Kid Jace had other ideas. I don't know if you are aware of this, but that brother of yours has a soft spot in him for horses and dogs, and I guess for women, too. Especially those he finds chained to trees. Before you could whistle a 'whip-poor-will,' ol' Jace yanks out his Colt and shoots both them Choctaws deader than last week's breakfast fire."

My head came up at that. "He killed them?"

"I don't reckon they keeled over from heart attacks."

I tore my eyes away from George's to stare out across the

land, but I wasn't really seeing it. I remember getting a kind of tight feeling in my chest as George's words sank all the way in. It was another sobering revelation, and even more troubling to my mind than learning Jace was a cattle rustler, as I could sort of see a reason for his thievery. But killing men, just pulling your pistol and shooting them down like rabid skunks—which some folks might think they were, I'll admit—was far more disconcerting. It made me realize just how little I knew about Jace, and left me wondering how much Mama knew. Did she truly think her oldest child was a victim of a rich man's vendetta? Or was she aware of the facts behind Kid Jace's burgeoning reputation? And if she did know, then why in Hades had she sent me out here with instructions to stay with him after he was found?

It was a puzzle, all right, but one I knew I wouldn't be able to work out on my own. Me and Jace first needed to sit down by ourselves and talk it over, so that I'd know all the whys and wherefores. Then I'd have to ponder it alone for a spell, get it all straightened out in my head. I was hoping to do that when Jace got back from Tucker, but when he finally did show up it was just scant minutes ahead of a posse of Kermit Watson's hired guns, and there wasn't time to do any pondering after that.

SESSION FOUR

If you're ready to start recording again, I'm ready to pick up where we left off before lunch. Like I was saying then, me and Black George and Milly Bolton were sitting there keeping one eye on those beeves and the other on the horizon in case . . . well, just in case.

I was still mired down in what George had told me about Jace killing those two men over in Choctaw country, so I was caught off guard when Milly hollered—kind of a polite way of saying it on my part—that Jace was returning. It wasn't surprising that she spotted him first. She was still sitting her pony up on that low hill watching the cattle while me and George were keeping track of them from where we'd planted our butts in the grass, letting our horses graze and our thoughts wander.

Jace had been gone for a couple of hours by then and we weren't expecting him back until after dark, but all of a sudden Milly let out a screech that set the hairs across the back of my neck to scrambling. I jerked upright, not knowing what was going on, but George was off the ground and in his saddle in a flash, halfway up the hill to Milly's side before I had my wits gathered. By the time I got mounted and joined them, they'd already decided the risk wasn't imminent. I saw Jace out in the near distance and knew something was out of whack, though. He was pushing that leggy gelding of his faster than a smart man ought to without good cause. By the time he reached us, the sorrel was showing a lot of lather around the cinch and across its chest, although it didn't seem overly winded. I guess by that time in his career Jace was making it a point to ride good horses.

"The deal's gone sour, boys," he announced tautly, reining his horse aside and walking him back and forth in front of us to keep the gelding's muscles from stiffening up. "Watson's already got men in Tucker."

"Son of a bitch," George mumbled; then, "How many?"

"I saw three of them lazing around down by the cattle pens along the Rock Island tracks, but Carter says there were eight or nine of 'em nosing around town last night. Says they came in on the train yesterday and rented horses at the livery."

"Then Carter isn't buying any more beeves?"

"Not from us. I told him where we had these stashed and said he could come out and rope a few from time to time, and we'd settle up later, but he said he wouldn't."

George snorted. "He'd say that no matter what, but he'll do it if he can, and keep the money for himself."

"That's likely," Jace agreed. "Nothing we can do about it, though."

"Then the hell with Carter Falling Bear," George said. "What're we gonna do now?"

"I've been thinking about that," Jace replied, bringing his horse to a stop in front of us like an army officer addressing his troops before a charge. "I say our best bet is to hole up at the Notch until Watson gets tired of paying men to look for us."

"I'd imagine Watson and his men already know about the Notch," George said.

All this time, Jace and George had been talking like me and Milly weren't even there, like we were nothing but a couple of cow patties plopped down on top of empty saddles. I guess even though we both had a vested interest in whatever decision they came to, neither of us felt connected enough to the outfit to butt into the conversation, but at mention of the Notch I decided to throw my two cents' worth of opinion into the pot.

"They wouldn't try going after us there," I said with youthful assertion.

George took it for what it was worth and gave me a dismissive glance. I stayed strong in my confidence, though, and stared right back at him. Hell, I don't guess there were many folks in that part of the country that hadn't at least heard of the Notch. Back in those days it was as famous locally as the Hole-in-the-Wall and Robbers Roost were farther west. Rumor had it that the Notch was located so deep into the Arbuckles that no lawman had ever seen the place, which I kind of figure now was more hoorah than fact, since the Arbuckles just ain't that big a mountain range. On the other hand, and considering the reputation of the desperados who frequented the hideout, I suspect a prudent lawman might decide to look elsewhere if he thought the men he was chasing had taken refuge there. In my mind that same logic would apply to Watson's hired guns, if they had any sense about them.

"It doesn't matter if they do," Jace said in response to George's comment and ignoring mine altogether. "They'd not have enough guns or guts to try to root us out."

George didn't argue the point, although I'm not sure he agreed with it, either. Jutting his chin toward the grazing cattle, he said, "What're we going to do with these beeves? Just leave them to fend for themselves?"

"You want to take them with us?"

Before George could answer, Milly lifted an arm and pointed west. Way off in the distance a thin cloud of dust was brushing the horizon. Beneath it I could make out a number of horsemen—maybe six or eight altogether. That was less than the number Carter Falling Bear had claimed were in town looking for us, but still enough to have us outnumbered. They were a couple of miles away yet, but coming on fast like they knew where they were going. I couldn't tell if they'd spotted us yet, but I knew they would as soon as we started moving.

"You still want to bring those shorthorns along?" Jace asked wryly.

George's grunted reply sounded like an answer and an opinion, all wrapped into one quick expulsion of air. Pulling his horse around, he set off at a swift lope. Jace heeled the sorrel after him, leaving me and Milly to make up our own minds what to do—not that I was seeing a lot of options.

We kept as straight a line as the country would allow until the evening's gloaming finally forced us to a walk. Watson's men kept up their pursuit but didn't gain on us, and as dusk closed in they gradually faded from sight. That was a relief to me, although neither George nor Jace seemed reassured by their disappearance.

"I'd rather know where they are than where they ain't," George mumbled when we finally hauled up. I didn't know who he was talking to and wasn't sure what he meant, anyway, so I didn't answer. No one else did, either. We rested our horses for a spell, then pushed on into the night. I reckon it must have been close to midnight before we stopped along a creek to make a cold camp. We watered our horses and staked them out close by and Milly laid out a meal of leftover beef and biscuits from the night before that we consumed without speaking. Afterward we rolled up in our blankets, and I'll admit I slept soundly.

George was up before any of us the next morning, rousting us from our bedrolls with gentle kicks to our feet. Well, gentle to me and Milly; he was rougher with Jace, who sat up with a curse and a glower at George's back as he walked away. Although the sun wasn't anywhere near rising, it was light enough to see by and we quickly brought in our stock and got them rigged out. George passed out jerky from his saddlebags—

poor fare for someone having grown up on eggs and grits and fatback—but common enough fare for men riding the owlhoot I was to learn.

After breakfast Jace rode off toward a nearby rise spotty with scrub oak and tangle. Milly went with him, leaving the pack mule behind. George told me to grab the lead rope, making that flop-eared jack my responsibility as we rode out to face the new day. I glanced back after a hundred yards or so and saw that Jace and Milly had dismounted and tied their horses to a low tree limb. They were walking slowly toward the top of the rise, but didn't appear to be in much of a hurry.

"What're they doing?" I asked George.

"Waiting for us to clear out."

"Are they going to watch for Watson's men?"

He gave me a searching look, then laughed softly and shook his head. "Yeah, that and a few other things."

"What other things?" I persisted.

"Christ, Elijah Two-Buck, even a green-as-grass youngster like you ought to be able to figure that out."

Well, I hadn't, not until that moment, which I'm still embarrassed to admit. I guess from the way Jace had been treating Milly, and then the way she'd glare back at him, I'd kind of figured they were like a cow and a mule hitched to the same wagon—both of them heading in a similar direction but never quite pulling in tandem, if you know what I mean.

George and I continued east that morning, straight into the rising sun. It was a nice warm day for late October, the sky clear blue and damn near cloudless. Although pleasant, I knew it wouldn't last much longer. Not with November looming so near.

Jace and Milly didn't catch up until nearly noon, when they galloped down on us from the northeast, where they must have circled wide to get the lead. Milly looked as sullen as ever, like she was waiting for me or George to make some kind of snide remark, but Jace was grinning broadly, and he sounded almost chipper when he announced there was no sign of pursuit. I noticed that George's expression didn't change.

"It won't take them long to pick up our trail," he predicted.

"Damn, old man, don't be so glum all the time."

George muttered a reply I didn't catch and heeled his black horse into a swift trot. Jace smiled big and gigged his own mount after him. Those two puzzled me, as did Jace and Milly. I couldn't get a handle on where they stood with one another, which made me doubt my own place within the group.

We kept on with Jace and George up front and me and Milly following. Milly came up alongside Minko long enough to yank the mule's lead rope from my grasp, then fell back to the rear of our stubby column. Up ahead, Jace and George were still going at it.

"Maybe they will," Jace was saying to George's earlier observation, "but there ain't no point in worrying about it until they show up."

"Unless they've figured out we're heading for the Notch, in which case they might already be ahead of us, waiting with their rifles cocked."

"Aw, hell, I swear sometimes you're a worse worrier than some ol' black mammy."

Well, that was the wrong thing to say. George spun his horse around to face Jace, and his dark eyes were flashing thunder and lightning. Jace pulled up sharp, his right hand partially raised toward the revolver on his hip, fingers splayed to grab it. George said nothing, and after a moment of taut silence, Jace spoke softly. "All right, I'll apologize."

George's reply was low and grating, like the words were being pushed out of his throat from behind without benefit of lubrication. "They'll come a time, Jason Two-Buck," he said, "when your apologies won't cut no ice with me no more."

"You just let me know when that time comes," Jace replied, his hand resting lightly on his holster.

"I won't have to let you know. You'll see it coming without me saying a word." Then he reined his horse around and kicked it into a gallop. I glanced at Jace to see if we were going to follow, but he shook his head.

"Let 'im go, little brother. He's gotta pound some of the mad outta his gullet before he becomes fit company again."

"Why'd he get so mad?"

"Ol' George has got a whole lot of cockleburs in his britches, and you never know when something you say is gonna get one to poke him in the ass."

It was beginning to seem to me that they all had an overabundance of cockleburs lodged in their drawers—George and Jace and even Milly. Some folks think an outlaw's life is free and easy, that you can just take what you want at gunpoint and not have to worry about the consequences, but first impressions weren't encouraging me to take up the lifestyle.

We kept on into the afternoon, angling a shade north of due east now. Jace rode up front, his spirits darkened by his earlier altercation with George Holly. Milly was keeping her bay horse close behind him, although she neither spoke nor offered him any noticeable consolation. As for me, I believe I could have fallen down a well and neither of them would have noticed my absence until something needed to be fetched or toted and I wasn't handy to do it.

From time to time I'd catch sight of George crossing a low swell somewhere ahead of us. He wasn't looking back, and Jace was making no effort to catch up. The whole bunch had turned as dour as old maids, and the mood began to gradually rub off on me, until I wished I'd turned right around after delivering Mama's message to Jace and gone back home to where life was normal and animosity was reserved for folks like Kermit Watson and his ilk.

It was late afternoon when we raised the western tip of the Arbuckle Mountains, perched on the eastern horizon like low-slung clouds. I figured they'd be our destination for the night, but just about the time we sighted them, Jace reined abruptly north. Within minutes we crossed a dry wash where I spotted the tracks of George's horse in the sand, letting me know they'd had a destination in mind all along.

The land began to change the farther north we traveled, twisting valleys and rocky outcroppings slowing our progress. By the time the sun settled down on the horizon like a weary old man sinking into his favorite chair, I was beginning to believe someone had kindled a fire between my butt and the saddle's hard leather seat. I had no idea where we were as we wound our way through another tangle of burr oaks mantling a low hill no different than the last dozen we'd crossed. What was different was catching up with George near the top, tucked back among the scrub and staring down into the valley below. It took but a moment to spot the object of his attention—a small log cabin with a corral to one side where a dun mule was standing with its muzzle nearly brushing the dirt, its ribs visible from nearly a hundred yards away, like a hide-covered washboard.

"There ain't no smoke coming from that chimney," George observed quietly.

"He's gotta be there," Jace said. "If he'd gone to visit his daughter he would have taken the mule."

"You don't reckon Watson's men beat us here, do you?"

"What would they want with an old man like that?"

"Information, if they thought he had any."

"Whose place is this?" I asked.

"Old Tom Red Corn," Jace replied.

It was a name I recognized instantly. Most folks back then

would have. For a long time Thomas Red Corn had been a vocal critic of the Chickasaw Nation's tribal legislature, along with a lot of the decisions that came out of that body of largely distinguished gentlemen. I remember Papa talking about how Red Corn would make a good governor someday. I think he eventually did run for some kind of office, but when his name got linked to a young girl's body found floating in the Washita River—a daughter of someone close to the Red Corn clan, if I recall correctly—the chocks got kicked out from under Old Tom's political ambitions quicker than a rattler's strike. He'd protested the charges of course, but politics were as crooked and underhanded then as they are today, and he'd lost the election by a sizable margin. Lost his will to fight, too, Papa claimed.

Mama thought it wasn't Red Corn's political defeat so much as the lack of faith in his claims of innocence that sucked the fire out of the old man's belly. Within a month of losing the election he'd sold off all his holdings in Tishomingo and taken his family into the Cross Timbers. Being just a young sprout during the height of Red Corn's prominence, I'd damn near forgotten about the old fire-breather.

After another few minutes of speculation, George slid a Winchester from his saddle scabbard. "I reckon one of us needs to ride down there and see if he's alive."

"I'll come with you," Jace said. He looked at me and Milly. "You two stay here until I wave you down."

"No," Milly immediately objected. "I'll come with you."

Jace cursed her and repeated his instructions to stay behind, then told her he'd bust a barrel stave across her shoulders if she didn't. Milly glared at him like he'd just sold her soul for a nickel—I'll tell you, for a long time that anger-filled gaze of hers was the only expression I saw, other than her slack visage as she went about her camp chores—but she didn't argue with him, and after a moment to make sure she wouldn't, Jace nudged his horse after George's black and they rode down into the valley's deepening shadows.

It wasn't long before both men vanished into the trees along the creek, leaving me and Milly alone and on edge. I didn't attempt a conversation. I'd already tried that a few times over the past couple of days and received no more than what I took for a hate-filled glower every time. Seeing no future in it, I'd quit trying.

After about twenty minutes I noticed movement behind the corral. For a moment I thought it might have been one of Watson's posse members. Then George eased his horse out of the trees and I relaxed. A few minutes later I saw Jace ride into the yard from a different direction and dismount. He didn't approach the cabin like I figured he would, but instead walked to a nearby woodpile and squatted beside what I at first thought was a length of gray timber. When he rolled it over, I saw it was a man.

Making a sound I later pegged as a gasp, Milly kicked her bay downslope toward the cabin, the mule following behind on its lead rope. With a brief curse, I rode after her. By the time we reached the valley floor and splashed across the creek to the opposite bank, Jace and George had both dismounted. One of them had opened the corral gate to free the dun mule and it was already standing knee-deep in the middle of a still pool as we passed, slurping up sun-warmed creek water like it was sweet wine. I glanced around briefly as I rode across the tiny dirt yard, taking in the weeds and the cabin roof in need of repair; a fence post in back of the corral had been broken at its base and was causing the whole rear section to slant outward.

I got down and looped my reins around one of the rails and walked over to where Jace and George were standing above the supine form of an old man with iron-gray hair fanned out under his head. I thought at first he was dead, which was why I jumped a little when he rolled his left eye toward me and blinked. I wasn't expecting that. He looked bad, though. Husk-dry and burned crisp after laying out in the sun for who knew how long—quite a spell, judging from his emaciated appearance. I noticed the right side of his face appeared kind of droopy, like a candle partially melted, and his right hand was curled into a claw.

Milly spoke first. "What's wrong with him?"

"Stroke, I expect," George said. "I've seen it before. Something to do with the heart or the brain, I'm not sure which. It kind of paralyzes them on one side. Look at how stiff his arm and leg is on that side."

"What causes it?" Milly asked. She was leaning over the old man, studying him like he was some kind of bug she'd never seen before.

"Damned if I know," George replied. "I've heard of a few who got better, but most of 'em don't. They just lay abed until they die."

Noticing the panicky look that came into the old Indian's good eye, I said, "Maybe we ought not be talking that way."

"Hell, he knows the hand he's been dealt," Jace said matter-of-factly. "Don't you, old-timer?" He knelt and patted the man's good shoulder, kind of like you might a hound that was no longer able to hunt. "Old Tom Red Corn, brought down by a weakened body."

"I wouldn't count him out yet," George opined.

"No, we won't do that," Jace agreed, standing and brushing his hand off like he was afraid he might have gotten some of the old Indian's affliction on his fingers. Catching my eye, he said, "Lige, go drag that blasted mule outta the creek before he gets the collywobbles." Then he looked at Milly, who instantly stepped back and shook her head.

"I ain't cleaning him up."

We all knew what she was talking about. You could smell he'd messed himself, and there were flies and other tiny critters swarming the stained wool of his trousers. But Jace was adamant. "It's a woman's job," he told her.

"I won't do it."

"You'll either do it or get your ass out of here and find someone else to torment."

She started cussing him then, not real loud or creative, but with vim enough to make up for any lack of artistry. Jace's expression hardened, but he didn't respond until she talked herself dry. When she was done, he lifted an arm and pointed to the cabin, looking kind of like a boiler about to explode.

"I hate you," Milly said vehemently.

"I hate you, too, you little shit. Now get your hind end in there and get ready. Me 'n George'll carry him inside, but after that he's yours to tend to." Looking around, he noticed me standing there gawking and snapped, "Damnit, Lige, go fetch that mule."

I hustled down to the creek, wading out far enough to take the dun by the cheek strap on his halter and pull his head up. He resisted at first, but then relented and allowed me to lead him back to dry land, water sluicing off his belly hair like a mudflow. I took him around back of the cabin and turned him loose on some good grass and he immediately lowered his head.

I lingered there to watch him graze, taking advantage of the solitude. Jace and Milly were still out front arguing about whose responsibility it was to look after poor old Thomas Red Corn, but I'd noticed when I came up from the creek that George was no longer in sight. I could hear him inside, rattling things around as if getting it ready for the old man. I waited until a puff of smoke popped out of the stovepipe, then walked back around front. Jace and Milly were no longer there. Neither was Thomas Red Corn. I didn't go inside, but wandered over to the corral to check the horses. I felt oddly bothered by the old man's fate. It didn't seem dignified that someone of his past reputation should be subjected to such an inglorious end. He'd been a warrior, damnit, and he deserved a warrior's death, not this slow withering away.

I was standing next to Minko with one hand wrapped gently in the pinto's mane when George exited the cabin and came over. "Get on your horse," he said, his expression grim, as it often was after dealing with Jace.

"Where are we going?"

"Red Corn's got a daughter nearby, a woman named Sarah McFarland. We're gonna let her know what happened to her daddy."

Getting out of there suited me, and I quickly freed Minko and booted a stirrup.

"Bring the mule," George instructed.

"The mule? Ain't we coming back with his daughter?"

"No, we'll stay at the McFarland place tonight, then ride on to the Notch tomorrow." He must have noticed my puzzled glance toward the cabin. "Jace will catch up with us at McFarland's. The girl's staying with the old man."

"For good?"

"That's what Jace says, although there's no telling how it'll all pan out. She's a bullheaded little thing, but so is your brother."

Well, I wasn't going to argue with that, although I'll admit the thought of never seeing Milly Bolton again triggered a strange feeling within my breast. Not that I was interested in her in any other way than as a curiosity. Nor had she ever made any effort to hide her own low opinion of me. But it did seem like a shabby way to leave, with neither a fare-thee-well nor a go-to-hell—whichever fit.

We mounted and I slipped the mule's lead rope from where

it was looped over a fence rail and the two of us rode away side by side. The sun wasn't but a peach-fuzzed cap sitting on the horizon as we guided our horses east along a creek-side trail. I glanced back one last time just before a bend in the valley took the cabin from sight, but there was no one watching our departure, no movement of any kind save for the gently purling smoke from the chimney. Feeling as low as a worn-out bootheel, I turned my back on the cabin and concentrated on what lay ahead.

SESSION FIVE

It was an hour's ride to the McFarland place. The sun was gone by the time we got there, dusk creeping in like thieves from the surrounding woods. The farm was as impressive as any I'd ever seen in that part of the Nation. There must have been ten acres of recently picked cotton east of the house and a cornfield of equal size to the south, with an orchard of peach, apple, and cherry trees in between. The house was log, but square-hewn and two-storied, and it looked as solid as a chunk of mountain granite sitting there in the shadows. There was a barn out back, along with other assorted buildings, and four big draft horses—Conestogas, judging by their size and color—in a pasture behind the barn. As large and prosperous as the place looked, I was surprised Red Corn didn't live there with his daughter.

We stopped about fifty yards out and George helloed the house, causing a pack of hounds in some kennels down by the barn to send up a tremendous caterwauling. A shadow flashed briefly across a curtained, lamplit window; a few seconds later a man stepped onto the porch with a shotgun clenched firmly before him. "Come on up here where I can see you," he called in a voice tinted with more wariness than welcome.

As we heeled our mounts forward, George whispered out the side of his mouth, "Don't make no too-quick moves, Elijah Two-Buck, and keep your hands where he can see 'em."

I nodded a curt "damn right," and placed both hands atop the tall horn of my Texas rig. As we drew closer the man inched

66

sideways until he was partially shielded behind one of the massive oak columns supporting the veranda. He looked like he was in his mid-thirties and had curly red hair, but you could tell there was a healthy dose of Indian running through his veins. He wore a working man's attire of sturdy jeans and a dark flannel shirt, and the toe of his right boot, poking out from behind the porch column where it caught a splash of lamplight from the open door, looked worn but clean.

"How do," George said amicably, reining to a stop some yards away; I quickly echoed the greeting.

"Howdy," the man replied cautiously, gripping his scattergun with a lot more firmness than seemed warranted, considering our open approach.

"We're looking for Sarah McFarland," George continued. "I believe she's Thomas Red Corn's daughter."

"She is."

"Then this is the McFarland farm?"

After a pause to consider his answer, the man nodded guardedly. "Yes."

I sensed George's growing exasperation with the man's reticence. "Would Mrs. McFarland be around?"

"Who's asking?"

"Just a friend," George replied. "We came from Red Corn's place, and—"

A woman appeared suddenly in the door behind the man, and George shut up mid-sentence. She looked older than the man, possibly as much as ten to fifteen years older; like the man, her hair was off-colored for an Indian, even one of mixed blood—kind of honey-blond in the lamplight behind her—but her flesh was dark, textured from hard work, her shoulders straight, jaw firm. Her voice was firm, too, when she spoke.

"I'm Sarah McFarland. Is my father all right?"

"I'm afraid he's had an accident," George began, but the

man with the shotgun cut him off before he could elaborate.

"What kind of an accident?"

Brother, you could just about feel the hostility radiating off that guy. George must have noticed it, too, because his eyes suddenly narrowed and his voice turned rough. "I'd be obliged if you wouldn't interrupt so much, friend."

"Henry," the woman admonished gently, stepping forward to place a hand over his arm. "Let him speak." Then, to me and George, she added, "There has been some robberies in the area recently and we're all feeling a little edgy, but we mean no disrespect."

"No, ma'am," George said. "None was taken. Fact is, being cautious is good policy in these parts." His gaze swung back to Henry. "As long as it don't get in the way of good manners."

"Of course," she agreed. "But . . . you mentioned an accident?"

"More of an affliction than an accident, I expect, but yes, ma'am, I'm afraid he's in dire shape. We're thinking it might have been a stroke or a—" He paused at the woman's low, indrawn cry, then went on more gently. "He is alive, ma'am, 'though he can't talk or help himself any."

"Is someone with him?"

"My partner and his woman are there. We carried him inside, but—"

"He was outside?"

"Yes, ma'am, for several days, it appears."

"Oh, dear Lord," she whispered, and quickly turned to reenter the house.

"Wait, you can't go out there tonight," Henry protested.

"Why ever not?"

"Because it's nearly dark and you don't know what kind of men might be lurking along the trail."

"We just followed that trail and didn't see a soul," George

said. Then an edge came into his voice. "Unless it's me and the boy here that you're talking about."

"It doesn't matter who I'm talking about," Henry replied stiffly. "This is a dangerous country, and especially so at night."

"You could go with her."

Henry's gaze narrowed. Despite our riding out of the way to fetch old Red Corn some help, it was obvious the younger man didn't trust us, either with the woman or his farm, and maybe especially not his farm, I thought.

"We didn't come here to steal anything," I blurted, and Sarah hurried back to Henry's side.

"Of course not," she said, looking me over as if taking my measure. Then she turned to Henry. "If their intent was to cause trouble, they wouldn't have approached the house so openly."

After a pause, Henry said, "All right, what do you want to do?"

"Emily and I will take the runabout and go to Father tonight. You can stay here and entertain these men." She looked at me and George. "I imagine you're both fairly famished."

"I reckon we could eat a little something," George allowed, keeping his eyes on Henry McFarland. You could tell he trusted neither the man's stance nor his words, and I felt the same.

"Henry," Sarah said. "Have Rissa fix these men something to eat, then tell Kiefer to harness Sweetie to the runabout."

"You take your rifle," Henry said sharply.

"I will," Sarah assured him, before hurrying into the house to get ready.

After another lengthy pause, Henry said, "You boys can turn your stock into that empty corral north of the barn. The water trough is full and there's hay in the loft or shelled corn in a bin in the entryway, your choice. I'll have our colored gal fix you a bite to eat. Come around back when you've taken care of your horses."

"We wouldn't want to put you out any," George said, ladening his tone with a heavy dose of sarcasm now that Sarah was gone.

"Oh, you won't be a burden, I'll promise you that," Henry said. Then he went inside and closed the door firmly behind him.

Exhaling with enough gusto to flutter his lips, George said, "That there is one first-class son of a bitch, Elijah Two-Buck."

"He's just worried about his wife."

"I will tell you something, if it wasn't for that woman's kindness, I'd be damn tempted to kick that boy's door in and teach him how to behave around his elders."

I didn't have anything to say to that, but I will now, just so you know. Back in the '90s in Indian Territory, race wasn't viewed the same as it is today. It wasn't the same there as it was in most places around the country, for that matter. Not that it didn't eventually get as bad, or maybe even worse, because it surely did. When Jim Crow came along it got real bad. But back in those earlier times it wasn't unusual at all to see a white man married to an Indian woman or an Indian man married to a white woman, and there was colored folks thrown all over the place, as well. So George saying he was tempted to kick in Henry McFarland's door and pound some manners into him wouldn't have raised many eyebrows back then. Not like elsewhere, and the South in particular, where he'd have been strung up before breakfast for such a remark.

Anyway, with Henry gone, me and George walked our horses down to the corral and turned them loose to roll. After feeding them some shelled corn and adding a little hay to the manger in case they got hungry again later, we found brushes in the barn and curried down all three animals. We even took time to trim their manes and tails and check their hooves and shoes, since the tools to do so were handy.

While we were doing that, some kid who looked a lot like Henry—Kiefer, I think they called him—came down and hitched a fine bay mare to a light runabout. He never said a word to us, but I saw him sneaking peeks our way from time to time, no doubt curious about who we were. Me and George paused in our chores to watch him drive that skinny-wheeled vehicle back to the house, where Henry and Sarah were waiting with a trunk and a couple of cloth valises that they stowed in back. Then a pretty girl—Emily was her name—came out of the house with a satchel that she crammed under the seat.

I'll admit I watched a little closer when she stepped around the rear of the runabout, passing through the light from a lantern Henry had sitting on the edge of the porch. Emily Mc-Farland looked a lot like her mama, who was a handsome woman in her own right. But Emily was younger and smoother, with an inviting plumpness that gave her the appearance of a down-filled pillow any man would love to nestle his head against.

Noticing the intensity of my gaze, George smacked my shoulder with the back of his hand. "A gal like that ain't gonna look twice at someone like you or me, Elijah Two-Buck."

"I'm not asking her to look at me," I retorted, and he laughed and went back to his chores.

By the time we finished caring for our stock and scrubbed our faces and hands in a basin alongside the summer kitchen behind the house, our meal was ready. The McFarland's cook, Rissa—short for Clarissa, I'd learn, tall and willowy and lightly chocolate colored, although with some kind of tribal scarring on each cheek that gave her a fierce appearance—had a small banquet set out for us under the arbor where the hired help ate. It was mostly leftovers from the McFarland's supper, I suppose, but a real fine spread nonetheless. There was fried chicken and mashed potatoes with gravy and fresh green beans and creamed corn—the first I'd ever tried of that, and mighty tasty in my opinion—and coffee without a trace of bitterness, and then damn if there wasn't blackberry cobbler with fresh cream for dessert. I'll tell you what, by the time me and George finished laying waste to the meal, we both looked like we were about to pop our britches.

We thanked Rissa, then George shooed me back to the corral. Said he wanted me to keep an eye on the horses, as he thought he'd smelled a skunk earlier and was afraid it might be rabid. Well, I was young and naïve—we've already established that—but I wasn't altogether stupid, so I tipped my hat to Rissa and left. Twenty minutes later, George showed up looking as sulky as a work-worn mule.

"Married?" I ventured.

"Said she wouldn't be interested even if she wasn't. Said I had a fiddle-footed look about me, and that she'd already been married to one man born to a wandering star."

"Sounds like she pegged you just about right."

"I wasn't asking her to marry me. I just wanted to do a little belly rubbing."

I laughed. "Maybe you'll have better luck down the trail."

"Not the trails we're gonna be riding," he replied, which scrubbed the grin off my face.

Now I've done enough talking for one day, so you can turn that recorder off and see yourself out, because I'm going to bed. Goodnight. I'll see you here again tomorrow morning.

SESSION SIX

I don't know about you, but I ain't gonna drink as much coffee today. I like to never got to sleep last night.

Anyway, getting back to my time with Jace, he showed up just after dawn the next morning looking haggard and ill-tempered, but he was alone, which surprised me and George equally. George asked if he wanted some breakfast—we'd had a good one earlier, thanks to Rissa—but Jace said he'd already eaten and was anxious to shake a tail. He said if we were coming with him we'd best get our horses saddled, else he'd leave on his own. Then he rode off a ways and fixed himself a cigarette while me and George walked down to the corral to ready our stock.

George was silent for the most part, but as we were lifting the panniers onto the pack mule he looked across the sawbucks at me and chuckled. "You reckon your brother had to tie that little gal down to keep her from following him?"

"You reckon there was enough rope at Red Corn's place to do that?"

George laughed and shook his head. "Tell you the truth, Elijah Two-Buck, I'm kind of sorrowful she ain't coming with us."

"She liked you," I said, recalling how she'd hand him his cup of coffee at the supper fire, or see he got a full plate of whatever it was she'd fixed us to eat.

"She liked you, too, she just never learned how to show it."

I paused with the rope we were using to tie down the cover in

73

my hand, staring at George and wondering if I'd heard him right. He looked at me and nodded, and I went ahead and tossed him the loose end of the tie-down. "I reckon you ain't been paying attention to what's been going on behind your back, riding up front with Jace and all," I said.

"Oh, I've been payin' attention, Elijah Two-Buck. The way she acted around you . . . and the way you acted around her."

"Hell, mostly I just tried to keep my distance."

"Uh-huh, you surely did that." Then he laughed like something funny had just occurred to him, and my face got unexpectedly warm. Scowling, I lowered my gaze to focus on snugging up my side of the diamond hitch we were tying.

With everything ready, we led our cavvy to where Jace was waiting on us. With the mule's lead rope in hand, I knew the little jack was going to be my responsibility from then on. Henry and Kiefer and a couple other youngsters—I'd find out later the McFarlands had eleven children altogether, ten of them male—stood at the entrance of a wagon shed to watch us ride off. I waved, but the gesture wasn't returned. Jace and George just rode out like the little goose-neckers weren't even there.

We moseyed along in silence all morning, Jace wrapped in a black gloom I swear you could almost see. Noon came and went without us stopping, and the sun was beating down on my shoulders like October was still weeks away, and not about to depart our company for another year. We were heading in a generally southeastern direction, intending to come into the Notch from the northwest, in case some of Watson's men were watching the trails between Tucker and the Arbuckles. We were a couple of hours into those winding canyons and timbered ridges when Jace abruptly hauled up. Me and George rode up to flank him.

"What do you think?" Jace asked.

"I ain't seen a thing worrisome to me," George replied.

"Me, neither," I piped in, and Jace smiled for the first time that day.

"Well, hell, I reckon that makes three for and none against," he told George, then reined back the way we'd come for a few hundred yards before turning off into a dense forest of oak and hickory. Thirty minutes later we came to a swift-flowing creek and guided our horses into it, riding upstream toward the higher peaks of the range. At first there was no trail along either bank, and then suddenly there was. We left the creek to follow what turned out to be a well-defined path winding through those tall oaks, passing beneath sunlit canopies of flaming red; the leaves that had already fallen blanketed the trail with a scarlet carpet that announced our presence in crackling heralds.

In time we came back to what I assumed was the same creek, although it was moving a lot faster here, tumbling over midstream boulders with a cheerful melody, the water so clear it looked nearly black. We followed it creek-side to where it spilled out of a notch in a nearly vertical cliff that must have towered seventy feet or more above our heads, then reined back into the water.

The gorge was narrow and sheer-sided, its walls blanketed in moss and bouquets of pale green ferns that seemed to jut from every tiny fissure, yet the entire passage wasn't more than thirty yards distance. After that it opened into a long, narrow canyon with rocky bluffs on both sides and a gently winding meadow down the middle; its flanks were covered with good oak and hickory about halfway up, before turning to stone and becoming nearly perpendicular. The place looked as impenetrable as a castle, but with good water and fine graze along the creek, you could easily see its appeal.

Jace pulled up just inside the Notch and twisted around in his saddle to study the precipice behind us. Finally spying what he was looking for, he said, "You gonna pass us on in, Bob?"

"Who's the kid?" a gravelly voice inquired, and a bearded man stepped out from behind some blackberry briars carrying a rifle up high where he could easily throw it to his shoulder if necessary.

"This is my brother Lige. I'll vouch for him."

Bob nodded. "Middleton came in last night. He said your brother'd joined you."

"We okay?" George asked.

"Yeah, go on in."

And that was my introduction to the Notch, one of the most nefarious outlaw hideouts between the Mississippi River and the Rocky Mountains. I'm kind of proud now to say I'd seen it, but back then I was feeling intimidated as hell. That Bob guy—that was Bob Hatcher, who had probably killed more men than the Jameses and Youngers put together. I recognized him from a police sketch hanging on the post office wall in Davis, and felt a chill creep up my spine as I turned my back on him.

A narrow trace ran along the creek and we followed that on into the canyon. Coming to a fork in the trail, Jace reined west and we soon began climbing toward where the slope became too steep for horses. Shortly below that lay a little flat patch of bare earth, powdery with old horse manure, the ground under it pounded solid as concrete. A couple of jackleg hitching rails had been set up on the far side of the flat and we dismounted there and tied up. Jace started up a footpath winding through rocks that had fallen from above, making his way toward what looked like the mouth of a cave another fifty feet overhead. When I started up after him, George called me back. Tipping his head toward Minko's saddle, he said, "Take your rifle, Elijah Two-Buck, and keep it close."

Billy Goodwin had offered similar advice, I recalled, and I slid the Marlin from its scabbard without asking why. We started up the path after Jace, and at the top there was a sure-enough cavern, its entrance a good fifty feet wide, its roof at least twenty feet high. There was a big chamber inside with boulders strewn around that must have fallen from the roof over the eons, and smaller cavities, some of which had been curtained off with blankets. A rough-planked counter had been set up to one side, and there were a few cobbled-together tables and stools scattered across the dirt floor in front of it. Lanterns sat on rocks and in small niches to provide illumination after dark, although there was enough ambient light coming in from outside that they weren't needed then. Toward the rear of the big room were two smaller openings that looked like regular cave entrances, the kind you'd need torches to explore.

There must have been a dozen men lazing around the cavern's front room, along with several women who fluttered between them like moths drawn to whichever flame was flashing the most money. It dawned on me about then that this was a saloon, right there in the middle of a hollowed-out chuck of granite, and of all the surprises I was in for during the next couple of days, I believe that was the biggest.

Jace was already leaning into the bar talking to a stubby white man wearing a bowler hat and red sleeve garters. Jace had his wallet in hand and was counting out money that he placed one bill at a time on top of the bar. The white-eye was watching him do it, lips moving as he counted along with Jace.

"That's Enoch Anderson," George explained quietly. "This is his place, his canyon, since he's the one who first found it, then sent word out to others. He'll charge us to stay here if we've got money, or expect payment the next time we come through if we're short this time. He'll know Jace has money, though."

"How would he know that?"

"The word's been out awhile about Kid Jace running cows off the Watson place."

I kind of flinched at that. I was still uncomfortable hearing

Jace referred to as "Kid Jace," since I still didn't want to believe there was any truth to the rumors I'd been hearing about him. But then something else clicked in my mind and I hesitated. "Then . . . that bunch the other day, those weren't the first cows he stole?"

George gave me a puzzled glance. "No, they weren't, nor the second or the third."

Well, that was a gulletful to swallow, but there wasn't going to be time to chew it down to manageable if I wanted to keep up with George, which I did. I followed him to the bar just as Enoch pocketed the wad of bills Jace had shoved across the counter toward him. The old man eyed me speculatively.

"This is Lige," Jace said, as if he'd already explained my presence.

Enoch shrugged and looked at George. "Your partner's already ordered a whiskey. You want one, too?"

"Might as well. Pour one for young Elijah Two-Buck, while you're at it."

Enoch reached under the counter and came out with a two-gallon glazed jug corked with a stub of corncob. Setting a trio of cheap tin mugs in a line on the counter, he pulled the cob and swiftly filled each cup to within an inch of its rim. "You'd better drink fast," he suggested. "Some of these cups has got leaks."

"Fast is best in these parts," Jace agreed, grabbing the nearest cup and taking a healthy swig. He sputtered some as he lowered it. "Lord God," he wheezed, looking at me and George as if he'd just accidentally shot his favorite horse. "Don't spill any on your boots, boys. It'll eat the leather and blister your toes before you can peel 'em off."

"It'll burn a hole through your britches come morning if you ain't careful when you break wind," Enoch added.

"I don't doubt it," Jace replied, looking flushed and uncomfortable. "By damn, Enoch, if you're charging for the burn, it's money well spent."

I peered into my cup, filled with a mostly clear liquid, which moonshine usually is, although this had little pieces of something swirling around near the bottom. Enoch's lips rolled back in a gap-toothed, yellow grin.

"Don't be shy, sonny," he said. "Whatever it was, it's well pickled and harmless by now." Then he laughed, his breath warm and putrid as it flowed across the bar into my face.

Aware of others around the cavern watching and waiting to see me take my first swallow of Enoch Anderson's rotgut 'shine, I raised my cup and took a big gulp of smoldering brimstone. Although it burned hotter than live coals, I'll confess I've tasted worse behind barns and hay sheds at weddings and dances and such. Jace grinned approvingly as I lowered my mug, then slapped my shoulder with what I hoped was proud affection.

"How much for the jug?" he asked, but Enoch shook his head.

"I'll sell you a quart for a dollar, but not the jug. I'll need 'em for future use."

"I expect a quart will do enough damage," George opined, but Jace shook his head.

"There's three of us now," he said, and tossed a couple of bills onto the bar. "Give us two quarts, old man."

Enoch's grin spread like a vulture's wings above a fresh kill as he scooped the cash into his pocket. He set a pair of Mason jars down in front of Jace and we took the corn and our mugs over to an empty table against the far wall. It was pleasant inside the cavern with just the three of us relaxing at a table, sturdy kegs for seats and a nice breeze flowing out from one of the deeper passages in back. Had it not been for the liquor it might have actually been chilly; as it was, we were all lightly sweating.

After draining the cups Enoch had filled, George leaned back in his chair and belched loud enough to produce an echo. "We gonna stay put awhile, Jason Two-Buck?" he asked.

"I'm thinking so, at least until we can figure out what that backstabbing bastard Watson is up to." He sniffed and wiped his nose with a knuckle; my own nose was dripping pretty steadily, too, compliments of Enoch's corn liquor. "The old man says J.R. McNeil has been asking about me," Jace went on. "He says he's still here, so I'll need to talk to him soon, but we can finish these squeezin's first."

"If we try to empty both of these jars in one setting, these squeezings might finish us first," I remarked, and Jace and George both swiveled their heads toward me in surprise.

"I'll be damned, Jason Two-Buck, I believe your little brother has finally found his tongue."

Befuddled, I said, "What do you mean?"

"I mean you ain't peeped more than half a dozen chirps at a time since you joined the outfit."

I looked at Jace for confirmation and got it from a grin. "Hell," I said, feigning indignation, "I just ain't had nothing to say before today."

Jace laughed, and George said, "I believe it's the liquor must've scraped the rust off your tongue, Elijah Two-Buck."

"I believe that's true," Jace added.

Well, maybe it had—the liquor, I mean—because after just one tin cup of the stuff I was feeling mighty big and tough all of a sudden. Like I could go after Kermit Watson myself and punch that troublemaking son of a bitch square in the nose. Maybe stop off on the way out of the Notch and set Bob Hatcher straight on who was the king of the roost while I was at it. Shoot, by the time we'd drained that first fruit jar I was laughing at just about anything and everything, including the spectacle I made of myself as I ran a finger around its rim to capture any wayward drops of liquor.

Yes, sir, I was feeling mighty bold as Jace twisted the top off that second fruit jar and filled our cups for maybe the third or fourth—or was it the fifth—time? I know I was feeling real good when he announced it was time we found a place to throw our bedrolls and take care of our horses. I kicked my chair back and rose with my chest puffed out and my head thrown back, and hardly felt the fall. I was just all of a sudden lying on my back with my arms spread wide, laughing my fool head off.

George and Jace were both laughing along as they helped me to my feet. George thrust the Marlin into my hands and the three of us headed for the cavern's entrance, the earth lurching mischievously under my feet as we staggered down the path to our horses. George had to get a shoulder under my backside to heave me into my saddle, while Jace stood across from him with slurred assurances of catching me if I overshot my target. I'll tell you what, we were all having a grand ol' time of it, but it's a good thing I was riding Minko, and not some prairie mustang. Minko had been swarmed over by kids ever since Mama purchased him, and was used to such shenanigans as I was putting him through that day outside of Enoch's saloon. Any other horse might've kick my fool head off its stump, the way—

SESSION SEVEN

Now, I'll tell you—and I don't care if it is being recorded—but the way that machine just squawks and stops like some truck driver stomping down on worn-out brakes when it runs out of space is enough to set a fella's teeth to shimmying. I'm not claiming I had much more to say on the matter of ornery horses and drunken men, but that kind of squeal can throw off a fellow's timing. If it does it again, I might be tempted to drag my Colt's revolver from the closest and put that damned Dictaphone of yours outta my misery.

That revolver, by the way, is the same one Jace gave me all those years ago, and if you can keep your machine running without running outta disks, I'll tell you how that came to be. But first I need to back up to what happened after me and Jace and Black George Holly left Enoch Anderson's rock-ceilinged saloon that afternoon. I'll confess I don't recall much of what remained of that day, although George assured me I was as awake and functional as any of them as we located a place near the lower end of the canyon, took care of our animals, then tumbled into our bedrolls.

I woke up the next morning with mushy brains and a churning stomach, convinced I'd contracted some horrible disease and would soon die—an outcome not all that unpleasant to contemplate, considering the way I felt. Jace was still tightly cocooned in his blankets, but George was squatting beside a small fire nursing a cup of what smelled like coffee. He was looking pretty used up, like maybe he'd kicked the jug and the damn thing had kicked him back.

I lumbered over in my stockinged feet and flopped down cross-legged in front of the fire, wondering at the awfulness of the taste in my mouth and if there could be anything worse; swallowing a three-day-dead skunk might have compared, but I wouldn't have bet money on it. George didn't speak, but he did pour me a cup of coffee that he first laced with a dollop of store-bought whiskey from a bottle he carried in his saddlebags. I felt somewhat better afterward, but still had the trots all morning. Like most young bucks just starting to kick up their heels, I swore right then and there to never again drink so much hard liquor in one sitting. Sadly, and also like so many youngsters such as I was, it was a promise I'd soon forget.

Later that morning we started improving our camp in anticipation of the wet weather George's knees were forecasting. I believe I've already mentioned how the days had been pleasantly warm for several weeks by then, which isn't unusual for that part of the country in October, but we all knew it was just a matter of time before winter moved in like an unwelcome houseguest. So while George chopped down saplings with a short-handled camp axe to frame a lean-to, I cut boughs from some cedar trees higher up the canyon wall and layered them inside as both mattress and floor. While we did that, Jace set out to find J.R. McNeil, who Enoch Anderson had mentioned was looking for him.

J.R. was a Chickasaw horse thief of some renown in that part of the Nation. Folks said he'd learned the trade from a Comanche over around Fort Sill, which seemed plausible as Comanches were noted for their talents in stealing horses. J.R. used to come around our home on Two-Buck Mountain from time to time when I was younger; this was back when Jace still lived there, when Papa was alive and Mama used to laugh, which seemed like ancient history at the time, and hardly seems real today, it was so long ago.

It took only a couple of hours to get our camp snugged up to George's satisfaction. He shingled the lean-to with bark stripped from a dying hickory tree, while I chopped enough wood to last us several days if needed. Later that afternoon, with the two of us sitting half asleep at the fire waiting for Jace to return from his powwow with J.R., there was a commotion in the trees between our camp and the creek, about sixty yards below us. We both sat up real quick and George put his hand on his revolver while I slid the Marlin across my lap. I didn't know who it might be, but I was fairly certain Jace wouldn't make that much racket, no matter how drunk he might be. We stayed seated, not wanting to present too much of a challenge in case whoever it was prowling around out there had been sent by Jace. Then, lo and behold, who do you reckon came stumbling out of the trees leading her horse by the reins?

"Lordy, a'mercy," George declared, and we scrambled to our feet.

Milly—you'd already guessed it was her, hadn't you?—led her little bay horse to the lean-to and flopped the near-side stirrup over the seat. She kept her back to us like we weren't even there, but when George spoke her name she flashed us a dark scowl as if daring us to protest her appearance. Then, still without speaking, she slid her saddle from the bay's back and set it down in front of the lean-to. After loosening her picket rope, she led her horse down to where we had Minko, Coal, and the pack mule staked out.

George shook his head. "Ol' Jace ain't gonna like this one bit."

"Why doesn't he like her?" I asked.

"Oh, I suppose he likes her well enough. It's just that she's latched onto his coattails like a cocklebur, and Jace likes his freedom more than he likes having a woman handy."

"Is that all?"

George smiled. "When it comes to man-woman stuff, Elijah Two-Buck, there ain't never a 'that's all' to any of it."

"If Jace feels that way, why doesn't she go home?"

"I expect she ain't got one to go to." We sat back down and George added more wood to the fire. Keeping his eyes on the capering flames, he said, "I didn't tell you the whole story about her, about how we found her. Shoot, I don't reckon I *know* the whole story, but I've pieced some of it together." He paused as if to gather his thoughts, then went on. "Milly Bolton was on her honeymoon when she was took by them two Choctaw devils your brother gunned down on Blue River. She and her husband, whose name I've never learned, were coming west in a wagon. They'd stopped along the Blue to rest their stock for a few days, but were planning on settlin' over around Duncan's Trading Post if the prospects there looked good. [*Editor's Note:* Although an exact location on Blue River wasn't given, it is approximately 130 miles from the mid-Blue to the town of Duncan, in Stephens County.]

"Them Choctaw devils told Milly's husband they had some good farmland not too far away that they wanted to sell, and convinced him to go with them and have a look. Well, they went off together, but when those two Choctaws came back, it was without her husband. They told her he'd fallen into the Blue River and drowned. They were lying, as anyone with half a brain could figure out, but Milly's man had taken their firearms and their mule, and left her with just an axe and a butcher knife for weapons, and a Jersey cow to look after.

"Them devil bucks claimed they wanted to help her. Said if she'd come with them, they'd take her to Durant where she could sell her cow, then write her folks to come get her. She told 'em no, being naturally bullheaded even then, I suppose, so they threw a rope around her and pulled her down. Afterward they chained her to a tree and gave up any pretense of wanting to help."

"Then Jace came along and rescued her?"

"That's about the size and shape of it."

"And she's clung to him ever since?"

"Tighter'n a tick in a hound's ear. Jace don't mind sharing a blanket with her time to time, and I guess she figures she owes him that much, but he'd just as soon she went away now."

George stopped talking then, and I had nothing to add. The magnitude of what Milly Bolton had suffered damn near knocked me off the chunk of firewood I was sitting on. My gaze strayed to where she was bent over her picket pin down near the creek, stomping it into the soft earth with the heel of her shoe. I knew, and surely she must have as well, that in such soil a picket pin wouldn't hold five seconds if her horse decided to spook. But I also knew better than to say anything, and when she trudged back up to the fire she looked as defiant as ever. Here, I suddenly realized, was a woman who would fight to her last breath to maintain her independence, no matter how skewed her view of what that meant might be. In my opinion she was stubbornly wrong to put up with the kind of treatment she had to endure from Jace, but I'll also admit that I felt a deep admiration for her strength and tenacity. Not that I'd dare voice it— she'd likely snapped my head off like a squirrel for the spit if I did—but it was there, and I think it was in George, too. I think we both stood a little in awe of Milly Bolton.

An uneasy silence fell over us that afternoon as we awaited Jace's return, but he never showed. Instead it was J.R. McNeil who rode into our camp shortly after sundown, sitting astride a steel-dust gray mare that looked like she could outrun a cottontail through a briar patch. We walked over to where he stopped his mare some rods away, it being considered impolite to ride a horse into a man's camp without invitation. Milly came along but didn't say anything, not even when J.R. told us Jace had left the Notch and probably wouldn't be back for several days.

"He left!" I echoed. "Where'd he go?"

"You'll have to ask him. He wanted me to let you know, and that's what I'm doing."

"Was there trouble?" George asked, to which J.R. laughed curtly.

"When ain't there trouble in these parts?"

"Did he say what it was?" I asked.

"He said to bring you this," J.R. replied, reaching into his off-side saddlebag and extracting a bottle of whiskey—the good stuff, not that horse piss Enoch was selling—and passed it to George. "Jace'll be back soon enough," he added. "He wanted to check out some rumors I picked up along the Washita the other day."

"Are you pulling out, too?" George asked.

J.R. nodded, and a sly grin crept across his face. "I gotta see a man about a horse."

"You've gotta dodge a man about a horse, would be more believable," George replied, and they both laughed.

"That could be," J.R. acknowledged. "Listen, if you boys need fresh mounts, I ought to have a few good head in about a week. If you're interested, I can swing past here and give you first pick."

"It's tempting, but I can't guarantee we'll be here," George said.

"Well, I'll swing past, anyway." His expression turned abruptly doleful. "You might change your mind . . . if you're still here." Then he reined away, his mare stepping out in a lively fashion, as you'd expect the mount of such a qualified horse thief to do.

"What did he mean by that?" Milly demanded after J.R. had

ridden out of earshot.

"He knows more than he's telling," George said. He held the whiskey bottle—a half quart of Jim Pepper Premium Rye—up to the diminishing twilight. "I expect he left us this to soften the blow."

"It'll more likely soften your head," Milly said disdainfully.

"I don't doubt it," George agreed. He took the bottle back to the fire and eased down in front of it, his knees popping crisply in protest. Me and Milly joined him there, sitting silent as the night closed in tight around us. Despairing images haunted my thoughts, of hired gunmen and dangling nooses—they were still hanging cattle rustlers and horse thieves in those days—and of cell doors clanging shut on tiny cages. My mood was sinking fast, and I suspect George's was, too, because after a bit he hefted the bottle of rye to where its contents glowed amber in the firelight and said, "I expect we might as well get started, huh?"

"You can both drink yourselves stupid, if that's what you want," Milly retorted.

Acting as though he hadn't heard, George peeled the wax seal off the bottle's neck with his thumb, then worked the cork out and tossed it into the flames, announcing his intentions to the world. He started to reach for a cup, then shook his head in an angry, the-hell-with-it gesture, and he tipped the bottle to his lips. His Adam's apple bobbed half a dozen times before he called it enough and handed me the whiskey.

You remember the promise I'd made to myself just that morning, to never drink so much in one sitting again? Well, that resolve got shot to hell in no time. Milly wouldn't touch the stuff, and stared daggers at George the one time he offered her a nip. She poked up the fire and fixed a bait of rice and beans for herself while me and George worked on that bottle and speculated on what had lit such a hot fire in Jace's britches. It began as a serious discussion, but as the level of rye was lowered the conversation began skittering off in different directions. I recall us discussing J.R. McNeil's pretty gray mare and wondering where she'd come from—not likely from Indian Territory, was George's opinion—then moving on to horses we'd known or heard of, and the kind of mount we'd like to own ourselves someday. We both agreed we'd look over whatever string J.R. brought back to the Notch, then buy the best of the lot. It was pure boastfulness on my part since I didn't have enough money at the time to purchase a lame goat. I couldn't tell you how George was fixed for cash, but no matter what angle you looked at him from, you'd never mistake him for a wealthy socialite.

Not surprisingly, we both woke up the next morning feeling like death warmed over. With my eyes squeezed tight against the thumping in my brain, I repeated my vow to forsake alcohol in large qualities until the day of my funeral, which at that time didn't seem too far distant.

The sun was well up and lowering its weight solidly into the canyon when I crawled out of my blankets, but there was a nip in the air, too, that reminded me of George's prediction that the weather would soon change. For the second time in as many days, I walked over to the fire in my stocking feet. I didn't see my boots at first, until George jutted his chin toward the creek and I spotted them sitting on the bank above the stream's purling waters.

"You said your toes were hot," he informed me in a voice that sounded hoarse and painful, a feeling I was sympathetic to. I couldn't recall taking them off, though, or even approaching the creek after we started drinking—one more reason to find another pastime, I told myself.

"Where's Milly?" I asked, easing down in front of the fire. I'd already decided I could fetch my boots later, when my head wasn't quite so throbby.

"Ain't seen her."

I sat there awhile staring into the flames, my curiosity about Milly already waning as my thoughts lurched aimlessly down various alcohol-fogged corridors. After a time George finished his coffee and poured a second cup for himself, then gave me a questioning look. I nodded carefully, not wanting to jar anything loose between my ears, and he filled a mug and passed it over. Milly showed up not too long afterward, her hair wet from washing, her clothes still damp. She fixed a meal for all of us—more rice and beans, as our supply of meat had been whittled down to jerky dust and crumbs by then—and afterward me and George made the hike up to Enoch Anderson's saloon. And damned if I didn't buy another tin mug of forty-rod when I got there, although I was careful to nurse it along and not overindulge as I had the previous two evenings.

When George got into a poker game with some men I didn't know, a penny-ante affair with a four-bit limit, I wandered over to make myself comfortable on a low, time-smoothed ledge where I could watch the game from some yards away and still keep an eye on the lower end of the valley.

As the afternoon progressed, some of the poker players dropped out and others took their places, although there were never more than half a dozen participants at one time. George did all right for himself, winning more than he lost but not pulling in enough to make anyone mad. Toward evening Pit Middleton showed up. He gave me a glance with his good eye but acted like he'd never seen me before. Then he looked at George and tipped his head toward the bar. George nodded but played out his hand, then another, before folding and leaving the table. Although my curiosity was piqued, I stayed where I was.

George and Middleton took their drinks to the back of the chamber, where they stood talking for a good twenty minutes before Middleton walked away with an irritable expression clouding his features. George watched him exit the saloon, then came over to where I was sitting with my by-then empty cup. Easing down beside me, he said, "Did you hear any of that, Elijah Two-Buck?"

"Not a peep, although I noticed Middleton didn't look too happy taking his leave."

"No, he wasn't. I guess Jace talked to him last night before pulling out, but wouldn't tell him where he was going. Pit reckoned I'd know, and didn't believe me when I said I didn't."

"Why would he ask about Jace if he already talked to him last night?"

"He said his boys are gettin' restless and want to move on before Kermit Watson shows up with his posse."

I sat up a little straighter at that. "Do you think Watson'll come here?"

"It ain't likely. I doubt if he could find the place without someone to guide him, and that'd be a death sentence for the man who did it." He looked at me. "That's something you might want to keep in mind, Elijah Two-Buck. Lots of folks have heard about the Notch, but not many know where it is, and a lot fewer have ever seen it. That's the way Enoch means to keep it, even if he has to bury a few souls now and again to keep its location secret."

"Hell, I ain't gonna tell anyone."

"I didn't figure you would, but thought I ought to mention it just in case."

"So what's Middleton going to do?"

"He says they'll hang and rattle awhile. Says Jace talked to him last night about putting together another outfit, but didn't say what it'd be for."

The flesh across the back of my neck rippled coolly. "I thought we'd come here to hide out and stay out of trouble."

91

"Plans change, Elijah Two-Buck."

After a pause, I asked, "Do you think it's because of what J.R. told him?"

"I'd expect so."

"Then it'd be something Watson's up to?"

"More'n likely. It ain't no secret he's sworn to see Jace hung, and the men who ride with him, too."

"Meaning you and me?"

"Maybe not you, not yet, but probably me and a few others. That ol' boy is on the warpath recent-like, and ain't likely to rest until he's got the whole bunch of us either strung up high or buried deep."

"Who else is he after?"

"Pit Middleton and his crew'd be near the top of Watson's list."

I thought about the men I'd met that night on Cottonwood Creek—Three Thumbs Boy, Farrell Crow, Strong Wolf, and that white-eye with the dingy beard called Quintin Haus—and realized with a kind of sinking in my gut that they were likely all camped nearby, sharing the same tight-walled valley refuge with me and George and Milly Bolton. All of us just waiting for Jace to show up and lead us . . . well, no one knew where he intended to lead us. Not then, anyway.

SESSION EIGHT

It occurred to me while you were changing the disk on your recorder that you're probably not all that interested in those days we spent at the Notch. At least not after Pit Middleton got his hackles up over George not telling him what Pit thought George ought to have known about Jace, but didn't. Sure as hell there wasn't anything exciting going on. If you didn't want to make the climb to Enoch Anderson's cliffside saloon to partake of the few amenities available there, then about the only other alternatives were mumblety-peg if you were ambitious, or napping if you weren't.

Nowadays folks read about men like Pretty Boy Floyd and John Dillinger and them and think an outlaw's life must be one of constant excitement—of fast horses back then and fast cars today; of fancy women with lustrous hair, alabaster skin, and shiny red lips; and wagonloads of money stolen from crooked bankers or railroad executives. In my limited experience riding the owlhoot, it wasn't like that at all, and others I've talked to have said the same thing. Men like Black George Holly, J.R. McNeil, and even Bob Hatcher, the little he'd deign to talk to me later on, when things got so desperate for the Kid Jace gang.

But that's all getting ahead of myself, putting the cart before the donkey as they say. What I was getting at is, there's no reason for me to chatter on about all the nothing that happened there in the Notch, so I'm just gonna skip on ahead to when Jace finally reappeared five days later. That's when all the hell that blew up around the Nation over the next few weeks got started.

I didn't even know he was back, none of us did, although I guess he'd showed up the night before and spent some time at Enoch's before making his way along the valley floor looking for recruits. It wasn't much past dawn, the sky still soft gray and the air chilly enough that we were all wearing our jackets as we huddled close to the fire, when Jace rode into camp. He pulled up in front of the lean-to where me and George slept—Milly had built her own small shelter across the fire from us, either for propriety's sake or because she didn't want to be trapped inside a lodge with men who had been drinking rotgut whiskey, if you catch my drift. George's expression never changed when he glanced up to see Jace sitting his tall sorrel staring down at us, but I think my chin might've sagged a couple of inches. The look on Milly's face was more of dread than joy.

Jace didn't say a word at first. He just sat there staring at Milly. Then something seemed to spark inside of him and he got down and came across the ground in long strides, grabbing a stout limb off the stack of firewood as he passed and cocking it over his shoulder. Milly must have known what was in store for her, because she immediately began scooting backward.

"No," she pleaded, and raised an arm protectively above her face.

Jace didn't hesitate. He swung that club low under Milly's arm to whack her solidly across the ribs. She let go of a low, guttural cry, and fell over backward. Rolling swiftly onto her hands and knees, she tried to scramble away, but Jace wouldn't allow it. Following close behind, he brought his club down twice more across her back.

I'd shouted out a protest the first time he struck her. When he hit her a second time I surged to my feet. George reached out as if to grab my arm, then pulled his hand back when he saw the look on my face.

"You had a heap of bad mad swirling around in you that mornin', Elijah Two-Buck," he would eventually confess to me, but at the time all he said was, "Don't, Lige," in an urgent undertone.

But I'd be damned to hell and back before I let that kind of behavior go on. I was across that camp in two quick leaps, latching onto Jace's wrist when he reared back for his next swing. I yanked hard and he spun around with a savage growl, a demon's rage burning so violently in his eyes that my grip instinctively loosened. He jerked his arm free and turned again to raise the club above Milly's bowed form.

"Goddamnit, Jace, no!" I shouted, grasping his shoulder.

He shrugged my hand off and whirled, and the blow he'd intended for Milly caught me upside my head. He didn't hit me hard enough to blow out the lights, but it rattled my senses real good. I staggered back a few paces before catching my heel on a root and going down hard on my back with my arms splayed to either side, staring up at the early morning light that seemed suddenly misty, like a fog had crept over the valley while I wasn't looking. I was blinking rapidly as Jace came over to see if I was dead. He didn't speak, not to me, but after a bit he turned to where Milly lay curled on her side like a doodlebug and grated, "I told you to stay at Red Corn's."

"They didn't want me."

"They didn't have any say in the matter. I told 'em you were staying, and that's damn well what I meant." He raised his club again, and Milly whimpered and turned her face to the ground.

"Jason," I said, struggling to my feet.

"You stay outta this, Lige."

"What would Mama say about hitting a woman?" I asked, using a trump card that had always worked well with us kids in the past. Its effect on Jace that morning sends chills down my spine even today.

"Mama's *dead*," he cried raggedly.

I'd been walking toward him with my fists clenched in determination, but stopped cold as his words slammed into me with far more force than what he'd given my head with that club. For one crazy minute the woods seemed to spin around me, blurring into a kaleidoscope of light and dark. Then my muscles relaxed and my shoulders slumped toward the ground.

"She's dead," he whispered.

"Lord a'mercy," George breathed. He was standing now, looking on in horror. I don't know if he'd ever met Mama, but he surely knew about her from me and Jace.

"Wh . . . what happened?" I asked numbly.

Jace turned away from Milly, and the heavy limb he'd been using on her slipped unnoticed from his fingers. He walked over to the fire to stare into the flames. "It was Kermit Watson, that day Mama sent you looking for me."

I nodded, remembering. "Yeah?"

"He had what he called a posse with him, but they weren't lawmen. They were just . . . just killers. Hired guns."

My pulse was pounding in my ears and my jaw trembled. I spread my feet wide, bracing myself against Jace's words.

"He had his men surround the house, then sent one of them, a dirty back-shooter named Ambrose, up to the house to talk to Mama. He told her they were looking for me, that I was wanted for rustling and suspicion of murder. I guess word about those two Blue River Choctaws," here he glanced at Milly, although there was no regret in his expression for what he'd done that day, "had somehow gotten out." He shrugged. "Lord knows I ain't kept it a secret.

"Anyway, this Ambrose said he knew I was there, and that if I didn't surrender, they'd start shooting. Mama told him I hadn't been around since spring, but he kept insisting I was there, hiding inside the house. He wanted to search it, but Mama got mad and wouldn't let him. I guess he finally believed her, because after a bit he waved Watson up."

"That damn coward," I whispered.

Jace shrugged like it didn't matter, and I guess it didn't. Not in the long run.

"When Watson sent Ambrose back to the barn where the others were hiding, Mama came outside. They stood in the yard talking for a long time. They were arguing about something. Mama finally told Watson to get off her property and never come back. Told him to leave her boys alone, and to be satisfied with all that he had. She was talking loud enough by then that Watson's men could hear her. After a while, Watson stormed back to the barn. They say he was so furious his face was damn near purple." Jace paused a few seconds, then finished with, "He had a cannon."

My head shot up at that. "A what?"

Jace didn't reply right away, but he did raise his gaze from the fire to look at me. As he did, I recalled that cart I'd seen crossing the bottoms along Lick Creek the day I'd left, and the faint rumbling I'd heard descending the far side of Two-Buck Mountain later that afternoon. Like a distant thunder, I'd thought at the time, and my gut tightened with the realization of what it had actually been. While I was riding away, men had been . . . they'd been—

I should apologize for that, and I definitely thank you for turning your recorder off for a few minutes. I'm not usually . . . well, anyway, it was George who spoke first, after Jace finished telling us what had happened. I still remember the disbelief in his voice, the slackness in his expression as he stared at Jace.

"A cannon?" he echoed.

Jace nodded. "One of those little Grasshoppers. Watson

ordered it out of New Orleans, figuring to do a Ned Christie on us." [*Editor's Note:* A "Grasshopper" was a lightweight field cannon used by British forces during the American Revolution and the War of 1812; when assembled it could be maneuvered into place with a pair of poles attached to the rear carriage, which, when in use, sometimes resembled the rear legs of a Grasshopper, thus giving the gun its unique nickname.]

You probably already know about Ned Christie and what they did up there on Ned's Fort Mountain, so I won't go into any detail about that, other than to say I agree with Jace that that's likely where the bastard got the idea. [*Editor's Note:* Ned Christie was a Cherokee accused of killing a U.S. deputy marshal in 1887. Although subsequent evidence strongly suggests Christie was framed for the murder, his suspicion of the federal court under "Hanging Judge" Isaac Parker caused him to flee rather than risk a trial. Christie managed to evade capture for five years before he was surrounded in his home by lawmen in November of 1892, eleven months before Kermit Watson's attack on the Two-Buck home in the Chickasaw Nation. When traditional methods failed to break an extended siege at Christie's heavily fortified cabin, a cannon was brought in; it was also unable to breach the massive twin walls of the Christie home, and ultimately dynamite had to be used to destroy one of the walls. In the ensuing fight Ned Christie and at least two associates—one of them a seven-year-old boy—were killed. For readers who wish to know more about Christie and what became known as Ned Christie's War, an excellent source of information is Devon A. Mihesuah's *Ned Christie: The Creation of an Outlaw and Cherokee Hero.*]

"After some shouting back and forth [Jace continued], Kermit's men started shooting. Mama and Rachel and Noah fired back and kept 'em pinned down for several hours, they say. Then one of Watson's men caught a bullet through the neck

98

and died before he hit the ground. I guess Watson figured that gave him the authority to wheel out that little Grasshopper. They fired three or four cannon balls against the house, but those thick logs Papa used stood up real well. They say those cannon balls left some pretty big dents in the wood, but that the house stood firm, so Kermit ordered his gunner to bring out a grape shell. [*Editor's Note:* Two-Buck probably means *grapeshot,* a shell not unlike a shotgun shell that unleashes numerous rounds of smaller balls, although in this description the item in question was an explosive shell, a sort of bomb within a bomb designed to explode upon impact with its target.]

"They had the cannon down there in the barn's entryway, back in the shadows but with a clear view of the house. They, uh—" Jace stopped, his words jamming up in his throat with a terrible harshness, his face a mask of anguish like I'd never seen before. Taking a deep breath, he forced himself to go on, but the words were strained now, like barbed wire strung so tight it hummed when plucked.

"They fired just two rounds after that. The first one took the door off its hinges. Blew it right off. They say someone inside screamed, Becky, I'd guess."

My own throat tightened. Becky was just six that year, probably terrified by all the gunfire and chaos erupting around her. She wouldn't have understood—how could she?

"Then they fired a second round," Jace said. "It, uh, that one went straight through the door and exploded inside."

I felt something within me wrench violently, like muscle torn loose from bone, a sundering I knew would never completely heal, and to this day it hasn't. "Was . . ." I began, then stopped, not sure what I wanted to ask, or how much I wanted to hear.

"They were killed," Jace said, his voice strangely calm now, his expression smoothing out as if in wonder.

"All of them?" George asked, and Jace nodded.

"All of them. Rachel, Sally, Noah, even . . . even little Becky."

"And Mama?"

Jace nodded a final time. He was staring into the fire again as if he could see them deep down in the flames, looking up alive and smiling. After a couple of minutes I asked about what had become of them, their bodies and all, and he told me the Harpers had seen to the burials. "Laid them to rest under the same oak tree where we buried Papa," he said.

Knowing Sam and Alice Harper, I had every confidence the family, my family, had been interred properly and with dignity. It was comprehending the magnitude of what Watson had done that continued to elude me. "How can he do that?" I asked in the stillness following Jace's narration. "How can he get away with murdering a woman and her children?"

"He'll hire an attorney who'll claim his posse was legal, and that the fault was your mama's for . . . resisting." George replied.

"Resisting what?"

"Whatever he wants to claim, I expect. Hell, I don't know, Elijah Two-Buck, but him and his lawyer'll come up with something." He shook his head at the injustice of it. "Likely he'll tell the Lighthorse it was between two white-eyes, meaning him and your mama, and they won't have any jurisdiction over the crime. Then when the federal deputies show up, he'll claim it was between him and Jace, who is Chickasaw, and that it's an Indian matter. By the time his lawyers get done muddying up the waters they won't be nobody able to sort it out." His voice turned bitter. "Or likely try very hard."

I didn't say anything to that, nor did Jace, and Milly hadn't spoken at all. For a long time the four of us just stood there in petrification, our whole world—mine and Jace's, at least—pulled down to that one tiny patch of earth. Then I walked over to the edge of the trees, keeping my back to the others so that they couldn't see my face and the pain that was twisting it into grotesque forms. I leaned into a hickory tree to keep from falling over, and after a bit Milly came over and stood next to me; she placed a hand gently on my shoulder, but didn't say anything, and for that I was grateful. I think what I appreciated most was just her being there, her gentle touch that let me know I wasn't as alone in the world as I felt at that moment.

After what seemed like hours but probably wasn't more than thirty or forty minutes, judging by the canyon's still-gray light, we gathered back at the fire. Somewhere on his rambles Jace had rustled up some pinto beans and rice and a slab of venison—the latter purchased from a hunter along the Washita River, he claimed—and Milly fixed a simple breakfast that we ate while standing. It was a wanting meal, the meat edging toward bad and the coffee as thin as tea, and George allowed that we'd need to reoutfit soon if we planned to stay holed up much longer.

It was that which finally pulled Jace out of his mournful ruminations. "We ain't stayin'," he said brusquely, and although he didn't elaborate beyond that, I think we all understood what was coming. We just weren't sure yet how it was going to unfold.

After breakfast me and Milly took the dirty utensils down to the creek to wash. I noticed Milly's expression wasn't as tight as it usually was, like she wasn't as on guard about what I might say or do. I considered asking her if that was the first time Jace had ever attacked her like that, but couldn't seem to find the words. Or maybe it was the courage to utter them that I lacked. Either way, I let the matter drop. Regrettably, as soon as I did, thoughts of Mama and the others came slamming through me in a wave of grief that nearly felled me to my knees.

Around noon, Pit Middleton and Three Thumbs Boy showed up on foot. The way they plopped down at the fire without a by-your-leave indicated they'd been invited. They said howdy to Jace and nodded a greeting to George, but ignored me and

Milly like we were clods of dirt. With a white-eye's impatience, Middleton bulled immediately into what was on his mind.

"What's your decision, Kid?"

Kid! There was that name again. I kept forgetting it was how a lot of people in the Chickasaw Nation referred to him.

After eyeing the older man thoughtfully for a couple of minutes, Jace said, "I've already told you my decision."

"You also said you hadn't talked it over with your nigger or your brother." His gaze slewed toward Milly. "Or the girl. What's she doing here, anyway?"

"That gal's none of your business, and George ain't my nigger," Jace replied stonily. I thought he was going to say something else, but George suddenly swelled up like a puff adder about to strike and cut him off.

"I ain't nobody's nigger, Middleton, and you'd best remember that."

Middleton shrugged dismissively, and Jace went on. "They're in or they're out, it's their call. Whatever they decide won't change my mind."

"Maybe you ought to tell us what it is you got on your mind," George suggested.

After a pause, Jace said, "Yeah, I should have already told you." He looked at George first, then me, but didn't even glance toward Milly. "You boys don't have to be a part of this if you don't want to, but I'm going after Watson."

"We figured that much," George replied.

"I reckon you did, but you ought to know that I'm not going after him the way you might think. I'm not going to hunt him down and kill him like the dog he is. I want him to suffer first, the way he's made us Two-Bucks suffer. Kermit Watson has stole just about everything of value we ever had, me and Lige here. And he stole my freedom and good name by having me arrested for something I didn't do."

Jace was talking about Watson's accusation that he'd stolen the man's racehorse, resulting in Jace spending three years in Leavenworth for the crime. But he was also talking about our family, about Papa all that time ago, and Mama and the others that Watson had as much murdered, no matter who had actually lit the cannon's fuse.

George understood that as well, so what he said next puzzled me. "The Lighthorse is going to call for federal marshals to look into this, Jason Two-Buck. That's something you gotta remember."

It was also something we'd already discussed. Hell, it had been George himself who'd claimed Watson's attorneys would sour any legitimate investigation into my family's murders.

"A bunch of federal officers ain't gonna give a hoot in hell about what that bastard did, not if there wasn't no bank robbed or train held up," Jace said, and Middleton and Thumbs nodded quick affirmation.

"I ain't even sure it'd be a federal matter," Middleton added. "Not with their mama being married to a Chickasaw man."

"Them kids was Chickasaws, too," Thumbs said.

"I ain't tryin' to sort out the legalities," George replied. "I'm just saying Watson is white, and they'll be federals poking around out here for a spell. Whatever you got planned, you'd best keep that in mind."

"I don't care who's poking around," Jace said stubbornly. "It won't change my intent."

"Just what is your intent, anyway?" Middleton asked.

"We're gonna grab that devil by his horns," Jace said savagely, "and we ain't lettin' go 'til he hollers 'Quits.' We're gonna rob that bastard dry, take everything he owns and either kill it, burn it, or give it to someone who needs it."

Watching his face, hearing the hollow intensity of his words, I felt a chill worm its way across the back of my neck. This was a

Jace I'd never seen before. Judging from the expression on the faces of George, Pit, and Thumbs, I didn't think they had, either.

"How do you reckon to do that?" Middleton asked cautiously.

"Watson owns stores in Davis, Erda, and Tishomingo. He's got that bank in Erda, and he owns a big chunk of the Chickasaw Express Company, plus all of the cotton and tobacco his sharecroppers farm for him along the Washita."

"Hell, I'd be all for hitting that Erda bank," Middleton said, "but we can't steal twenty tons of cotton or tobacco."

"Then we'll burn it. We'll burn his whole damn harvest and the sheds it's stored in, like he did to our buildings on Two-Buck Mountain." My head came up at that. Noticing, Jace said, "They did, Lige. After they carried Mama and the others outside and left 'em in the yard for the Harpers to find, Watson ordered his men to burn down everything. Had them trample the garden with their horses, too. It's like the son of a bitch wants to wipe us, wipe all sign of us, off the earth."

"Jesus," Middleton whispered. "Well, I can understand your feelings, Kid, but I won't stick my neck out just to watch a barn burn. There has to be something in it for me, or I won't do it."

"There will be," Jace assured him. "We're gonna start with his stage line, then we'll hit his stores."

"What about that bank?"

"I ain't forgettin' it, but we're gonna rob his coaches first. I want him to bleed out slow, so that he can see it coming."

Middleton looked like he was going to balk, until George said, "I reckon there'll be less chance of federal officers getting involved if we do it that way."

"Yeah, I suppose," Middleton allowed after a moment's reflection. Then he leaned forward with his elbows on his knees. "How much do you figure Watson's got in that bank, Kid?"

"I don't know, and I don't much care. I'll need some of it for horses and supplies and such, but you and yours can keep

104

what's left."

"Couple thousand, at least," Thumbs ventured.

"Hell, I bet it'd be closer to eight or ten thousand," Middleton replied, an eagerness coming into his eyes that instantly flashed across the fire to Thumbs. To me, it appeared as if both of them were about to start drooling.

Jace was looking at me. "You don't have to come along on this, Lige," he said, then jutted his chin to George. "Nor you."

"Are you asking us to stay out of it?" George inquired.

"No, but once it starts, there's a good chance it won't end well. Right now neither of you have dodgers on your heads. If you stay, that'll probably change pretty quick." [*Editor's Note:* A "dodger" is an antiquated term referring to a wanted poster; by October of 1893, there was a $500 reward posted for the capture and conviction of Jason "Kid Jace" Two-Buck; no similar reward could be located for George Holly.]

"What happens after Watson is wiped out?" George asked quietly. "Assuming we can do it."

"I ain't looked that far ahead yet," Jace admitted. "I guess if Watson's gone, either dead or flat broke and living in a cave somewhere, there won't be much reason for us to hang on here. If it gets that far, maybe I'll ride down to Mexico and see what kind of future I can make for myself there."

"What about Elijah?"

"He can come with me if he wants to."

After a pause, George said, "All right, Jason Two-Buck, I'll stay and ride the river with you. Let's see where it takes us."

Jace nodded, and I thought he looked relieved. Turning to me, he said, "What about you, Lige?"

"I'm staying," I replied without hesitation. I wanted to get my hands on that devil myself, wanted to twist him down like a bulldogged steer to see him lying in the dirt, bleeding and broke.

I guess, when I look back on it, Kermit Watson is the only man in my life I ever truly hated.

SESSION NINE

Word spread quickly through the Notch that Kid Jace was putting together a new outfit, but we didn't get nearly as many takers as I figured we might. I think maybe it was the brashness of Jace's plan that cowed a lot of them. Oh, they understood his motives, and I suspect most of them shared his feelings toward the Watsons of the world. Hell, we'd all been trampled under a rich man's boot at one time or another. But as a rule, outlaws like easy targets; pudgy bankers and timid shopkeepers are more their style, and they'll usually shy away from anyone they think might fight back.

I'd heard Kermit Watson called a lot of things over the years, but he wasn't fat, and I doubt if he'd ever been timid in anything he did. It just wasn't in his nature. Nor did anyone in the Notch doubt that he'd shoot to protect what was his. Or hire it done if that was more practical. That's something else I've noticed about the Watsons of the world; they don't like to get their hands dirty if they can avoid it.

Another thing that probably held a lot of men back was Jace's determination to focus on just one target. He wasn't proposing a raid on a bank or train, followed by a quick getaway. What he intended would probably be a drawn-out affair against a single but well-equipped enemy, meaning not just Watson, but everything the guy's money could buy—like guns, and the men who knew how to use them. The odds against us would be steep, even I recognized that.

By nightfall we still had Pit Middleton and his crew—Three Thumbs Boy, Farrell Crow, the Kiowa known as Strong Wolf, and the white-eye who called himself Quintin Haus—but only two other men had materialized. One was Harvey Judd, a Texas-born Negro who used to ride with the Bill Eisner gang, robbing and waylaying folks across the Nations until Eisner was gut-shot in the middle of a holdup some years earlier and died not long after in a Cherokee jail. Judd was gray-haired, slope-shouldered, and crippled in one leg from a bullet just above his knee, caught in the same scrape that had cost Eisner his life. But even with that gimpy leg he was as game as any man I've ever met, before or since; there was just plain no back-down in that man, not from anyone.

The other fellow was one I've already mentioned. Bob Hatcher, if you recall, was the gunman who'd challenged us when we first rode into the Notch, and he was a stone-hearted killer by all accounts. George said he'd probably gunned down thirty men over the years, and I've heard as high as one hundred, although that seems excessive, even for a man of Hatcher's reputation. [*Editor's Note:* According to historian Malcomb Combs, Hatcher is credited with nine confirmed killings, and was strongly suspected by the U.S. Marshals Service in the deaths/murders of five others.]

Earlier that afternoon Jace had sent me up to Enoch's saloon to buy several quarts of his best whiskey, although I doubt that there was much difference between his best and worst. I had a half cup of the stuff after supper that night, while we were all sitting around the fire making plans, and it still tasted worse than raw turpentine as far as I was concerned.

I won't even try to list every idea that got tossed around that evening, other than to say that except for me and Milly, everyone had a proposal they were convinced was the best in the herd; some had three and four. Jace sat listening to their counsel for a couple of hours, trying to be polite, I guess, but I could tell he'd already made up his mind. Finally he made a short, cutting motion with his hand, and everyone immediately quieted down.

"Here's what we're gonna do," he said bluntly. "We're gonna hit two coaches at the same time." He meant stagecoaches from the Chickasaw Express Company, of which Kermit Watson owned the controlling interest.

"Why at the same time?" Middleton asked, scowling.

"Number one, because I said we are, and two, because we don't need ten men to hold up one stagecoach." He paused as if waiting for Middleton to reply with something combative; when he didn't, Jace went on. "George is gonna take five men west of here and catch the coach outta Ardmore two days from now. The rest of you will come with me and we'll stop the line somewhere east to Caddo. I've got it figured to hit both of them at the same time, give or take a few hours. Anybody got any questions?"

Bob Hatcher glanced briefly at George, then looked Jace square in the eye. "I reckon I'll ride with you, Kid, unless you don't want me. If that's the situation, I'll cut my pin now and move on."

"Meaning you won't ride with a Negro?"

"Oh, I don't mind riding *with* niggers. I just won't ride *behind* one."

I was kind of surprised when, after a long pause, Jace relented. "All right, you're with me. You, too, Pit. Lige and Thumbs," Jace's gaze swept the rest of us, "Farrell Crow and Harvey Judd, you four will go with George. Anybody got anything else to complain about?"

No one spoke, and that was it, so damn simple and quick it didn't hardly seem real. Rising, Jace said, "I'm turning in, boys. We'll be riding out of here at first light. Them that ain't with us can stay behind." Then he walked away, but not before dropping the cup he'd been drinking his whiskey from in the dirt next to Milly's knee, where she'd been sitting back a ways listening to the men talk and likely wondering where all their planning was going to leave her.

After a while Hatcher stood and moved off in the opposite direction. One by one, the others followed, scattering into the trees to find their own camps. Finally only me and George and Milly were left at the fire, until Milly, keeping her eyes lowered, picked up Jace's cup and took it down to the creek to wash. When we were alone, I glanced at George, and I don't believe I've ever seen a more worried or melancholy expression on a man's face.

True to his word, Jace was in his saddle by first light the next morning, following the creek toward the Notch's solitary access. The rest of us came behind in single file, shoulders hunched to the deepening cold. There were a couple of men at the entrance when we got there, one of them up high where Bob Hatcher had been the day me and Jace and George rode in. For a minute I thought maybe they wanted to join us, but when they waved us on through I realized they were doing the same thing Hatcher had, standing guard against Lighthorse posses and U.S. deputy marshals. I reckon if we'd been there much longer, Enoch would have expected me and George to put in our time as sentries, as well.

We wound back through the deep forest to the wagon trace we'd followed east from Henry McFarland's farm. There, Jace and George rode off a ways to palaver in private. When they came back, George gathered his crew with a quick wag of his finger and started off to the west. I lingered for a few seconds, but Jace was deep in conversation with Hatcher and Middleton and was paying me no mind, so I quick-like heeled after the others.

About fifty yards or so down the trace, I glanced back to see Jace leading his bunch east at a swift trot. That was no less than what I expected. What nabbed my attention was seeing Milly sitting her little bay in the middle of the road, the pack mule held close beside her on a short lead. I started to pull up, thinking maybe her horse had turned balky, but as soon as I did she reined in my direction and gave the bay a swift jab with her heels. I started to holler at George, but he'd already spotted what was happening. Catching my eye, he grinned and winked like he'd just shared a joke I apparently hadn't heard. Then he pivoted back to face the horizon, leaving me to ponder this unexpected turn of events with all the insight of an average sixteen year old—meaning I hadn't a clue what had happened to pry her off of Jace's coattails.

Milly caught up and fell in beside me but didn't speak or even glance my way as far as I could tell. That suited me, as I figured anything I might say to her would only earn me a scathing glare in return.

We continued on past noon, curving gradually southward around the western terminus of the Arbuckle Mountains. The air was noticeably cooler now than it had been when we came this way the last time, just after abandoning those Durham cows over by Tucker. There was a lot more color up high, too— golds and browns and vivid reds where the oaks were edging into their brightest shades.

Toward evening we came to a farm where George knew the daddy, a Chickasaw sharecropper named Bluford who, along with his family, was butchering a couple of two-year-old barrows for winter meat. [*Editor's Note:* A "barrow" is a castrated male hog.] We hauled up at the edge of the yard while George rode in alone to negotiate a meal and a place to stay in exchange for our helping with the processing. Although most of the hard work—the killing, gutting, and skinning—had already been completed, there was still plenty to do with the boning and cutting, then storing the pork in two-gallon crocks and covering it with melted lard to preserve the meat against spoilage.

It turned out to be a good deal for everyone, as our extra knives made quick work of those two hogs, while Milly and the Bluford women set out a feast of fresh-cut corn, fried squash, souse, blood sausage, chops as thick as your palm, and two big frying pans of cornbread. There was both coffee and blackberry wine to wash it down with, and a sugary blackberry cobbler swimming in rich cream for dessert. I'll tell you what, we might have been a hungry bunch riding in—grub in the Notch had been largely skimpy and of poor quality—but by the time we waddled out to the barn and tumbled into our blankets that evening, I believe we were all about to pop a few buttons off our britches.

Milly slept inside with the Bluford's oldest daughter, a girl not much younger than she was. I could tell they did some cleaning up after us men retired to the barn, because the next morning at breakfast—more pork chops and ham, along with eggs and grits in cream—Milly's hair held a gleam I'd never noticed before. Her clothes looked recently laundered and freshly pressed, too. I'll say here that Milly Bolton bathed more than any woman I ever knew; it would be several more years before I'd finally figure out why.

And since I'm already getting off track here, let me tell you something about the kind of men I was riding with, so that you don't get the idea they were all rotten to their cores. While we were sitting around the big harvest table in the cabin's main room at breakfast the next morning, Three Thumbs Boy began putting on a performance for Bluford's two youngest kids, boys who couldn't have been more than four or five years old. Thumbs was acting like he wasn't aware of them watching, but you could tell he was, and he was having a fine ol' time showing off that extra appendage of his. He'd wiggle it back and forth like a worm on a hook, then use it to scratch inside his ear or dig around in his nose—he was crude to do that at the table, but a lot of men back then were, and still are—or use it to push his scrambled eggs onto the spoon he was holding with the same hand. Those boys were enthralled by his antics, too, owl-eyed and slack-jawed, and not a peep out of them the whole meal.

I'll tell you, that little digit of Thumb's was an oddity to attract anyone's attention. It sprouted from the top of his regular thumb like a wilted flower, maybe an inch and a half long but no bigger around than a slim pencil. The thing that made it unique was its suppleness. Although joined solidly at its base, it could bend at mid-joint like any other thumb at the table that day; I'll guarantee those Bluford boys weren't the only ones watching the show that morning.

Anyway, it was a pleasant interlude in an otherwise gloomy time, with good food and good company, and I think we were all in a better mood when we rode out that day. We were heading due south now, toward the road linking Ardmore and Tishomingo, the railroad having not yet reached the latter destination. We camped that second night in a brushy draw—a cold camp on cold ground, with cold pork chops and chilled canteen water for our supper—and the next day George led us to where a well-graded road crossed a shallow flow of water he called Camp Creek. It was about midmorning when we got there. After a few minutes staring at the muddy ford and the road beyond it, he motioned for us to follow him behind a hill a couple of hundred yards away where we wouldn't be spotted by passersby.

"We might as well make ourselves comfortable," George announced as he stepped down from his saddle. "We'll be here a spell."

"How long of a spell?" Farrell Crow asked.

I haven't said much about Farrell yet, have I? Even though he and Thumbs seemed like good friends, I doubt that you'll ever find two more disparate individuals. Where Thumbs was short and chunky and not quite as sharp as a cheap folding knife, Farrell was long and lean, a keen observer of the world around him. About the only thing those two had in common was that they were both young, male, and Chickasaw, and in that part of the country the latter was a damn sight more important than the two formers.

George eyed Farrell thoughtfully for a minute, maybe wondering if the younger man was challenging him, but Farrell's expression remained only mildly curious, without threat.

" 'Til the coach shows up, I reckon," George finally replied. "It'll be a few hours yet, if it's on schedule."

Farrell nodded and got down with the rest of us and loosened the cinch on his saddle, as I did with Minko. I took the bridle off too and hung it from the saddle horn so the pinto could graze. George sent Harvey up to the top of the hill to watch for the Ardmore stage while the rest of us scattered out under some nearby trees. Farrell and Thumbs immediately lay back in the tall grass like they planned to catch up on lost sleep. Or pack away some extra in case things went bad with that Ardmore stage. Milly led her bay horse and the mule well away from the rest of us before she also settled down to wait. George sagged down nearby and rolled a cigarette, his expression distractedly pensive. As for me, I had about two million questions ricocheting around inside my skull, but I kept them penned up as I could tell George was deep in contemplation and likely wouldn't be receptive to a greenhorn's inquires. Shortly after noon Harvey wandered down from the hill and announced the stage was on its way.

"Be here in thirty minutes or so, the way it's poking along," he stated.

Well, we all stood and readied our mounts, and I'll admit I was as nervous as a mouse in a snake's burrow. The others were acting like they were all going out on a lazy Sunday afternoon ride without a care or concern to muddle their thoughts, although I'd eventually learn they were as anxious as I was, just more adept at hiding it.

Although no one summoned Milly, she must have noticed our actions because she showed up before most of us had scaled our saddles. Spying her, George said, "You stay here, girl."

"I can help."

"I know you can, but you stay here anyway and keep a tight hold on that mule. That's your job."

"Any fool can hold a lead rope," she argued.

"But it's you I gave the job to."

Milly's jaw slid back and forth at that, but she finally nodded and pulled the pack animal up next to her. The way she was gripping the halter rope, I figured that mule stood a better chance of escaping a corral full of grizzly bears than it did of breaking away from Milly.

Taking a deep breath, George let his gaze sweep over the rest of us like a slow-moving wind. "This is it, boys. Let's go make some history."

I didn't know what he meant by that, but it turns out it was something Jace had cooked up on his ride back to the Notch, after learning about Watson's attack on our farm. Jace wanted to hit Watson hard, and by robbing two of his stagecoaches at the same time, he'd let the world know the Kid Jace gang was a force to be reckoned with. It would also be—at least as far as we knew—the first anyone had ever robbed two coaches at the same time. [*Editor's Note:* Two-Buck seems to be correct. Despite an extensive search, the editor was unable to locate any reference to two stagecoaches being held up at different locations at approximately the same time and by the same gang.]

We rode back around the base of the hill to the east side of the ford. A low banner of dust hung above the horizon half a mile west of us, the Chickasaw Express coach rolling along under it at a leisurely clip. Pointing to some bankside scrub north of the road, George told Farrell and Thumbs to wait in there.

"Stay back in the brush until we get the coach stopped, then come out where they can see you. Make sure you have your pistols drawn when you do."

Now, to me, that last part seemed a little unnecessary, but I'd soon learn you can't count on much of anything when it comes to robbing folks at gunpoint. Nerves have a way of tripping up the best-laid plans, so it's generally good policy to have everything spelled out beforehand.

George sent Harvey Judd into the shelter of some low willows south of the road with the same instructions, then gave me a gloomy eye. "You're to stay with me, Elijah Two-Buck."

I nodded and slid the Marlin from its scabbard. I didn't have to check to make sure there was a round chambered. I'd already picked up that habit of the owlhoot.

When the others were out of earshot, George said, "I reckon you know you look a lot like your brother." When I allowed that I did, he went on. "Jace wants to take advantage of that, and maybe confuse the Lighthorse, if not Kermit Watson. You and me ain't gonna be wearing bandannas over our faces like the others. We'll have our mugs hung out where everyone can see 'em. Then at some point I'm supposed to call you Jace. Or Kid Jace, if I can make it sound natural. You savvy what I'm getting at?"

I nodded solemnly. Or maybe queasily would be a better description. So far the law didn't know me from a shoat in a drift of hogs, but that was going to change real soon. If not with this robbery, then not long after, when folks realized Kid Jace's little brother had turned outlaw. I thought about that for a minute, especially about what Mama and Papa would have said had they been alive. But you see, they weren't. They were both of them dead, and all because of one man.

"How you feel about that?" George asked quietly.

"As long as it's that son of a bitch Kermit Watson we're robbing, I ain't got no qualms about it."

George nodded as if satisfied. "That's good, because that's all we're robbing. Any passengers they got riding the line, we're to let them go unharmed." He chuckled, I guess at the relieved expression on my face. "That make it easier for you to swallow, Elijah Two-Buck?"

"Yeah, I reckon it does," I admitted. I could hear the stage drawing closer now, the rattle of harness chains and creak of the thorough braces. George jerked his head to the rear and we rode off about thirty yards, east of the crossing and north of the road.

"Soon as that coach gets down in the creek and out of sight, you and me are gonna gig our horses out in front of 'em," he explained tersely. "With any luck, they won't even know we're here until they pop out on this side of the ford."

I nodded. I think outwardly I was doing all right, but I'm not ashamed to confess that my throat felt as dry as moldy hay, and that my palms were slick with perspiration despite the cool autumn air; especially around the Marlin's checkered wrist, where I was holding on tight with my right hand, its steel butt gouging into my thigh. I remember how odd it felt, sitting there preparing to commit armed robbery when only a couple of weeks earlier I'd been home, me and Noah prying bots out of our milk cow's hide while Mama and Rachel were at the house wrapping up the season's canning. Even now there's a kind of dreamlike quality to that day, my first deliberate step over the line into outlawry.

"Here she comes," George said, and I blinked and looked up just as the lead team in a six-horse hitch surged up out of the Camp Creek crossing.

George was already spurring his black horse into the middle of the road. I smacked my heels into Minko's ribs and that little paint horse took off after George's Coal like he'd been born to rob stagecoaches. We reached the middle of the road about the same time the driver and messenger—messenger is what they often called the guy who rode beside the linesman; most of them usually carried a shotgun, but this guy was toting a Winchester—heaved up into view. The driver shouted a startled warning, and before either me or George could tell them to haul up and raise their hands, that damn messenger shouldered his long gun and let fly. Out of the corner of my eye I saw George leave his saddle like a—

SESSION TEN

Like a sparrow leaves a branch.

There, I finished my sentence, and to hell with that machine of yours. I swear I'm gonna take a sledgehammer to that persnickety son of a bitch before you've got this story all the way recorded.

Anyway, like I was saying before you ran out of disk, that messenger let off a round that swept poor ol' George Holly out of his saddle, and left me sitting there like a toad on a stump. In all my imagining of what might happen that day, George getting shot before the driver even got his rig stopped never even entered my mind.

That driver, his name was either Matthew or Matthews—first or last, I never caught—immediately started hollering for the messenger to quit shooting. [*Editor's Note:* An article from the Erda *Eagle* dated November 3, 1893, lists the name of the driver as Kyle Matthews, but only offers the last name of the messenger, referring to him as "young Donahue."]

"They ain't wearin' masks, you blasted fool," was one of the things the driver shouted, and, "Put that damned rifle up before you shoot someone else," was another. There were a few choice curse words sprinkled around in the mix, too, but they wouldn't really advance the story any.

I noticed right off that the messenger was youngish, probably no more than a year or two older than I was—white faced, grass green, and scared yellow—but at Matthews's command he im-

119

mediately raised his Winchester's muzzle and took his finger off the trigger. That obviously worked to our advantage, because by the time the driver got his rig stopped and realized his mistake, Harvey Judd, Farrell Crow, and Three Thumbs Boy had flushed their horses out of the brush and had the coach surrounded.

While Farrell took charge of the one-sided transaction with the driver, I leapt from Minko's saddle and knelt at George's side. The bullet had taken him in the chest, not square but high and to one side. Although he was awake, he wasn't really aware; his face was kind of gray and his eyes were wide and glassy-looking. Putting my hand on his shoulder, I came close to asking one of the stupidest questions you can ask a man who's just been shot: *Are you hurt?* Fortunately, I clamped down on the words before they could slip out.

"George?"

"Damn, Lige," he hissed, forgetting, I suppose, that he almost always called me either Elijah or the whole thing—Elijah Two-Buck.

"How bad is it?"

He chuckled, although there wasn't much spirit in it. "It gets your attention."

I took out my Green River and, as gentle as I could, started slicing the fabric of his shirt back far enough to see the wound. Over by the coach there was a lot of angry shouting and slamming of things like doors and messenger and such. Men and women were spilling out the north-side door like they were getting booted in the butt from inside, which I later learned they were. Harvey had crawled in the opposite side and was herding them out with stern commands and a cocked Colt. I saw some of it, but not all, and when I was able to get a look at George's wound, I quit paying attention altogether.

Truth to tell, the damage didn't look as bad as I'd feared it might. There was a small hole rimmed with purplish flesh and a little oozing blood, but no splintered bone or pumping streams of coral that might have indicated a severed artery. I eased him onto his side to have a look at the exit wound. It was naturally larger than where the bullet had entered—probably twice that size—but it was still fairly modest. I wish now I'd taken note of the messenger's rifle, as I'll bet it was a smaller caliber, but at the time it never even occurred to me.

I was still examining the tiny crater in his chest when rapidly thudding hooves broke my concentration. Glancing over my shoulder, I saw Milly galloping up with the pack mule in tow, the mule high-headed and crazy-eyed, while Milly's expression leaned more toward grim. She swung down from her saddle before her horse had come to a complete stop and flung the reins over the bay's neck so that he wouldn't step on them. The mule snorted his opinion of the situation and stalked off to sulk. "Move," was Milly's curt command, and I happily obliged.

"Lige," George rasped, lifting his head to find me.

"I'm here."

"Don't let them hurt the passengers. Jace was real clear about that."

"I won't."

"And Lige." His head sank back to the ground like it was too much effort to keep it raised. "Burn the coach."

I hesitated only a moment, then nodded my understanding. Jace wanted Kermit Watson to suffer, and setting fire to a fifteen-hundred-dollar Concord stagecoach was going to hit the bastard where it would hurt the most. With rifle in hand, I walked over to where Farrell and Thumbs had five passengers and the driver clustered some yards off the road. Harvey was still at the coach, pistol-whipping the messenger something fierce until I hollered for him to stop. He did, but only for a moment. The messenger was pressed back against the front wheel, his elbows hooked over the upper arc of the rim, his face torn and bloody.

After a puzzled glance my way, Harvey lifted his revolver for another slashing blow, and I repeated my command for him to quit. This time I raised the Marlin level with his midsection for emphasis.

"What the hell's the matter with you?" he demanded.

"I said to let him go."

Harvey pulled his left hand away from the messenger's chest, and the guy dropped like a sack of bloody stones. "I'd advise you to lower that rifle, sonny, before I forget who you are."

I shook my head in stubborn anger. "We're not hurting the passengers."

"He ain't a passenger."

"We're not hurting him or the driver, either. Damnit, I mean it."

"Who says we ain't hurtin' the driver or messenger?" Farrell demanded from over near where the paying customers were looking on with a kind of stupefying dread, like they were anticipating the same treatment before their ordeal was over.

"Kid Jace." I said it loud and flat, so that there wouldn't be any misunderstanding.

Now, if you recall, me and George were supposed to work that into the conversation anyway, so that the driver and passengers would think I was Jason Two-Buck, and that this was his crew. I reckon tossing Jace's name out like that did it, too, even if it wasn't intentional. More important, it also reminded Farrell and them who was in charge, whether Jace was there or not.

It must have gotten through to Harvey, at least, because he grudgingly stepped back and holstered his revolver. Then he did something that confounded me. He yanked his bandanna down so that everyone could see his face. After an uncertain pause, Farrell and Thumbs also pulled down their masks, and Farrell said, "This here is the Kid Jace outfit, and we're robbing the

Chickasaw Express. You folks won't be hurt unless you do something stupid to cause your own pain, like that messenger over there did." He tipped his head toward the crumpled form lying next to the Concord's front wheel, and it was like there was a wire attached to the chins of the driver and his passengers, the way they all yanked their heads in that direction at the same time.

Harvey had meanwhile crawled up into the driver's box to poke around under the seat. After a minute he came back down and walked over to the driver. "Where's it at?" he growled.

"Where's—" he began, then shut up real fast when Harvey drew his revolver.

"You ain't gonna have a messenger ridin' a coach that ain't got some kind of valuables on it," Harvey said.

Deciding against heroics, the driver nodded toward the vehicle's rear boot. "In there, a little red-leather trunk tucked behind the other luggage. There's a padlock on the hasp but I don't have the key." Jutting his chin toward the messenger, he said, "He doesn't, either."

Harvey told him he'd better not be lying, then stalked around to the rear of the coach and began unbuckling the boot's cover. While he did that, I pulled the hitch pin, loosened the tugs, and drove the harness stock out of the way. Then I dragged the messenger over by the others—he was out cold by then, but thankfully still breathing—before returning to the coach and climbing inside.

Those Concord stagecoaches were nice. This one had plush leather seats dyed a soft tan color, green roller shades above the windows to keep out dust or rain, and brass carriage lamps fixed to the inside walls for light, should they be late getting in. Not finding any luggage or purses, I drew my sheath knife and started slicing the seats open to reveal the packed cotton batting inside. After drawing out several handfuls that I fluffed up into nests, I backed out the door and went to see what the others were up to.

With Thumbs keeping his revolver trained on the driver and passengers, Farrell had clambered up top and was tumbling the passengers' luggage to the ground. Harvey did the same with what he found in the boot. Then both of them kicked the trunks and valises away from the coach. Harvey had found the little red chest the driver had mentioned and was cradling it in his left arm like an infant. It was about ten inches long and six-by-something elsewhere, and seemed pretty light, the way he held it. When our gazes met, Harvey nodded his icy go-ahead, and I went back to unscrew the bases from the lamps and pour the coal oil over the shredded seats, the floor, and along the sidewalls. Then I stepped back . . . and hesitated.

"Light it, kid," Farrell said, and I pulled a match from my vest pocket, struck it on the iron rim of the rear wheel, and tossed it inside.

The fire caught with a low but volatile whoosh, the flames quickly engulfing the loose batting, then slithering up the inside walls like a dozen writhing serpents. I stepped back from the crackling blaze and glanced almost guiltily at the driver, but he just shrugged. I guess after what he'd witnessed happening to the messenger, he was content to let us do what we wanted and stay out of it.

That coach burned a lot quicker than I would have expected, and I've sometimes wondered if it wasn't all that polish they used to maintain the wood's rich, ebony glow. I watched until the flames were darting out the windows, reminding me of departing travelers waving a final goodbye, then walked over to where Milly was kneeling at George's side. I thought he looked a little better; still shocked and weak, but not as bat-eyed as he'd been earlier. Hunkering down opposite Milly, I asked how he was faring.

"He's been shot," she replied tartly; her old snarly attitude returned under a full head of steam.

"I know he's been shot," I flared. "Can he be moved?"

She gave me a wary look, taken aback, I suppose, by my testy reply. Her expression was similar to the look I'd seen on Harvey's face when I ordered him to quit pistol-whipping the messenger, although in his case I suspect the fact that I was Kid Jace's brother added some iron to my command.

Those two little incidences didn't put me in charge of the outfit, though. I learned that sometime later—after we'd sent the driver, his passengers, and the messenger, who had sort of regained consciousness, hoofing it back to Ardmore—when I suggested we take George to either the Bluford farm or the Notch to recuperate.

Farrell Crow immediately shot down both destinations. He said it wouldn't be fair to the Blufords to lead a posse to their door after they'd been so kind in feeding us and putting us up in their barn for the night, and the Notch was out of the equation altogether, to which Thumbs and Harvey both quickly concurred.

"The Notch ain't a place to run to if there's a bunch of badge-toters hound-doggin' our scent," Harvey said. "Old Enoch'd shoot the whole bunch of us if we showed up at his hideout right after robbin' a stagecoach."

"We'd stand a better chance against a posse than we would Enoch," Farrell added.

"Then where can we take him?"

Me and Farrell and Harvey were standing a few yards away from George by then, over near where Thumbs was hanging onto the cheek strap of the Express team's ncar-side leader; the horses were still in harness, as we'd decided to take them with us as soon as we agreed on a destination. Hearing a low mumble from where George was lying with his head in Milly's lap, his chest and shoulder bandaged with an extra shirt from Farrell Crow's kit, we all looked his way. With our attention arrested, George motioned us closer.

"We're supposed to meet Jace on the Greasy Bend," he said, looking at me but speaking to all of us.

"I know, but that's too far away for a man with a hole through his middle," I said.

"Ain't got no choice," he replied huskily. " 'Sides, it ain't all that bad." He made a vague motion toward his chest. "If it was, I'd know it. Put me on Coal, and if I get to feeling poorly I'll pull out and let you boys go on without me."

"We're not going anywhere without you," Milly stated firmly.

Reaching up, George lightly patted the back of her hand where it rested atop his shoulder. "It'll be all right, Milly Bolton. You can stay with me if I have to quit the bunch. We'll let the others go on without us. I don't reckon I could be in better hands than yours, anyway."

Milly's eyes grew suddenly moist. "You're going to be all right," she told him, and if determination had anything to do with it, he was as good as cured right there.

I went to fetch George's horse, and with Farrell and Harvey's help we got him in his saddle. I offered to lead Coal behind Minko, but George said no.

"The day I can't handle my own pony is the day I hang up my spurs," he asserted, although still in that grating tone that told me he was hurting, whether he'd admit it or not.

I handed George his reins, then climbed into my own saddle. Off to the west I could see the Chickasaw Express passengers, tiny figures trudging through the dust toward Ardmore. It was going to be a long and footsore day for those folks, but it'd also be one they'd remember for the rest of their lives. And once word got out about what Kermit Watson had done to my family, maybe those folks would understand why we did what we did, and hopefully appreciate that we didn't take anything from them except time and a little shoe leather.

Thumbs had tied up the loose ends of the harness to keep the horses from stepping on something and breaking it or tripping and falling, then strung them out one behind the other like a string of pack animals. Swinging astride his own mount, he led the Express horses over to where the rest of us were waiting.

Say what you want about Kermit Watson, but he ran a first-class stage line, and those horses showed his dedication to quality. They were fine animals, every one of them, even if they were all sporting the corporation's *C-Bar-Ex* brand, representing the Chickasaw Express Company.

We had to go slow on account of George, which I could tell was worrying Harvey and Farrell. Even Thumbs kept looking over his shoulder every few minutes as if expecting immediate pursuit, no matter that it would take those folks from the coach the rest of the day to hike back to Ardmore.

Me and Milly rode up front with George, both of us keeping a vigilant eye on him. He seemed to be hanging on all right, despite occasionally spitting up some blood that he'd wipe from his lips with the cuff of his shirtsleeve. You could tell he was hurting, though. Talk is cheap when the pinched look on your face tells a different story.

It was full dark by the time we reached the Washita. That river runs mostly southeast across the Chickasaw Nation, but where we came upon it that evening its course angled more north to south. I wasn't sure which way to go from there, but Farrell said, "upstream," so that was the direction I took. We followed the right-hand bank until we came to a ferry shortly after midnight, and I once more pulled rein. It was Farrell who gigged his horse forward to hail the cabin. Silence greeted his shout, so he tried again, telling the ferry operator we wanted to cross. As you might expect, the guy wasn't happy being dragged out of his blankets in the middle of a frosty night.

"Come back in the morning when it's light," he hollered. Then, as if in afterthought, "It's fifty cents for a horse and rider. If you don't have the cash, you'll have to swim across."

I glanced at the river. The Washita was low enough at that late date that we likely could have found a place to cross without having to swim too far, if at all. The reason we didn't was because of George, who, as the evening progressed, had taken to clinging to his saddle horn with both hands, his face dipped toward Coal's withers.

After a growled curse, Farrell shouted, "We're six, but I'll pay you five dollars to take us over tonight."

Ain't it funny how hard cash speaks its own language. After a brief silence, the guy allowed that he'd do it. "But I'll need to see the money up front," he added, which I considered a savvy request.

"I've got it right here," Farrell returned. "Come on, damnit, we're in a hurry."

The front door creaked open and the ferryman eased outside. He was carrying an unlit lantern in one hand and what looked like a double-barreled shotgun in the other. He set the lantern on the porch, then moved the shotgun to both hands, although he was careful to keep its muzzles pointed skyward. Without taking his eyes off of us, he called over his shoulder, "That's right, honeybunch, you keep that buffalo gun pointed right at 'em, and the first one reaches for a pistol, you start shooting."

To our rear, Harvey Judd hawked up a choking guffaw. "Hank, you old skinflint, you ain't married, and you ain't got no honeybunch. Hell, there ain't a woman in these parts'll have you unless she's blind and can't smell."

After an uncertain pause, the ferryman said, "Harvey, is that you?"

"Yeah, it's me." He took his hat off and heeled his mount

forward so the ferryman could see him better in the waning moonlight.

"Darnation, you old coot, why didn't you sing out sooner? You could have kept me from making a fool of myself."

"I could've sang out from Texas and you'd have still have found a way to make a fool outta yourself. How you been, you damned horse thief?"

"Middling, mostly." Hank leaned his shotgun against the cabin's front wall and stepped out into the moonlight with just his lantern, though it remained unlit. "What brings you this far west?"

"Just passing through, but we've got an injured man we need to get across the river."

"Well, hell, come on down and climb aboard." His gaze raked the knot of us in a calculating manner. "Now, which one of you boys was it promised me five dollars?"

"That would be me," Farrell groused, dragging a leather poke from his coat pocket. From his tone it occurred to me that he might not have intended to pay Hank anything, that he might even have contemplated robbing the man outright, or at least chiseling him out of his fare. I suspect it was Harvey's acquaintance with the ferry operator that doused the flames of that idea.

Hank, meanwhile, was staring past Farrell to where Thumbs sat his saddle with the string of coach horses in tow. "You said six. You didn't mention any extra horses."

"Five dollars is plenty, no matter how many horses we've got," Farrell said, an edge coming into his voice.

"Well, we sure as shootin' ain't gonna get all of you and them horses across in one trip, I can tell you that right now."

"Then we'll make two trips," Farrell said, his fingers paused inside the poke, his words reminding me of ice hardening over stone.

My impression of Farrell Crow up until then had been largely positive. He'd seemed like a decent sort, mild-mannered and quick to smile, and he'd remained patient and friendly with Thumbs even when the chubby Chickasaw's prattle chafed the rest of us. I'd kind of imagined him drifting into outlawry in much the same manner I had—not something I'd set out to do, but something chance had tipped me into without my really seeing it coming—but that night I witnessed a coldness in the man that seemed to reach out from his core, and I thought: *Here's someone I'd never want to cross.*

Hank must have sensed it, too, because he quickly nodded and said, "Yes, I suppose we'll have to," and you could tell he was no longer thinking about being paid for that second trip, either. "Well, let's get it done," he added briskly, and led us down to a splintered slip where his low-hulled ferry was berthed.

Harvey and Farrell followed close behind, and I noticed Farrell had returned his poke to his pocket without paying. I wasn't anticipating the subject of money to come up again, but was smart enough by then not to involve myself in the negotiations.

We dismounted and led our horses onboard one at a time, all save George, who seemed to have drifted away from cognizance for a while. By turning our mounts sideways to face downstream, we got everyone on for the first crossing except Thumbs and the coach horses. It was cold out there on the river, where a stiff breeze seemed to drift along with the current. I could see my breath against the pale band of the water, and Minko's, too. I mention that because right about then I peered up at George and noticed sweat just a'drippin' off his face. He was aware of me looking at him and tried to speak, but no words came out.

"We'll stop on the other side," I told him, but he shook his head and wet his lips, and this time managed to squeeze out a short sentence.

"I can do it."

"I know you can. I just ain't sure we need to."

"No, keep goin'. We'll be there by dawn. Jace can take over after that."

I patted his knee. "It won't be much longer," I said, and he nodded and closed his eyes. I felt sorry for the guy, I surely did, but the decision to stop or keep riding was his to make. Me, I had no choice. By that time I was feeling like a twig in floodwaters—no idea where I was going but with a dread inside that no matter where it led, it wasn't going to end well.

SESSION ELEVEN

Me and Milly stayed next to George all the way across the Washita, ready to grab him if he looked like he was going to topple from his seat, but Hank brought us into the far shore with barely a nudge. George didn't even look up as I led Coal to solid ground, which was worrisome. Nor did I like the way he kept slipping in and out of awareness, if not unconsciousness. From time to time Milly would glance at me across the withers of George's black horse, her deep brown eyes large and solemn in the moonlight, but she kept her thoughts to herself.

We waited on the far bank while Hank went back to fetch Thumbs and the harness stock. It didn't take but twenty minutes before we were all together again. I was kind of anxious about what might happen after Thumbs came ashore, wondering if Hank would demand his fee or if Farrell would refuse it, so I was surprised when Farrell pulled several bills from his pocket and handed them over.

"That's ten dollars," he told Hank. "For the ride, and for you to forget you gave it to us."

Looking even more relieved than I felt, Hank quickly pocketed the money and started backing toward his craft. "I never saw a soul," he assured Farrell, then scuttled in and pushed off for home.

Farrell laughed softly and pulled his horse around. I mounted and reined over next to George and spoke his name, but he didn't respond. He was still clinging tightly to his saddle, though. Watching from a few yards away, Harvey said, "Take his reins, Lige. If it looks like he's gonna fall off, we'll have to tie him down, but it'd be better for him if we don't." He looked at Farrell. "You know where we're supposed to rendezvous with Kid?"

"Yeah, it's up the road a piece."

"Lead out," Harvey instructed, and Farrell headed for a narrow track winding back into the trees. The rest of us fell in behind him. Way off to our left I heard the low rumble of thunder—the real thing this time, and not some maniac's Grasshopper cannon—and knew we were in for a soaking. Glancing over my shoulder to where George swayed loosely atop Coal's saddle, I hoped we'd reach some kind of solid shelter before it arrived. The last thing George needed that night was to be caught out in wet weather.

It was another couple of hours before we left the Erda Road to plunge into near total darkness beneath a canopy of brittle autumn leaves. [*Editor's Note:* Although no mention of an "Erda Road" could be located outside of the Two-Buck transcript, the route described here seems to correlate with the current Greasy Bend Road of Johnston County.] The trail took us in a more or less westerly direction, although I'll admit it was hard to keep track of our route through such thick timber. The clouds had rolled in to obliterate the moon, hanging low enough that I could feel their moistness against my cheeks. Had the sun been up I'm sure it would have revealed a soupy fog creeping through the trees.

It didn't seem quite as dark by the time we reached a shallow cove several miles into the timbered ridges. Farrell led us to the far side of the little glade and dismounted. I paused a moment, looking around to see what I could of our surroundings and was kind of surprised that I saw anything at all; the night was about done, dawn coming on timidly through a gray mist. Even in such poor light I could tell it was going to be a decent place to hole up for a while. There was a nice spring coming out of a rocky ledge to the north, good grass for the horses, and plenty of old, downed timber for firewood.

Milly spread George's bedroll out under the trees while me and Farrell eased him from his saddle. We laid him down on his blankets and covered him up, then set about building a small lean-to over him. Although neither as large nor as tight as the one George had constructed in the Notch, it would keep the worst of the rain off of him, and it wasn't long before it started, a fine drizzle carried slantwise on the breeze.

While Thumbs fashioned hobbles out of the long reins from the stage to secure the harness stock, Harvey and Farrell saw to the rest of the horses. I noticed them talking between themselves and glancing our way now and again, but didn't think anything of it at the time—another lesson learned the hard way.

Even as tiny as it was, it didn't take the others long before they crawled into the lean-to with us. After studying George for several minutes, noticing the gray hue of his flesh and the sheen of sweat across his forehead despite the cool temperature, Harvey said, "That old man's in bad shape. He'll likely expire if something ain't done."

"He just needs rest," Milly replied defensively. "He's worn out after riding all night."

"What he needs is a doctor, someone who knows how to patch a bullet hole and bring down a fever."

"There's a doctor in Erda," Farrell said. "At least there used to be." He and Harvey exchanged glances, and I got an uneasy prickling across the back of my neck, like a heat rash after a hot afternoon putting up hay.

"How far away is Erda?" Milly asked hopefully.

"It ain't far," Farrell replied. He jutted his chin toward the narrow path we'd used coming in, the one that would take us back to the main road. "Another few hours, I'd judge. A man could be there and back before dark easy enough."

"Why don't you do it?" I said.

"He ain't my friend, but if he was, I damn sure would." Farrell was looking at me, his gaze vaguely threatening, and I knew that my hunch had been right. He had something unscrupulous in mind. When I glanced to where Harvey had dropped that little red trunk taken off the Chickasaw Express coach, Farrell chuckled. "We ain't gonna run off with your money, boy. We ain't even gonna open that box 'til your brother shows up."

"Thumbs can go with you if you're worried about it so much," Harvey offered.

"Me?" Three Thumbs Boy glanced out at the falling rain, his breath puffing like tiny, darting ghosts in the damp air. "Hell, he ain't my friend, neither."

"Yeah, but you bein' along'll mean Lige won't have to worry about us hightailin' outta here with that chest," Harvey logicized.

I didn't reply, not right away. I sensed the trap they were trying to haze me into and knew I'd have to tread carefully to avoid triggering it. Glancing toward Milly, observing the naked fear in her eyes, I knew she'd also seen through their attempted ruse. Taking a deep breath, I said, "No, I reckon not."

"You're gonna let him perish because you're afraid to trust us?"

Meeting Farrell's gaze, noticing for the first time the underlying savagery in his eyes, I recalled how I'd earlier thought he seemed like a decent fellow. It just hammered home all the more how much I had to learn yet about making my way in a hostile world . . . and wonder if I'd live long enough to do so.

My voice taut with stubbornness, I said, "I'm staying. One of you will have to go." I looked at Harvey. "You can do it. Take

135

Thumbs with you. That way you'll know me and Farrell won't run off with whatever's in that chest. You know, until Jace shows up."

Harvey got mad at that. So did Farrell, although he hid it a little better. Thumbs was looking from one to the other of us like he didn't know what was going on, so I knew they hadn't included him in their plans. Muttering a curse, Harvey shoved to his feet and stalked into the trees. After a couple of minutes, Farrell followed. Milly just sat there staring into the fire we'd kindled in front of the lean-to, its flames hissing in the rain. Her face looked so pale you might have thought someone had slit her throat and drained the blood from it.

"Why don't you want to go?" Thumbs asked me, but I didn't reply.

"Someone has to," Milly whispered without looking up.

"I'm not going to leave you here alone with those two."

At that, Thumbs said, "Oh," and bobbed his head; he'd finally figured it out. After a pause he stood and went in search of Farrell and Harvey. I pulled my rifle across my lap, although I worried a long gun in such cramped quarters wouldn't be very practical if the three of them came at us from different directions. I glanced at George, but he was all the way out of it by then. Watching the fitful rise and fall of his chest beneath the damp blankets, I knew we'd never get him back in the saddle to take him with us to Erda. Not without killing him. Hell, I wasn't sure we hadn't already pushed him too far.

"You and I will have to go together," I told Milly.

"Then who will take care of George?"

"They will. They'll have to if they don't want to get crossways with Jace."

"They won't care. Men like that never care about others, only themselves. Farrell Crow would back-shoot anyone here for a ten-dollar gold piece, including Jason. So would Harvey

136

Judd." Her lips twisted into a brief grimace. "So would Thumbs, if Farrell told him to."

"Maybe we wouldn't have to go all the way into town. Maybe we could find a farm along the way and borrow a wagon."

"Are there any farms between here and Erda?"

"I don't know," I admitted. I'd never been to Erda. Mama had done her shopping and trading in Davis, and only rarely made the long journey—six days, round trip—into Tishomingo, and that always from the north, bypassing the smaller burg by a good many miles.

Leaning forward, Milly stared past the edge of the shelter to where Farrell, Harvey, and Thumbs had reappeared and were standing close to their picketed horses, their shoulders hunched to the strengthening rain. Easing back, she slid a leather pouch around on her belt where she could more easily reach it. I didn't mention that pouch earlier because I hadn't seen a need to, but it was something she always kept close. It was brain-tanned and fire-smoked, with a cloth lining and a strip of beadwork along the flap. From it I'd seen her pull some small scissors, a comb, a little tin of soap, and whatnot. Female stuff, I'd always figured, and nothing I would have considered useful until she slid one of those stubby four-barreled Sharps pistols from its depths.

Judging from the size of its bores, I figured the gun for .32 caliber—small for most purposes, but plenty big enough for close-in work. [*Editor's Note:* If Two-Buck is correct in his estimate of the pistol's caliber, then the weapon Bolton carried was more likely a Sharps and Hankins model, a later rendition of the earlier, .22 and .30 caliber brass-framed units produced by Christian Sharps before his partnership with William Hankins.]

"Where'd you get that?"

"Jason gave it to me. He told me to keep it out of sight unless I needed it."

"That was smart thinking," I said approvingly. "Jace must've known what kind of company we'd be keeping."

"If he was such a good thinker, he wouldn't have saddled us with men like Farrell Crow and Harvey Judd."

Well, she had a point there, although I wasn't going to acknowledge it, let alone argue with her about it. "I'm still glad you have it," I replied. "I've been worrying my rifle might be too awkward if they came at us amongst all these trees." I started to reach for the pistol, but she quickly yanked it out of reach.

"I'm not giving this to you."

"Then what are you going to do with it?"

"I'm going to use it to keep Crow and Judd away while you and Thumbs go find a doctor."

"The hell! I'm not leaving you here with those two."

"We don't have a choice, Lige. George needs a doctor. Crow and Judd won't go, and I wouldn't trust Thumbs to find one by himself. That leaves you, but if you take Thumbs along, I at least won't have to worry about him."

I started to ask if she knew what those two had in mind—meaning Farrell and Harvey—then recalled what George had told me about how he and Jace had found Milly chained to a tree over in Choctaw country. It sobered me to realize she probably had a better idea of what they were capable of than I ever would, but was still willing to take the risk for George's sake.

"If you leave now, you can be back before dark," she said. "I can keep them away that long."

Gritting my teeth against the protest I wanted to utter, I glanced out to where Farrell, Harvey, and Thumbs were still standing close to their horses. Farrell met my gaze with a smoldering rage I could damn near feel from thirty yards away. Harvey had managed to light a cigar despite the dampness and was staring across the cove as if he were the only living creature for miles around. Thumbs had his back to the wind, his hands thrust deep into the pockets of his rubberized slicker; he looked miserable in the chilling rain but was too stupidly loyal to Crow to come in out of it.

"Lige," Milly pleaded softly.

"All right." I leaned back and took a deep breath, knowing that if anything happened to her while I was gone, it would create a purgatory I'd have to live in the rest of my life. "How many cartridges have you got for that little pepperbox?"

"A full box, save for what's already chambered."

"You got all four barrels loaded?"

When she said that she did, I glanced skyward. The sun was a faint glow through the clouds. It was late morning by then. If Farrell was right and Erda was only a few hours east of us, I'd likely be back well before dark.

Our gear was stacked to one side of the lean-to, covered with a piece of oilcloth. I dragged my saddle out of the pile and shouted for Thumbs to grab his. "You're coming with me," I told him.

Farrell's head reared back in surprise, and the cigar came close to tumbling from Harvey's lips. Thumbs started to protest, but Farrell leaned close and said something I didn't catch and he shut up. I carried my rig over to where Minko was standing with his head lowered to the rain and quickly cinched it down. I didn't boot the Marlin, though. I kept it handy, not trusting Harvey or Farrell at all, and having little enough to spare for Thumbs, as well. Thumbs saddled his mare and we both stepped into our hulks, but before we pulled out I rode over to where Farrell and Harvey were standing.

"If you hurt her," I said, "I'll kill both of you."

Farrell laughed. "That's kind of bold, ain't it, squirt?"

"You ain't killin' nobody, boy," Harvey added menacingly.

"You'd have to kill me to stop me," I replied. "Then you'd have to kill Milly and George, too, and when you're done with them, you'd have to deal with Kid Jace, and Jace won't be as easy to handle as me or George or Milly. Jace'll put a bullet through both your skulls and not lose a minute's sleep over it."

That struck a chord, with Farrell especially. His face turned dark as mud and he started to reply, then abruptly swallowed back whatever it was he was going to say. From his expression, I judged the taste was harsh.

"Maybe you'd best go find that doctor now," Harvey suggested rigidly, and I nodded and reined away. I'd done what I could under the circumstances, and had to trust that Milly could handle them until I got back.

Jerking my head for Thumbs to follow, we left the soggy cove in silence. I glanced back only once. Farrell and Harvey were still in the rain with their horses; at the lean-to, Milly was sitting next to George, holding the Sharps pistol in her lap.

SESSION TWELVE

It haunted me for a long time, wondering whether Farrell Crow had deliberately lied, or if he'd been honestly mistaken when he claimed it was only a few hours from the cove where we'd gone to roost to the little hillside town of Erda, Indian Territory. The truth is, it was closer to six, and closing in on midafternoon by the time me and Thumbs got there. I was simmering hot enough to warm a plate of beans by then, although there wasn't anything I could do about it short of hauling Minko around and racing back the way we'd come. And I wouldn't do that until I found a sawbones for George . . . assuming the town even had one.

The rain had tapered off but the sky was still gray and overcast, the clouds so low it seemed you could almost reach up and scoop out a handful of the stuff. The cold was deepening, too, like it was burrowing in for an extended stay. Erda's single main street—part of the road between Hank's Washita ferry and Tishomingo—was slick with mud as we made our way to the central business district. From what I could see, Erda seemed fairly typical for the times. There was a dry goods store and a couple of groceries, a wagon repair shop, two liveries, a feed and grain, a haberdashery, and several law offices. This being Indian Territory, there were no saloons—folks back in Washington wouldn't want us redskins getting ahold of anything that might set us off on a scalping frenzy, you understand?—but there were billiard halls and smoking parlors and other such

141

places where men could gather, and most of them would sell you a drink if they knew you or felt confident you weren't accepting bribes from the Lighthorse or U.S. marshals' office.

Had the threat of more rain not seemed so imminent I might have tied up outside Talbot's Billiards Palace. Instead I opted for the Erda Livery on the far side of town, dismounting out front and leading Minko in through the wide double doors. It was noticeably warmer inside, the lingering result of the recent high temperatures and the presence of livestock. I unbuttoned my heavy coat and was loosening the wool scarf around my neck when a potbellied man with a bulbous nose stepped out of a small office just inside the main doors.

"How do, gentlemen," he greeted.

"Howdy," was my reply. Thumbs had swung down from his mare and followed me inside, but ignored the hostler's greeting. He'd been acting surly all day, no doubt put out at having to accompany me into town when he would have rather stayed back with Farrell and Harvey. I noticed he was also keeping his right hand thrust deep into the pocket of his coat, as if embarrassed by the peculiarity of his extra thumb. I found that kind of surprising considering the way he'd flaunted it back at Bluford's farm, and had made no effort to conceal it in the Notch. Three Thumbs Boy was an odd duck, all right, but at that moment I had little interest in what was sparking his aloofness.

"Lodging is fifty cents an animal per night," the hostler continued in what sounded like a familiar rote. "That includes hay and water. Grain is ten cents extra. If you want to spend the night with your horses, that will be another fifty cents, but there is no smoking inside. I have hay stacked at the other end of the barn."

"Nobody gives a damn about your hay," Thumbs replied irritably.

"We're not staying," I interjected before the stableman got

his dander up and refused to cooperate. "We've got a hurt man back down the trail that needs a doctor."

"There is no doctor in Erda. The nearest medical man is in Tishomingo. We do have a barber who can set broken bones, if that is what ails your friend."

"If he's got any broke bones, it was done by a bullet," Thumbs said, staring at the guy as if daring him to question the cause. I wanted to punch Thumbs for his unprovoked aggression, but feared it would only worsen our situation.

"It was a hunting accident," I said. "He dropped his rifle while putting the sneak on a deer."

A scowl rippled the hostler's brow. "Which direction did you come from?"

"North of here," I replied, spinning another quick windy.

After a moment's reflection, he shrugged. "It does not matter. I only ask because there was a stagecoach held up east of here yesterday, and the one from Ardmore also runs late."

"I wouldn't know about that," I said, then changed the subject. "You mentioned a barber who might be able to help us?"

"Yes, his name is Charlie Plummer, but I do not know how much help he would be for a bullet wound. You would have to ask him about that."

"We passed a barbershop coming into town."

"That is his. Charlie is our only barber."

I offered the guy my thanks and was turning away when my gaze passed over the door to the livery's small office. I halted abruptly. Burned into the wood just below the paned glass window was a mark I recognized well. Jutting my chin toward it, I said, "Is that Kermit Watson's K-Bar-W brand?"

"It is. Mr. Watson owns the livery." A crooked smile tipped a corner of his mouth. "Mr. Watson owns much of Erda. Too much of it, some will tell you."

"That son of a bitch owns too much of everything, far as I'm concerned," Thumbs growled.

"Many in town would agree with you," the hostler replied, but said no more. I think he must have sensed Thumbs's desire to start an argument, and I admired that he wouldn't let himself be goaded into one.

Thanking the man for his information, I led Minko outside. Thumbs followed along. "That guy is a jackass," he said as we prepared to mount.

"Why?"

"The funny way he talks, for one thing."

"I noticed he knew when to keep his mouth shut."

"That's 'cause he didn't want it filled with my knuckles." Thumbs got a foot in his stirrup and swung into the saddle.

"Just let me do the talking from now on."

"The hell with you. I got as much right to flap my gums as anyone else."

"Not today," I said, and reined away before he could reply.

Plummer's Barbershop sat on the north side of the street in a tiny board-and-batten structure partway up the side of the hill—twenty-two steps from the hitching rail to the front door, by my count—with a red and white barber's pole of soft pine affixed to a wrought-iron bracket above the entrance. We found Charlie Plummer inside, stretched out in his chair and sound asleep, although he woke up quick enough at the jingle of the bell above the door. He slid out of his chair with a sheepish look on his face, like he was feeling guilty at having been caught napping.

"You boys needing a haircut?" he asked, trying to look bright-eyed and beaver-eager but not quite pulling it off with his sleep-heavy lids and a trace of spittle at each corner of his mouth.

"We need to talk to the head head-shearer," Thumbs said, crowding in on my heels.

144

"I am he," Plummer answered, knuckling drool from his lips.

"He?" Thumbs looked momentarily baffled. "We're lookin' for a guy named Charlie Plummer."

"Yeah, that's . . . I'm Plummer."

When Thumbs hesitated, I jumped in. "Guy down the street said you do some doctoring."

"If it isn't too difficult." He shrugged. "I'll do what I can no matter how serious the injury or illness, but I've never had any real medical training."

Thumbs was craning his neck, searching the shop. "I don't see a brand."

"A brand? What do you mean?"

"Kermit Watson's brand. I want to know if you work for him."

"Let it go, Thumbs," I said softly.

"The hell I will," he replied, still simmering over my rebuke at the livery. But if I was worried Plummer might take offense at Thumbs's abrasiveness, I needn't have been.

"Well, Watson owns the building, but I'm the barber and it's my business." His gaze darted suspiciously between us. "You boys don't work for Watson, do you?"

"No, we've just heard of him," I said.

"What we've heard is he's a tightfisted bastard and a son of a bitch," Thumbs added, and Charlie laughed, uncertainly at first, then with more vigor as his guard eased down.

"That old skinflint's got his brand on a good chunk of this town," he agreed, more or less echoing what the hostler had told us. "Which one of you boys needs a doctor?"

"Neither of us," I said. "We've got a man hurt west of here. We're hoping you can come take a look at him."

"How bad is he hurt?"

Figuring the cat was already out of the bag on that one, I said, "He was shot."

"Accidentally," Thumbs added smugly.

"Well, if you can bring him in I'll do what I can, but I can't leave town today. There're two women about to give birth, and Erda's only got one midwife since Daisy Highwater moved to Tish-town."

"Since when does a woman need a doctor to have a baby?" Thumbs asked, and to be honest, it seemed like a legitimate question. I know Mama had given birth to all of us Two-Buck kids without benefit of even a midwife, although now that I think about it, I don't suppose she would have turned one away, had someone been available.

"Well, these are both shaping up to be difficult births."

"How the hell can you know something like that?" Thumbs persisted.

"You can tell."

"How?"

"Dang it, you just can. Look, you bring your friend in here and I'll do the best I can for him, but I can't leave Erda today."

"He can't be moved," I said.

"That bad, huh?" He seemed to ponder it a moment, then said, "Tell you what I can do. I'll sell you some stuff that'll help ease his pain. Then if he gets to feeling better, you can bring him on in."

"What kind of stuff?" I asked, but Plummer was already on his way across the room, heading for a cabinet fastened to the back wall. I followed him over, watching as he sorted through a clutter of pasteboard boxes, corked bottles and vials, and tins of pills stacked atop one another like tiny ricks of cordwood. Taking a half-pint bottle from a middle shelf, he handed it over.

"That's laudanum," he explained. "Give your friend a tablespoon of that every . . . oh, I don't know, every three or four hours likely won't hurt him. Just don't give him too much or it could stop his heart."

"He's got a pretty high fever," I said, examining the russet-

146

colored liquid inside.

"That should help the fever some, but mostly it'll take away his pain. Or else dope him up enough that he won't notice it."

"Hey, I got me some recent aches, too," Thumbs said, showing a sudden interest in the cabinet's interior. "What else you got in there?"

"You can have some of this when George is better," I told him. I was eager to start back to the cove now that I had something helpful to offer. The last thing I wanted was a protracted argument between Thumbs and Plummer over narcotics, but the barber seemed eager to please. Or maybe he just needed the money.

"I've got more laudanum, or I can give you something more specific. What are your symptoms?"

Thumbs tapped his chest. "Got me a tightness right in here."

"For ailments of the torso I generally recommend Dr. Cook's Cherry Pectoral Relief." At Thumbs's hesitation, he added, "It is regarded highly by my patients for its abatement of stress, as well as minor aches and pains."

"Well, that's what I got, aches and pains." After a pause, he said, "Aw, hell, give me a bottle and let's see what it does."

Plummer pulled a quart bottle from a lower shelf and handed it over. I could tell he was trying to avoid looking my way. He knew as well as me that Thumbs wasn't seeking relief from any physical malady. "That'll be two dollars," he said, and Thumbs's eyes popped wide.

"For just this little bit?"

"Well, for both, I guess."

"Pay him," I said, pocketing the laudanum.

"You pay him."

"Goddamnit, pay the man, Thumbs, and hurry it up. We're gonna run out of daylight soon."

Thumbs grumbled but shelled out two dollars. I left as soon

as I saw he would, hurrying down the steps and swinging astride my horse. I was already heading out of town by the time Thumbs exited the barbershop. I didn't look to see if he was following. I didn't care. It was a six-hour ride back to the cove where I'd left Milly to fend off Farrell Crow and Harvey Judd by herself, and I knew darkness would catch me on the road, no matter how fast I tried to push Minko over the rain-slickened trace. I leaned forward in my saddle as if that might somehow quicken the pinto's gait, while bleak images of what I'd find when I got there ravaged my thoughts.

SESSION THIRTEEN

I was right about me and Thumbs not getting back to the cove before nightfall. Sundown caught us well short of our destination, and with the heavy cloud cover, full-blown darkness followed soon after. If Minko hadn't veered off the road of his own accord, I'd have likely passed the narrow trail to the clearing altogether.

My nerves were fiddle-string taut as we threaded our way through the thick timber, the now sodden carpet of leaves muffling the thud of Minko's hooves. Thumbs was somewhere close behind me, having galloped his mare recklessly out of Erda to catch up after we left Plummer's barbershop. As we drew nearer the clearing I began to wonder if I shouldn't have let him enter the cove first, so that I'd have all three men in front of me should my fears prove true. I'll admit I was expecting the worst, but the pitch-like darkness that greeted our arrival was disconcerting. Halting Minko at the edge of the timber, I slid my thumb over the Marlin's hammer. Almost reluctantly, I called Milly's name; she replied instantly, and my breath seemed to explode from my chest.

"Where are you?"

"Here."

Now, *here* could have been anywhere in that lightless, rainy bowl, but I gave Minko his head and he ambled across the clearing like he'd been this way a thousand times before. I

149

wasn't letting my guard down, though, not yet. "Where are the others?"

"They left this afternoon, but I was afraid to light a fire."

"They left?" My hand twitched on the reins and Minko stopped. After a moment's reflection, I nudged the gelding with my heels and rode on in. As I stepped down, I could just make out Milly's form in front of the shelter, a darkness only marginally lighter than the surrounding night. "How's George?"

"He's sleeping. Did you find a doctor?"

"Erda doesn't have a doctor, but they had a barber who sold me some medicine that ought to help."

"He needs a doctor, Elijah."

I didn't reply to that, didn't want to reveal my exasperation at her comment. She wasn't telling me anything I didn't know, but, damnit, I'd been half sick with dread all the way back from Erda worrying about what might be happening to her. What had she expected me to do, ride all the way into Tishomingo in search of a physician?

I looped Minko's reins around the slim trunk of a sapling and I felt my way over to the lean-to. I was anxious to get a fire started, to add a little light and warmth to the camp, and to spoon some medicine down George's throat. Hearing a rattle of tree limbs from across the clearing, I spun around with my rifle raised partway to my shoulder, but it was only Thumbs, complaining about the darkness and his mare's clumsiness among the trees. My pulse was still clipping along at a swift beat as I eased the Marlin's hammer to half cock. I'd no idea where Farrell and Harvey might have gotten to, but doubted if they'd drifted too far.

"Two-Buck?" Thumbs shouted. "Where are you?"

"Over here," I replied—basically the same unhelpful reply Milly had given me—then bumped up against the lean-to and stopped, my fingers exploring the crosspiece above the entrance as I tried to find my bearings.

"What kind of medicine did you bring?" Millie asked.

"Laudanum," I said, then, "We need a fire. I can't see a damn thing."

Milly immediately started rummaging through her stuff for matches. She'd apparently already laid out some dry kindling before dark, because it took only a couple of minutes to touch off a nice blaze. With its light flickering against the rear of the shelter, I moved in for a closer look at George. He was asleep, as Milly had said, but he seemed restless; his legs were twitching and you could see the rapid movement of his eyes under his lowered lids. He was still sweating, too, his forehead glistening.

"He's been like this all day," Milly said quietly, standing close enough that our shoulders touched gently through our damp clothing. Although she seemed unaware of the contact, it surged through me in a galvanic jolt that just about curled my toes. "He started mumbling just before sundown like he wanted to say something, but I couldn't tell what it was."

I did a bit of mumbling myself, which seemed to amuse her, judging from the faint smile that crept across her face. Then Thumbs poked his head inside, looking half drowned and as irritable as a bee-stung bear, and Millie leaned back a few inches, breaking her contact with my shoulder.

"Where's Farrell?" Thumbs demanded, and Milly told him the same thing she'd told me. Scowling, Thumbs ducked back out into the night. He showed up again ten minutes later, toting my gear along with his own. "I took care of your horse for you," he informed me, like I'd forgotten Minko was standing out there still under saddle.

"Appreciate it," I replied mildly, and helped him stow our rigs inside with the rest of our gear.

"Figured somebody better, 'fore he stood there all night waiting for you to show up."

"I didn't forget him. I was looking in on George."

"Well, I didn't forget him, either. I take care of my horses."

"We all appreciate it, Thumbs," Milly said. "Come inside and have a seat. I'll fix us a bite to eat."

Thumbs grumbled something unintelligible and squeezed inside the tiny shelter, sitting down as far from George as he could get. Milly warmed up some ham and beans—grub George had bartered for from the Blufords in exchange for our helping them butcher their hogs—and we sat in front of the fire and ate and tried to warm up.

Thumbs seemed unusually quiet. In part I knew he was exhausted. We all were following our long flight after robbing the Ardmore stage with a wounded man in tow, but I also think Farrell Crow riding off without him had drained some of the bluster from his breast. Without his old pard, Thumbs seemed somehow less than what he'd been before.

Later on, after Thumbs had turned in, I asked Milly if they'd given her any trouble and she said they hadn't. "I believe they wanted to, but when I let them see my pistol they changed their minds. It wasn't long after that they rode off."

We debated waking George to give him some laudanum, but decided to let him sleep. With the fire dying down, we rolled up in our blankets with Milly on one side of George and me on the other, and it wasn't but a few seconds before I drifted off.

The night passed uneventfully, as did the following day. Me and Milly were both growing more and more fretful about Jace, as he should have reached the cove before we did. I told Milly what the Erda hostler had said about a stagecoach being robbed east of there and tried to reassure her the theft had gone smoothly.

"If there'd been any shooting, he would have mentioned it," I said.

"Maybe a posse caught them?" she fretted.

I didn't have a reply for that, which I think she appreciated. Too much optimism would have betrayed my own apprehension.

Thumbs stayed close to the camp, instead of going out to look for Farrell and Harvey. Although he got into his cherry elixir from time to time, he didn't abuse it as I'd feared he might. I've known a few dopers over the years, and some of them can get kind of loopy, but Thumbs never did. He turned out to be more helpful around the camp than I would have expected, too, as if without Farrell Crow's influences he was starting to pattern his behavior after me—scrounging firewood and looking after the horses, even helping some with the cooking. The fact is, the guy was becoming almost likable—which was just one more reason to dread Farrell Crow's return.

I want to say something here, get it down on your Dictaphone so that anyone who listens to these recordings or reads a transcript of them later understands what I was feeling. I haven't made much so far of how Mama and Rachel and them were killed, but I don't want you thinking their memories weren't always there with me, like anvils dropped on top of my heart. There wasn't a day gone by, not an hour, that I didn't think of them. Sometimes it'd be a recollection of some incident that included one or another, or even all of them. Maybe of us sitting around the table of an evening and talking, or working together in Mama's big garden behind the house. I'd see them clear as day and hear the echo of their voices, and it'd be like a knife twisted deep inside of me. And there was an emptiness, too, a feeling of desolation so intense it liked to rip me apart. So, yeah, I might not be talking about it over much for your recordings, but just don't start wondering if I'd forgotten them, because I haven't. To this day, I haven't.

Anyway, George finally woke up around noon of our second full day in the cove, kitten-weak but with his fever broken and

153

his gaze quite a bit brighter. He asked where we were and Milly brought him up to date on all that had happened. Turns out the last thing he remembered clearly was that Ardmore stagecoach coming up out of the Camp Creek ford.

Milly fixed him some mashed rice in pork broth and fed him a warm meal, then pulled his old bandages off to clean the wound. The lesion had quit its slow oozing, which was reassuring, but it was obvious he wasn't going to be fit to ride anytime soon. Not without it tearing open again. In that regard, I guess it was a good thing Jace and his boys hadn't shown up yet.

It was cold enough the next morning that our breaths were visible anytime we left the vicinity of the fire. On top of that, the rain refused to let up. It wasn't steady, but off and on with little breaks in the clouds that occasionally allowed some blue sky to show itself, but then it would close in again and rain would start rattling the lean-to's roof, making our lives miserable. I kept hoping it would clear off for good, but when it hadn't quit by midafternoon of our third day there I decided to set out on foot to hunt for fresh meat. I wanted a deer if I could find one, figuring its liver would do George more good than the weak broth Milly had been feeding him, but I didn't see so much as the snowy flicker of a tail all afternoon. By dusk I'd resigned myself to taking whatever I could find, and finally got a shot at a hen turkey just as the light started to fade.

Thumbs plucked the bird and Milly roasted it, and we had a nice little meal. Afterward, Milly again stripped the bandages from George's chest. This time she left the wrappings off, the wound exposed to the air. She said it would heal quicker that way, and no doubt George seemed more comfortable without the bindings. He was just dozing off when a voice helloed us from across the cove. Me and Thumbs grabbed our rifles and faded quick-like into the trees, which brought a laugh from the guy who'd hailed us. I hadn't recognized the voice, being caught off guard and all, but the laughter was as familiar as the back of Minko's ears, and I stepped back into the light as Jace rode up and dismounted. His smile disappeared when he spotted George sloped against his saddle in the lean-to.

"Where have you been?" I asked, putting out my hand, but Jace brushed past it without even a glance. He knelt at George's side, leaning forward to examine the uncovered wound.

"What happened?"

"What generally happens when a man takes up lawless ways," George replied casually.

"It was the messenger from the Ardmore stage," I said, standing at the lean-to's entrance.

Smiling, George said, "Don't work yourself into a lather, Jason Two-Buck. I ain't dying yet."

"You'd damn well better not be." Jace rocked back on his heels with a slow expulsion of air, and it struck me that these two were more than just friends. They were like brothers, maybe even closer than Jace and I were. The realization stung.

Standing next to me, Milly said, "Elijah asked where you've been."

"We've been taking care of business," Jace replied brusquely.

"While we've been sitting here wondering if you were dead or in jail?"

"Well, now you know." He stood and glanced around the camp. "Where's Crow and Judd?"

"They're gone," Milly said. "They came at me while your brother was in Erda getting medicine for your friend, but I showed them my pistol, so they left."

Jace's eyes narrowed. "The Sharps? That ain't your pistol."

"You want it back?"

I had to grin at the fire in her words. You couldn't keep that gal's spirit dampened for long, no matter how hard you tried.

"Yeah, I want it back," Jace told her, and she pulled the little four-barrel from her belt pouch and chucked it over. Jace snatched it out of the air left-handed, then just stared at it for a moment as if not knowing what to do. Finally he tossed it back. "You'd better hang onto it," he said, and she slipped the pistol back into her pouch without a word. They were a confusing duo.

I was aware of the others out in the shadowy cove, caring for their mounts and gathering damp firewood. After a bit someone kindled a fire maybe twenty yards away. I recognized Pit Middleton in its light, Quintin Haus and Strong Wolf at its periphery, but Bob Hatcher was nowhere in sight, and I asked Jace about him.

"Bob's gone off to Texas. He ain't riding with us no more."

Although curious to know why, I sensed the timing wasn't right. It was plain something was eating at Jace, though. Something bigger than Hatcher's departure or George's injury, and I wasn't surprised when he told Thumbs to go over to where the others were gathered around Middleton's fire.

"This is ours," he added gruffly, and Thumbs shrugged and walked off without protest. He was a confusing one, too.

"What are you so bristly about, Jason Two-Buck?" George queried.

"Who says I'm bristly?"

"Goddamnit, a jackrabbit told me. What happened?"

Jace took a deep breath, then spiraled down cross-legged on the same piece of canvas Thumbs had been sitting on. "We robbed that Caddo coach slick," he began. "Burned it afterward, too, like we planned, so I figured while we was in the area we might as well go into Caddo and do the same with the Chickasaw Express office. That's when things went bad."

"How bad?" George asked.

"That son of a bitch Hatcher killed one of the stable hands, and no reason for it, either."

"Just . . . killed him?" I said, stunned by the casualness of Jace's confession.

"Bob said he wasn't moving fast enough, but hell, he was just a kid, scared half outta his wits. Anyway, Quint Haus and Pit Middleton already had a fire started inside the Express office and Strong Wolf was runnin' the livestock outta the barn, so there was no way to stop it then. Some kind of lawman, a marshal or something, came out to investigate what all the ruckus was about, and Hatcher shot him, too. Hit him a good one in the leg, and he went down hard, then crawled into an alley." Jace paused, shrugged, and added, "After that, we came here."

George tipped his head back and swore softly. "The Lighthorse ain't gonna ignore that," he said.

"I know."

"Robbing a white man's coach is one thing—"

"I said I know," Jace snapped, but George wouldn't be put off.

"They'll consider it a personal insult."

"Goddamnit, that's enough," Jace lashed out, but by then the conversation had taken on a life of its own.

"What do you mean?" I asked George.

"I mean there's a big difference between law and justice, Elijah Two-Buck, and one don't always line up with the other. I'm guessing the Lighthorse have stayed out of this so far because they know what Watson did to your mama and siblings, and they likely ain't called in the U.S. marshals for the same reason, although I expect Judge Parker'll hear about it eventually. But killing that stable hand puts a crimp in our defense." [*Editor's Note:* "Hanging Judge" Isaac Parker has been mentioned here before; he was a federal judge for the Western District of Arkansas, which encompassed the Indian Nations of

157

what is now eastern Oklahoma. Parker earned his sobriquet as "Hanging Judge" due to the number of men he sentenced to the gallows. In his twenty-one years on the bench at Fort Smith, Arkansas, Parker sentenced 160 men to their deaths, although a significant number of these had their sentences commuted or their cases retried by the United States Supreme Court. At his death in 1896, only 79 individuals were actually executed. Ironically, Judge Parker openly opposed capital punishment.]

George had grown quiet as he contemplated the crackling embers of our fire. Then he fixed his gaze on Jace. "How long do you reckon we got, Jason Two-Buck?" When he didn't reply, George turned to Milly. "Maybe you'd best wrap me up again."

But she didn't reply, either. She was glaring at Jace like he was the worst kind of slug ever to crawl out from under a rotting stump. He seemed oblivious to her silent condemnation, though. Like George, he was also staring into the low flames of our fire with a faraway look in his eyes, listening to the hiss and pop of the wet wood and seeing . . . hell, who knew what he saw in there? Mama, maybe? Or that stable hand in Caddo? For that matter it could have been our own futures he was looking at—mine and his and George's and Milly's. I doubted if he was giving much thought to the others, Pit Middleton and them. They were there for the money, and would likely scatter to the winds if they didn't anticipate any more coming in—which brought something Jace had said our last night in the Notch to my mind.

"What are we going to do next?" I asked. "Are we still going into Erda?"

Jace looked up, blinking. "Milly said you went there for medicine?"

"Uh-huh."

"Did you see the bank?"

"Yeah, it's a brick building in the middle of town, south side of the street."

"What about a city marshal?"

"I noticed a little stone building with bars on the windows I figured for a jail, but I didn't see any sign of a lawman. If it was a jail, it didn't hardly look big enough to have an office inside of it."

"They could have the marshal's office somewhere else," Jace mused. "Or they might just use the building for drunks and petty thieves. Erda's close enough to Tishomingo to send for the Lighthorse if they catch a real hard case."

"Then you still plan to rob the bank there?"

"Yeah, I sure as hell do, little brother. We're gonna take every nickel Kermit Watson has in there, then burn it to the ground like we did that stable in Caddo."

"What about the other people who have money there?" Milly asked.

"All the better, because Watson'll have to make good on it."

"He won't," George said. "He'll put the blame on the Kid Jace gang, and tell everyone who lost money that they're shit outta luck."

"He might try, but folks won't let him get away with it. Not with that big farm he's got outside of town. They'll slip out there in the middle of the night and help themselves to as much of Watson's beef and tobacco crop as they like. Take his corn and cotton, too."

"I doubt it," George said. "Folks don't think like you do, Jason Two-Buck. They're not as full of hate as you are."

"That's 'cause they ain't been hounded like I have, like my family has."

"I won't argue that, but if you rob the Erda bank, it won't be just Kermit Watson you put the hurt to. It'll be honest folks who'll take the brunt of it. Might be some of them will lose their homes or business because of it, too. Is that what you want?"

Maybe at some other point in Jace's life, George's words would have taken hold and meant something, but that night above the Greasy Bend, they were like pebbles flung against a speeding locomotive. I saw a familiar stubbornness take over his expression—the same hard set to his jaw, the identical thinned lips and furrowed brows, as I'd seen so often on Mama's face— and I knew he wouldn't change his mind. Jace was going to rob that bank if he had to do it by himself. But of course, he wouldn't. The others would go along because they wouldn't care if their crime created hardship for the people of Erda. And I'd go for the same reason I'd trailed along with him so far . . . because, good or bad, the outlaw known as Kid Jace was my brother, and I wouldn't abandon him.

Not yet.

SESSION FOURTEEN

Strong Wolf didn't go into Erda with us. He told Jace all he wanted was the harness stock we'd taken off the Ardmore stage. After some deliberation, Jace told him to take them. Farrell Crow—he and Harvey had showed up shortly after dawn the next day, both of them hungover from drinking bad whiskey with that ferryman I'd earlier thought Farrell wanted to shoot—argued that we'd need those horses for relays to escape any following posse, but Jace stuck to his guns.

"All he wants is some horses to take back to the reservation to show his pards how rich he is," Jace said. "We can't sell 'em around here with Watson's brand on their hips, so we might as well let Strong Wolf have them."

"Damnit, they'll be our relays, Kid. We'll use 'em in Erda and run 'em like hell for an hour or so after we leave town, then switch to our regular mounts and leave any lawmen following us high and dry on worn-out stock."

"I doubt they'll be a posse," Jace said. "Erda's too small, so we won't need relays. Besides, I already told Strong Wolf he can have them."

"You think those government agents on the Kiowa reservation ain't gonna take notice of an unfamiliar brand, or that the military won't look into it?"

Jace's expression grew hard. "The fact is, I just don't give a good damn. Strong Wolf wants those horses and I'm giving them to him. What happens after that is no concern of mine."

Gritting his teeth, Farrell walked back to where the others were gathered around Middleton's fire. I never heard what became of the horses they cut loose from the Caddo stage, or the ones Strong Wolf had freed from the Chickasaw Express stables just before the buildings were set aflame—I'm assuming the fear of pursuit kept them from taking time to haze along any extra stock—but Strong Wolf seemed as happy as a cat in a cage full of canaries to have those six we'd taken from the Ardmore coach. The last I saw of him, he was riding northwest out of the cove with the harness stock strung out single file behind him on lead ropes. As far as I could tell, he never looked back. [*Editor's Note:* Although there were several Strong Wolfs listed in the records from the 1890s on both the Kiowa and Comanche reservations, no mention could be found of a man with that name being investigated for the theft of the Chickasaw Express Company's horses.]

Strong Wolf was barely out of sight when Farrell returned with the others to demand that the little red leather chest we'd taken off the Ardmore stage be opened and its contents divvied between us. I've learned over the years that there are times to hold your ground and there are times to concede. I guess Jace understood that even then, because he just shrugged and said, "Bring it over."

Harvey went to fetch the trunk and we all gathered around to see what kind of treasure it contained. Even Milly wandered over as Harvey set the chest on the ground close to our fire. Jace used our stubby camp axe to break the lock. I think we were all either puzzled or disappointed when he flipped the lid back to reveal a jumble of envelopes inside; I know I fell into the former crowd. Most of the envelopes sported official-looking seals, but as Jace thumbed them open one by one it soon became apparent there was nothing spendable within. After shuffling through the entire stack, he laughed and tossed them back into the busted trunk.

"Stocks and bonds, letters of intent, and other useless crap," he announced. "As worthless to us as a Confederate dollar."

Maybe more so, I reflected, as I knew there were still folks around the South who would honor Confederate script out of pure stubbornness. Farrell reached down to scoop up a handful of the documents, but you could tell by the way he handled them that he couldn't read. Neither could Harvey.

"Then you won't mind if we toss these into the fire," Farrell said to Jace, as if to call a bluff.

"You can wipe your hind end with 'em for all I give a damn," was Jace's careless response. He turned his back on the others and walked over to where George was sitting up in the lean-to, a cup of coffee in his hands, a blanket draped over his shoulders against the chill. Me and Milly went with him. Squatting next to the older man, Jace said, "You reckon you can sit a saddle without passing out?"

"I expect I can."

"He'll tear his wound open if he does," Milly said in alarm.

"Stay out of this," Jace replied curtly.

"I'll be fine," George assured her with a gentle smile. You could tell he was fond of Milly, and that she was growing fonder of him as time went on, too. She was certainly treating him better than she had when I first showed up. George looked at Jace with a question in his eyes. "What happened to the money from the Caddo stage?"

"There wasn't any, none that belonged to Watson, anyway."

"Is that why Hatcher quit?"

"Yeah, I guess he didn't believe me when I said we wouldn't rob the passengers. I just about had to shoot him to keep him away from them. It made him mad, though, which I figure is why he shot that kid in Caddo."

"To get back at you?"

"He'd see it that way." Jace shook his head, and there was pain in his eyes for the loss of another innocent life. Revenge, I was to learn, is a complicated business, and seldom goes the way you plan for it to.

"Let it drop, Jason Two-Buck," George urged gently. "You've put a big enough dent in Watson's wallet, now let the law take care of it."

"No! I want that sonofabitch begging for coins in the street. I want him barefoot, and rooting through trash heaps for his meals."

"Then take the fight to him. Quit dragging others into it."

Jace shook his head. "I'll take the fight to him and never said I wouldn't, but not until I've made him hurt the way he made Mama and Papa hurt. Lige, too, forcing him to ride the owl-hoot with common saddle tramps like us, when he should be home milking cows and shucking corn."

George sighed and eased the blanket from his shoulders; it crumbled around his waist, revealing the butt of his revolver that I hadn't been aware he'd strapped on again. "Then I expect we'd best get riding, because if the Lighthorse won't touch Watson, they'll sure as Hades be comin' after us. I doubt the federal marshals will be too far behind 'em, either."

"Let's get mounted," Jace said, pushing to his feet.

Tight-lipped and skeptical, I brought Minko and Coal in and curried them down as best I could with the only brush we had. Milly started breaking camp, stowing our gear in the panniers while Jace saddled her bay and got the sawbuck cinched tight to the mule's back. George just stood out of the way and concentrated on breathing easy and not overexerting himself, which I thought showed uncommon good sense considering the severity of his wound.

The sun was just peeking over the tree-whiskered lip of the horizon when I crawled into my saddle that morning. Most of the others were already mounted, as well, sitting their horses close to one another while their horses fogged the air around them with their breaths. Reining Minko to the side while Jace and Milly settled George atop Coal, I found myself eyeing the others with a new perspective; I was part of the gang now, no longer an outsider or Jace's tagalong little brother. It dawned on me that we were a pretty mixed lot. Pit Middleton and Quintin Haus were white; Black George Holly and Harvey Judd were Negro; Farrell Crow was a full-blooded Chickasaw, while the rest of us—me and Jace and Three Thumbs Boy—were all mongrels to one degree or another. I didn't know anything about Milly Bolton's past then, but felt confident she was full-quill Indian. But not Chickasaw; don't ask me why I felt that way because I couldn't tell you, I just did.

With George astride Coal and Milly sitting her bay with the pack mule at her side, Jace rode over to where I was sitting Minko off by myself. "I've got something for you," he said, opening the mouth of a burlap sack hanging from his saddle horn. He took out a gun belt and holster and handed it over. "Strap that around your middle," he said. "Your Marlin's gonna be too bulky for what we gotta do."

I was just about speechless as I accepted the belt and slipped the revolver from its holster. It was a nickeled Colt with a five-and-one-half-inch barrel—a .45, I saw from the cartridges in the belt's loops. I eased the hammer back, and for a moment I thought the dang thing was broken, it cocked so smooth and easy.

"Watch that trigger," Jace advised. "It's got a real fine pull." [*Editor's Note:* A trigger's "pull" is how much pressure is required to fire the weapon; in target shooting, a lighter, smoother pull usually results in better accuracy.]

I stuttered what might have been a thanks, although I doubt if it was needed. They could all see the grin plastered across my

face like a circus broadside. At that point in my life it was probably the best gift I'd ever received. I didn't question where it
had come from, either. I felt fairly certain Jace hadn't purchased
the gun from a store, but I was also confident he hadn't taken it
from a working man—not that any working man I ever met
would have been able to afford such a fine revolver. No, one
way or another, that firearm—like Strong Wolf's horses—had
come from Kermit Watson's pocketbook.

"Strap it on," Jace said, and I did, wrapping the belt around
my waist and cinching it down. I was feeling almighty proud for
a moment, until I noticed a sadness in Jace's eyes, and my
excitement leveled out in confusion, but he reined away before I
could say anything. Tossing the empty burlap into the tramped
grass next to the empty lean-to, Jace dropped his gaze on George
and Milly, a brooding weight I suspect they both felt.

"You two head on back to Thomas Red Corn's place and
wait for us there."

"I can ride, Jace, if that's what's worrying you," George said.

"You won't be able to ride the way we'll have to after leaving
Erda. No, go on back to Red Corn's and take the woman with
you. We'll swing past on the way through and pick you up."

Although Milly's face reflected the thunder of her feelings,
she must have sensed the resoluteness in Jace's words, and kept
her mouth shut. After a few seconds, George nodded. "All right,
if that's what you want."

"I wouldn't have said it otherwise."

George and Milly left following the same trail Strong Wolf
had taken with the harness stock. Jace waited until they were
out of sight, then motioned me to follow him over to where the
others were waiting. As I came up beside him, he whispered,
"Watch your back around this bunch, Lige." Then, "Watch
mine, too."

I told him that I would, and didn't ask why. Those men who

rode with what became known as the Kid Jace gang had turned surly after two stagecoach robberies where nothing of value had been gained. The only reason they were still with us was because of our next target.

Halting a few yards away, Jace said, "You boys ready to hit that bank in Erda?"

The men stared at him with flat, hard expressions, all of them cold, wet, miserable . . . and out of patience. Finally, Middleton said, "You got a plan for that bank, Kid?"

With Bob Hatcher no longer with us, Pit had scooted back up to the position of toughest hombre in the bunch—at least that was his opinion. I'm not sure Farrell Crow or Harvey Judd shared it, but for the moment they seemed willing to let Pit do the talking.

"Yeah, I've got a plan," Jace replied, and succinctly laid it out.

It being my first bank job, I couldn't say how it compared to the methods of other, more experienced outfits, like Bill Doolin's Wild Bunch, which was even then raising hell all over Kansas and Indian Territory, but it sounded all right to me, and no one raised any objections.

It started raining again about midmorning and continued off and on all the way to Erda. We pulled up about half a mile east of town and Jace gave me a questioning look as if to ask if I was going to be all right. When I nodded that I would, he gave the order for the others to scatter and come into town from different directions, while I waited under a big oak alongside the road with Quintin Haus. Even with my coat buttoned and my collar turned up around my neck, I could feel myself trembling. I wanted to believe it was from the cold rather than nervousness, and even asked Haus if he was feeling skittish, but he just snorted and said, "Pit'll keep things under control."

I bristled at the implications of his remark. Pit Middleton

wasn't in charge; this was the Kid Jace gang. On the other hand, I didn't see any point in arguing about it, not with what awaited us in town. So we sat our horses not ten feet apart and said nary a word to one another until, judging that enough time had elapsed, I nudged Minko with my heels and headed for town. After a couple of minutes, Haus grudgingly followed, although by the time we got there, he made sure we were riding in side by side.

Approaching from the west, the Edgerton Wagon Works was the first business we came to. It sat on the right-hand side of the street, a low, sprawling building with a tin roof and a chinaberry tree out front. The huffing of a bellows and the clatter of steel on iron from within told me the smithy was hard at work. I guided Minko over beneath the tree where I'd have some shelter from the rain and loosened the two lower buttons of my coat, pulling its tails back so I could more easily reach my new revolver. Quint took a position on the opposite side of the street.

Charlie Plummer's Barbershop sat across from Edgerton's but was another thirty or so yards closer to the center of town. Although I didn't see any sign of Charlie, there was a thread of smoke curling from the chimney above the shop; it made me wonder if he was sacked out in his reclining barber chair again, warm and comfortable and snoring the morning away.

Farrell Crow showed up at the far end of the street, an equal distance on that side of town as Haus and I were on this end. Halted in front of a clapboard residence, he was filling his pipe as if he had all the time in the world. From a distance you couldn't tell he'd spent the last few days drinking corn liquor with Harvey Judd and Hank at the latter's ferry, but get within ten feet of him and you couldn't miss the results of his recent spree. Farrell Crow was one mighty sick bird, far worse than Harvey appeared in my opinion, and had looked like he was ready to puke all the way into town. It amazed me he was holding up as well as he appeared.

Harvey was nowhere in sight. Jace had sent him around to cover the rear of the bank and prevent anyone from escaping that way, and to keep the law from entering, in case some badge-toter got wind of what we were doing and tried to slip in through the back door.

Not long after me and Quint and Farrell got into position, Jace appeared from a side street, he and Pit Middleton and Thumbs walking their horses toward the bank as calm as you please. They pulled up out front and Jace and Pit got down and handed their reins to Thumbs. Although my fingers itched to draw the Colt, to have it ready just in case, I kept them resting lightly atop my saddle horn so as to not draw any unwanted attention our way. So far everything seemed to be going just as Jace had predicted, and I was beginning to think we might pull this off without trouble. Then, out of the misty rain, Bob Hatcher appeared from an alley across the street from the bank. He jogged his tall gray horse over to arrive just as Jace and Pit were starting up the steps and in that same instant a voice behind me barked, "What the hell do you think you're doin'?"

SESSION FIFTEEN

I flinched more from the voice behind me than the unanticipated appearance of Bob Hatcher, although I'll admit both were equally startling. Twisting around in my saddle, I found a burly Negro in a leather farrier's apron standing between me and the entrance to the wagon shop. He wore a sweat-damp calico shirt with the sleeves rolled up over massive forearms. For a few seconds I was so taken aback by the rumbling bellow of his voice that I failed to respond to his question. My silence didn't set well with him.

"I asked you something, boy. You gonna answer me, or sit there like a damn fool?"

Well, that lit a fire in my belly. "How do you figure what I'm doing here is any of your business?" I retorted, and he immediately pointed to the ground behind Minko's rear hooves.

"Your horse just shit in my yard."

I looked, and sure enough he had. A horse humping up a little to defecate is something you get used to after a few days in the saddle, so I'd hardly been aware he was doing it. Still, it didn't seem like anything to get all twisty about.

"I reckon he felt the need," I said, and that didn't sit well with him, either.

"You think that's funny?"

"I ain't thinking about it at all."

"I'm tired of people letting their stock crap all over my yard."

I looked at the sign above the wide double doors of his shop.

170

"If this is a wagon factory, you ought to be used to having livestock around."

"If you're buying a wagon, your horse can shit anywhere it wants. If you ain't, then get your ass down here and clean up this mess."

Normally that kind of brusqueness would have raised my hackles to near ceiling level, but the fact is, after my initial burst of irritation, I became more puzzled than angered by the man's outrage. It occurred to me that somebody must have recently riled this fella if he was ready to raise hell with a stranger over a simple pile of manure. Still, I had my own business to attend to, and didn't plan on leaving my saddle to clean up a bunch of horse apples.

"I'll get to it in a minute," I said, even though I had no intention of doing so. I just wanted the guy to shut up and go away. Turning my back on him, I saw that Hatcher had already stepped down from his gray and was climbing the steps to where Jace and Pit had stopped to wait for him. That wagonsmith had no intention of letting the matter drop, though.

"You'll do it now, or I'll by God kick your skinny little ass from here to next Sunday," he informed me.

I continued watching Jace and Hatcher, and didn't reply. I suppose I was hoping he'd just give up and go away, but I wasn't to be that lucky. Growling something unintelligible, he stalked into his shop. Down the street, I could tell Jace and Hatcher were in a heated argument. Pit Middleton had moved to an upper thread and was watching the altercation with a hand on his revolver. So far no one seemed to be paying them any mind. I suspect the sprinkling rain had something to do with that, as the few folks I did see on the street were keeping their heads down as they hustled from one covered location to another. Still, I knew somebody had to be watching. In a small town like Erda, there was always a busybody or two to keep an eye on the goings and comings of the community, and a bunch of strangers showing up at the same time wouldn't go unnoticed, I don't care what the weather is doing.

I think I might have mumbled a curse when the wagonsmith showed up again, carrying a heavy scoop shovel, the kind commonly used to toss grain from wagon to bin or vice versa, although it comes in handy for cleaning up after horses and mules, too. Holding that shovel up like a holy man's staff, he said, "Get down here, boy, and clean up after your horse."

Well, I was nervous and scared and out of patience for such a foolish and uncalled for request, and to my discredit I told the guy what he could do with his shovel. It wasn't polite, and it sure as hell wasn't smart, and I guess for that smithy it was the final straw. He strode toward me glaring like he was about to do battle with ol' Beelzebub himself, and I knew if I didn't stop him, he'd drag me out of my saddle and likely cuff my ears as he would any wayward schoolboy. Rather than let that happen, I palmed my new Colt and sent a bullet into the belly of his scoop shovel. It struck steel with a clang and a ring, and the smith jerked his hand away like the thing had burst into flames. Rocking the Colt's hammer back a second time, I centered the muzzle on the Negro's chest and said, "I ain't cleaning up any messes today, mister, I don't care whose horse left it. Now go away and leave me alone, before somebody gets hurt."

The guy's eyes grew as wide as a pair of Morgan silver dollars. He looked at me, then at his hand, which he was slowly shaking like it had gone numb—no surprise there, having had an implement shot out of it—then took a hesitant step backward and looked around as if coming out of a trance. For the first time he seemed to notice Quintin Haus sitting his horse across the street with that big Winchester of his butted to his thigh. Down the street, Pit Middleton cursed loudly and headed for the bank's front door. Jace and Bob hurried up the steps after him, and all three disappeared inside. With Thumbs left alone out there hanging onto the extra reins, it struck me that he might as well have been holding up a sign telling the citizens of Erda what we were doing.

"I'll be gone to hell," the wagonsmith breathed, more of an exclamation than an expletive, as he wasn't even looking at me when he said it. Then he hustled back into his shop. I glanced helplessly across the street at Haus, who shrugged in reply. Things were starting to unravel, but hadn't gone far enough yet for us to do more than hold our positions.

At the other end of the street, Farrell Crow was coming forward at an easy lope. He'd stashed his pipe somewhere and drawn his revolver, but wasn't pointing it at anyone. My pulse quickened as I reined Minko into the middle of the street. Haus joined me there, both of us watching the bank like we might a magician just before he pulled something unexpected out of his topper. Turns out what I should have been watching was the wagon works, because while I was focusing on the bank, that smithy had reappeared carrying one of those massive goose-guns, the kind that can bring down a few dozen or so ducks at a time. [*Editor's Note:* Two-Buck is probably referring to what was commonly known as a punt gun—a large-bored shotgun used by lodges and resorts to supply fowl for their guests; although some punt guns could weigh as much as 100 pounds and were measured in yards rather than feet, the more common variety could be shouldered and fired a much smaller charge.]

I guess if it wasn't the good Lord looking out for me that day, then it was pure luck that had Quintin Haus glance to the rear just as the wagonsmith started to raise his undersized howitzer. Had the smithy unloaded his shotgun into my back, he'd have likely cut me in half. Instead, Quint threw a round with his Winchester that took the bulky Negro square in the gut, folding him over and dropping him to the muddy ground in front of his shop.

I appreciated that first shot, but not the second, when a quick spurt of blood erupted from the base of the smithy's neck and his head flopped loosely to the side. He was dead before he toppled, and there was no doubt about that—none whatsoever. I don't recall if I've already mentioned this, but Quint's rifle fired a .45-75 cartridge, not unlike what the old-time hiders used for buffalo, and I don't care how big and solid you are, nobody is going to survive a neck wound from a large-bore gun like that.

The echo of Haus's rifle was still rumbling wagon-like down the street when Farrell Crow popped off a round from his revolver. Powder smoke wreathed his shoulders in tattered ribbons as he spurred his mount into a run. He sent another bullet through the window of a hardware store across the street from the bank, and a couple of men who had ventured onto the boardwalk immediately ducked back inside. Unfortunately, others were quickly showing up to replace them, stepping out of doorways all up and down the street to investigate the shooting. More than a few were carrying their own collection of rifles, shotguns, and revolvers, and I figured things were about to get lively in downtown Erda.

Spotting movement at the front door of the barbershop, I saw Charlie Plummer scanning the street. He looked puzzled by all the shooting until he spied me and Quint; his gaze locked onto mine with undeniable recognition, and he ducked back into his shop. At my side, Quintin Haus said, "Hell's fixin' to bust loose, Two-Buck."

Like I couldn't see that for myself. Like it hadn't started unraveling the second that blacksmith came at me with his shovel. Then Plummer showed up again with a revolver and things got serious real fast. I snapped off my shot before Plummer did his, which caused him to jump back just as he pulled his trigger, sending his bullet skyward. I missed too, and I'll confess I was glad I did. By this time gunfire was rattling windows all up and down Erda's main thoroughfare, and in front of the bank, Thumbs's mare was dancing back and forth, fighting the bit and wanting to bolt; its nervousness was lapping over onto Jace and Pit's mounts, as well. Only Hatcher's gray stood firm, high-headed from all the chaos breaking loose around it but rock solid otherwise, its hooves planted in the soft mud like fence posts—a well-trained horse if ever I saw one.

The sound of gunfire increased as more townspeople jumped into the fray, and powder smoke swirled in the damp air. With Jace's well-planned robbery falling apart before my eyes, I began returning fire in earnest, although at that point I was being careful not to actually shoot *at* anyone. So far the town's only casualty that I knew of was the big Negro Quintin Haus had shot, and I was hoping we could keep it that way.

I fired my Colt dry, then punched out the empties and reloaded from the row of extra cartridges carried in loops on my gun belt. A bullet whizzed past my cheek from somewhere down the street, close enough that I swear I felt the feathery disturbance of its passage. Charlie Plummer was also keeping up a steady firing in my direction, and his bullets were beginning to come uncomfortably close. I didn't know how much longer we could keep this up before someone—possibly even Plummer—became determined enough to actually *aim* his weapon and squeeze off a shot, rather than just poke his gun around a doorframe and jerk the trigger. I remember it was right about in there, with all hell shaking off its shackles just as Quint had predicted, that it occurred to me to wonder: *What in the hell am I doing here?*

What were *we* doing there, trading shots with folks who'd had nothing to do with Mama's death, or the deaths of my siblings and father? Men and women who would have been as appalled by Kermit Watson's actions on Two-Buck Mountain as me and Jace were. Damnit, these people weren't my enemies! If anything, we shared an enemy, a common foe to each of us in his own way. Yet here we were fighting among ourselves like bobcats and badgers, when if we'd had a lick of sense between us, we would have joined forces and taken the fight to Watson, the whole damn bunch of us hauling him out of that fancy house of his and stringing him up in a tall tree for the crows to peck on.

But that wasn't going to happen, and barely a minute after those thoughts flashed through my mind, a bullet took a bite out of my hat brim, a little half-inch hole barely a finger-width from my left ear. That, my friend, is a mighty strange sensation, one I'll never be able to accurately describe, or remotely forget, but it sure did yank my thoughts away from the *whys* and *what-ifs* and back to Erda's main street, where lead was flowing like floodwaters. Down the block I saw Farrell Crow with his revolver holstered, laying down a steady fire with his Winchester at the Erda livery where me and Thumbs had first stopped to ask about a doctor for George. It looked like he had three or four people inside who were shooting back at him, judging from the clouds of gun smoke spurting from the stable's door and windows. Harvey Judd had showed up from his original back-of-the-bank position as well, and was throwing shots at various locations where townsfolk were holed up and fighting. Pit Middleton had exited the bank's front door and was standing on the top step firing at the hardware store across the street; and at the bottom of the bank's concrete steps, Jace and Hatcher were already climbing into their saddles, each with a bulky canvas bag hanging off their horns.

My gaze went back to the barbershop where Charlie Plummer was standing framed in its door. He was taking deliberate aim, and I knew then where that shot through my hat brim had come from. Like it or not, the time had come, and I swung my revolver toward him and snapped off three rounds as fast as I could thumb the hammer. My first missed by a wide margin, but the second and third showered him with splinters from the door's casing, and he fell back with a startled squawk. Swinging my Colt toward the hardware store, I methodically emptied its remaining rounds through the big display window. Then I holstered the revolver and slid the Marlin from its scabbard.

I was a decent shot with a handgun, having practiced often with Papa's old Remington, but I was a crack shot with a long gun, and as I've already mentioned, that Marlin was probably the most accurate rifle I've ever handled; even with Minko jumping around under me, I began making myself known to the folks of Erda. A man coming around the side of the bank trying to put a sneak on Jace with a shotgun fled back the way he'd come after I sent a round into the brick wall in front of his nose; another, holed up under a wooden boardwalk down the street from the bank, went scurrying in the opposite direction when I sent two rounds into the dirt at his side.

Farrell Crow and Harvey Judd were running their ponies down the muddy street stirrup to stirrup, firing at anything that moved. Pit Middleton came next, with Thumbs close behind him. Jace and Bob Hatcher were bringing up the rear. Townspeople began darting out to get off a final few rounds at the fleeing outlaws. Then Farrell and Harvey swept past, and Quint pulled his horse around and drove his spurs into its sides.

It was time for me to go, as well, and I wheeled Minko and let him have his head. As luck would have it, the pinto caught his stride just as Jace came up on my left, and the two of us rode out of town side by side, bent low over our saddle horns and whooping loudly—Jace in victory, me with pent-up relief as we raced out of range of Erda's rifles and shotguns.

Michael Zimmer

Excerpt from
Erda *Eagle Special Edition,* November 4, 1893

Armed Bandits Disrupt Peaceful Afternoon
by
Miss Clara Mumford

Our harmonious community was visited by gunfire and mayhem yesterday afternoon when revolver-carrying ruffians invaded or [*sic*] community intent upon robbery and disorder. At least seven unmasked individuals "shot up" Main Street as a contingent of three hoodlums entered the First Bank of Erda to abscond with nearly 900 dollars of hard-earned funds deposited there by the towns [*sic*] hard-working citizens. Bank Manager Ernest Woodbury assured us that the larger portion of the banks [*sic*] deposits were spared pilfering by teller Lone Calf Walker when he professed to lack the combination to open the rear safe, where the bulk of the towns [sic] assets are kept.

Not to be denied their "ounce of blood," the bandits opened fire on the good citizens of Erda, shooting indiscriminately at any brave individual who dared exit their home or business to assess the causation of gunfire. While several citizens received minor wounds, death claimed only one brave soul. John "Big Jack" Edgerton, a Negro and owner of the Edgerton Wagon Works, was murdered in a cold-blooded manner in front of his place of business when he attempted to intervene in the atrocity . . .

178

SESSION SIXTEEN

We left Erda at a dead run and didn't slow our flight until, maybe six or seven miles down the road, Pit Middleton spilled limply from his saddle.

Farrell and Harvey dashed on past with barely a glance; Thumbs, Haus, and Hatcher slowed only briefly, then spurred their horses back to top speed. But Jace stopped, and I pulled Minko in as well, riding back to take the sorrel's reins when Jace stepped down and went to Middleton's side. My throat tightened when Jace rolled the older man onto his back. The front of Pit's shirt was sodden with blood, a thick, crimson swamp that had soaked all the way down into his britches.

"Pit!" Jace gave the man a rough shake but it had no effect. Middleton was still breathing—you could see the labored rise and fall of his chest from twenty feet away—but he was unconscious and his face looked as pale as one of Mama's freshly washed sheets, his empty eye socket like a shallow well drilled into crusted snow. Jace looked up helplessly.

"There's nothing you can do for him," I said.

"We can't leave him."

"The posse will find him. They'll see he gets what help he needs, or a decent burial, if it comes to that."

"If he lives, they'll hang him."

"If we try to take him with us, he'll die certain sure," I replied pragmatically.

Taking a deep breath, Jace pushed wearily to his feet. "Maybe

179

you're right." He was staring down the road to where the others had already disappeared. What he said next surprised me. "When did you get to be so wise, little brother?"

I almost laughed in response. At that moment I was feeling about as brainy as a moss-covered rock; if I'd an ounce of wisdom anywhere about me, I sure wasn't seeing it that day. After a bit, I said, "We'd better git, Jace."

He was looking north now, across an overgrazed meadow where Pit's mount had bolted after losing its rider. The horse was staring back at us with its head thrown high, as tense as an overwound watch. If Jace had made an attempt to go after it I would have argued for letting it go, but no such suggestion was made. "We did this wrong," he said out of the blue.

"What do you mean?"

"We should've waited until later in the day, until just before the bank closed. That way we'd have had a whole night to make tracks."

"Maybe what we should have done was not robbed it at all."

"Yeah, I've been thinking that, too," he acknowledged glumly.

Middleton made a noise I can't really describe, but it brought both our gazes back to where he lay at the side of the road. His chest was no longer rising and falling, and his remaining eye had taken on the glaze all creatures get when the light inside is snuffed. After a pause, I said as gently as I could, "Jace, Pit's gone, and we need to ride."

I hadn't a doubt in my mind there was a posse on our trail, and knew the longer we delayed, the more apt it was to catch up. But Jace seemed stuck in a muddle of regret and self-doubt, and it struck me then that no matter what his reputation was—or what it would become—Jason Two-Buck wasn't cut out to be a desperado. Oh, he hated Kermit Watson to the core, and likely would have enjoyed gutting the man and his hired guns with a rusted meat hook, but as bloodthirsty as that may sound, he had too much empathy for others to keep up an outlaw façade for long. I figured that stable hand in Caddo had stripped away the tough outer shell of his hatred; Erda had poked the exposed flesh underneath and made it bleed. Pit Middleton . . . who knew what his passing meant to Jace?

I don't think he realized it at that point, but I felt confident the Erda bank job was our last. We wouldn't be robbing any stores or burning down any more buildings—no matter who owned them—and most important as far as I was concerned, we wouldn't be jeopardizing any more innocent lives. Kermit Watson, of course, was another matter. We still owed him for what he'd done to us and ours, and that included his hired guns if they got in our way; to me, that seemed only fair.

We probably stood there another five minutes, each of us lost in our own thoughts, so that when Jace finally spoke it took me a second to absorb what he said.

"Pit Middleton was a son of a bitch, Lige, but he deserved better than this."

"No, he didn't." I looked up, meeting Jace's puzzled gaze. "Pit got exactly what he deserved. Now we need to get out of here before we get what's coming to us."

He looked at me curiously for another few seconds, then slowly nodded consent. I handed him his reins and he climbed into his rig like an old man. I swear something died in Jace that day. I don't know if it happened in Erda or while standing there above Middleton's lifeless form, but the difference was indisputable—it haunted his eyes and weighed at his shoulders until they sloped earthward. Pulling his horse around, he started down the road after the others at an easy jog. I thought about nudging Minko up beside him but decided he needed time to himself to mull over everything that had happened over the last few days. I know I sure as hell did.

It was midafternoon and the rain had finally stopped when

we entered the cove. The others were already there, most of them dismounted and waiting with unconcealed impatience. Only Quintin Haus remained in his saddle, kind of tipped to one side like he had a boil on his butt. Blood had saturated his left pants' leg, and his expression was taut. When me and Jace got down, Farrell said, "Where's Pit?"

"Pit's dead," Jace replied stonily.

"You sure? I saw him flapping one of his arms when we rode past."

"Why didn't you stop?"

"This ain't my crew, Kid, which means it ain't my job."

Jace turned away without reply. "How bad are you hit?" he asked Haus.

"I ain't looked."

"The bullet went in just below his knee," Farrell said. "I took a peek when we got here, then wrapped some cloth around it to slow the bleeding." He gave Jace a meaningful look. "He'd probably better stay in his saddle."

Jace nodded that he understood. I reckon we all did . . . even Quintin Haus.

Dropping his reins, Jace walked over to where Hatcher was standing next to his gray, and both mien and manner told me the old Kid Jace had returned. Maybe not for long—at least that's what I was hoping—but enough to take charge again. He said, "You told us you were pulling out for Texas, Bob. Did you change your mind?"

"Yeah, I changed it."

"And now you figure you're entitled to a full share of what we took from the Erda bank?"

A muscle twitched under Hatcher's left eye. "You ain't thinkin' of trying to cut me out, are you, Kid?"

"I'm thinking about it. If we can't depend on you, we don't need you."

Hatcher's gaze turned to ice. For a second I thought he was going to pull his pistol. His hand actually inched toward it, but then stilled. He didn't relax, though. He was like a wire trap right before it's sprung, drawn tight with no more give at all. "Make up your mind, Kid," he said in an eerily calm tone. "I'm takin' my share, and I'll kill any son of a bitch who says I ain't, but I want to know now if I'm in or out."

After a long pause, Jace said, "You're in . . . until I say differently."

Hatcher smirked and kind of relaxed—I guess he thought Jace was backing down, but he wasn't.

"Don't push it," Jace warned in a voice so taut it didn't even sound like him. "Don't ever try to push it against me."

Hatcher didn't look away, but his cocky grin sure faded fast, reminding me once again that the name Kid Jace meant something in that part of the Nation.

Stepping past Hatcher, Jace lifted the canvas bag from the gray's saddle and carried it over to Crow. "You carry the money, Farrell."

Crow accepted the bag, scowling as he hefted its weight. "There ain't much here, Kid. Didn't you get in the safe?"

"There wasn't time, and the kid behind the counter said he didn't know the combination."

"Hell, they always say that. Put a gun up to his nose and he'll find it quick enough."

"That wouldn't have changed the fact we was runnin' outta time. We cleaned the tills and I got some cash and a bunch of papers from a tin box under the counter, but that's it. We'll count what's there later and divvy it up. Right now we need to keep moving."

"You think they're comin' after us?" Thumbs asked in a draggy kind of way. Noticing the glassy visage on top of the faint slur to his words, I suspect he'd been deeper into his bottle of Dr. Cook's Cherry Pectoral Relief than he normally went. Jace noticed it, too, but didn't say anything about it.

"I figure so," Jace concurred. "They likely won't have any trouble finding us, either. We've left a trail a five year old could follow."

"It's too bad we don't have those harness horses you gave to the Kiowa," Harvey said pointedly, reiterating Farrell Crow's old argument. "Fresh mounts would have helped."

"Yeah," Jace replied flatly. "It's too damn bad, ain't it?" He gathered the sorrel's reins and stepped into the saddle. "Mount up, and let's get outta here."

Well, I'll say this: If a posse did follow us out of Erda—and I still don't see how they couldn't have—I never saw any sign of it. Leaving the cove, we rode west through a dripping forest, following the same trail Strong Wolf had forged earlier with the harness stock, and that George and Milly had taken later. Their tracks were easy to read in the rain-softened earth, as I knew ours would be to anyone coming along after us, and I kept watching over my shoulder for pursuit through what remained of the day—so much for the free and easy life of a bandit.

I wondered if we'd head for the Notch after exiting that low caprock country west of Greasy Bend, but we didn't. I guess even Bob Hatcher and Kid Jace were fearful enough of Enoch Anderson's promise to shoot anyone who brought the law into his valley not to press their luck. Instead we rode southwest all that night and most of the next day, skirting well to the south of Thomas Red Corn's place, where I was hoping George and Milly were safely ensconced. It was early evening of that second day when we came in sight of Goodwin's trading post on Cow Creek. Although it hadn't even been a month since I'd last laid eyes on Billy's low-roofed store, it seemed like years. Like a lifetime, in many ways.

The trading post had a forlorn look about it, the way some

places do with winter coming on. The hitching rails out front were empty and the tents that had been scattered along the creek bank on my first visit were gone. The front door was firmly closed against the chill autumn air, although I noticed the smoke from the chimney was rising straight into the pale blue of the fading sunset. The rain had finally moved on for good, something we were all grateful for.

Jace halted us below a cutbank on Cow Creek and rode in alone. We waited as he entered, tense and fearful of an ambush, but he reappeared within minutes to wave us up. Everyone dismounted out front—about as stove-up a bunch of hooligans as you're ever likely to see after our long flight—and me and Thumbs took the horses to the big corral out back and saw to their care, stowing the tack in a small saddle shed next to the corral and making sure the water trough was full and clean; we fed them shelled corn, then rubbed down their sweaty hides with burlap sacking while they ate. Those ponies were worn to their frazzles as well, and in dire need to some solid rest. As aggravating as it was to concede, I knew Farrell had been right when he'd urged Jace to hang onto those horses we'd taken from the Ardmore stagecoach.

It was coming onto full dark and growing downright frosty by the time me and Thumbs finished our chores and went inside. Being first through the door, I stopped abruptly with my hand still on the outer knob when I spied Billy and Elizabeth and a quartet of older Indians—two men and their wives, I judged—standing at the far end of the counter in a clump of unhappy. Hatcher stood some yards away with his revolver drawn and sitting on the counter in front of him; the canvas sacks from the Erda bank lay to one side of it.

At a table in the middle of the room, Jace and Harvey were wolfing down stew from tin plates. Steaming cups of coffee sat next to them, and there was a big skillet of cornbread—what was left of it, anyway—between them. Quintin Haus lay slumped against the wall behind them, his complexion even paler in lamplight than it had been outside at noon. I didn't see Farrell, but heard someone rattling around in back and figured that had to be him.

Billy gave me a level stare but no greeting. The others, even Elizabeth, who'd treated me so kindly the last time I'd been there, barely acknowledged mine or Thumbs's arrival. I think Bob Hatcher had their full attention; considering the snarly looks the man kept tossing their way, I wasn't surprised.

"What's going on?" I asked Jace, edging the rest of the way into the main trade room with Thumbs hard on my heels.

Motioning toward an empty chair next to him, he said, "Have a seat, Lige. This ain't half bad."

"What is it?" Thumbs asked, elbowing past me to the table.

"Mutton," Harvey replied around a mouthful of cornbread soaked in molasses.

"It's goat," Billy corrected. "Compliments of Little Tall Man." He tipped his head to the shriveled old codger next to him, wearing patched clothing and badly worn brogan shoes coming apart between the sole and vamp; Little Tall Man's hair was as gray as a fresh-forged horseshoe, worn long and braided in the old way, a style I'd always admired but never attempted.

"Why do you have them corralled over there?" I asked, ignoring Jace's offer of a meal. Thumbs took the chair, instead, and immediately began spooning hot stew onto a clean plate.

"We need to keep things under control, little brother. It ain't nothing personal against them."

"I think it might be," I said. "This is Billy's store, and it's his home, so I'd think he'd take it real personal. So would Elizabeth."

Jace met my gaze, and his own sent a chill down my spine. What the hell had happened in the hour or so that Thumbs and

I had been outside taking care of the horses? Where was the Jace I'd seen yesterday, standing drained and forlorn above Pit Middleton body in the middle of the Erda road?

"We were wrong," Jace said, as if reading my mind. "Nothing's changed. It can't."

"Yes it can."

He shook his head. "No, I wish it could, but no." He motioned to the table, the food and drink strewn across it. "This is who I am, who we all are. Thieves and killers."

"You didn't kill anyone."

"Same as," he replied, and turned back to his meal.

"You didn't think so yesterday."

"Yesterday was different." He was bent over his plate, leaning close as if to absorb some of the stew's warmth into his cold cheeks.

"How?" I persisted, and Jace spun around in his chair.

"Goddamnit, Lige, shut up! Just shut your mouth!"

I froze, my lips parted in astonishment. I'd never heard Jace talk like that. It wasn't the words that shocked me, but the raw emotion behind them. The look on his face and the blaze in his eyes frightened me, and caught the others by surprise, too. Harvey stopped eating with his spoon half raised, and Thumbs reared back as if the cornbread had grown teeth and snapped at him. Even Bob Hatcher, standing at the counter, straightened a few inches, and his fingers slid warily over the walnut grips of his revolver. Then the moment broke and Jace's shoulders sagged as if a rod had been pulled out from between them, leaving only the flesh to hold everything together.

"It doesn't matter," he said quietly. He eased back around and looked at his meal, but kept his hands flat on the table. "Maybe you'd best go on home," he added.

"I don't have a home, remember? Watson took it."

"Then make one. Rebuild the cabin, or raise a new one. Take

over the garden. Mama would've wanted that."

"Bullshit," I said, and Harvey laughed.

"He's part of us now, Kid. Ain't no goin' back after what we done." He looked at me. "We just found out your buddy Watson has got spies all up and down the ol' Rocky Island, and a special engine with two cars to tote his men and their horses wherever they're needed. Soon's they get wind we're here, they'll come a'swoopin' down like vultures." [*Editor's Note:* The "ol' Rocky Island" Judd is referring to is the Rock Island Railroad.]

"Is that true?" I asked Jace.

"That's what Billy says."

"It's true," Billy confirmed. "Riders have been passing through here every day since you boys robbed the Ardmore stage. Watson gambled that you'd come back this way sooner or later."

"He's got men at Duncan's Store and in Tucker, and he's got scouts everywhere," Harvey continued. "There's Lighthorse behind us, too." [*Editor's Note:* Duncan's Store is present Duncan, Oklahoma; Tucker was rechristened Comanche in 1898; both towns are located in Stephens County.]

"How do you know all this?" I asked Billy.

"I don't, not for sure. It's what I've heard from others, though."

"He means the moccasin telegraph, ain't that right, storekeep?" Hatcher said with a taut grin.

The moccasin telegraph, in case you're not familiar with the term, is kind of like today's grapevine, a means of communication that took advantage of local populations. Going back to General Custer, who I mentioned when we first started these recordings, there were reports of his death reaching the folks in Bismarck way before the first official word of the massacre got there. [*Editor's Note:* In late June of 1876, after G.A. Custer's defeat at the Little Bighorn, the wounded soldiers were transported north to the Yellowstone River and placed onboard the steamship *Far West*. From there, traveling in both daylight and dark, the sternwheeler returned to Fort Abraham Lincoln, across from Bismarck, ND (then Dakota Territory), in a record 54 hours—a distance of 710 miles. By the time the *Far West* arrived, it's said that rumors of Custer's defeat were already circulating through the town.]

"Some," Billy allowed, referring to Hatcher's comment about the moccasin telegraph as the source of his information, "but most of it came from Watson's men, assuming they weren't lying to me."

Thumbs looked puzzled. "Why would they lie?"

"To keep us confused," Jace said. "To keep us circling around the territory, dodging badges that ain't there."

"We're going to have to have horses," I said. I was hoping we'd keep riding, maybe go to Mexico like Jace had mentioned in the Notch, but I knew we weren't likely to make it out of Indian Territory without fresh stock. "Ours are wrung out and won't be fit to ride for a couple of weeks."

Jace nodded but didn't reply. He started eating again, and I went over and sat down near him. "We're paying for this, ain't we?" I asked softly.

"Yeah, we're paying. I ain't so low-down yet as to steal from a friend."

That was a relief to hear; in my mind it meant he wasn't all the way gone, no matter how hard he was trying to convince himself that he was. Billy didn't help matters, though.

"But you'll hold us under a killer's gun before you pay, is that it?" he asked from across the room.

"That's about the size of it, storekeep," Hatcher said, his fingers tapping the grips of his revolver to remind them it was still there.

"I gotta have some time to think," Jace said, abruptly pushing his chair back and rising. He looked tired, I thought, as worn out as our riding stock, although I suspected it was going to take him a lot longer to recuperate than it would our horses. He wiped his mouth with his sleeve and headed for the door. I kind of thought he'd slam it shut behind him, but I barely heard the bolt catch as he passed from sight. Over at the counter, Bob Hatcher chuckled low in his throat, the sound as menacing as a dog's growl just before it—

SESSION SEVENTEEN

That damn recorder. I'll take pencil and paper any day. At least they don't run out of disk in the middle of the conversation, or make such a god-awful squawk when they do.

Anyway, what I was about to say was that Farrell came out of the back of the store not long after Jace exited the front. He was toting a heavy sack that he dropped on the counter next to the two canvas moneybags from Erda. Walking over to where Jace had been sitting, he flopped down and peered at the uneaten stew. "What's the matter with this?"

"Not a damn thing," was Harvey's reply. "Ol' Kid just lost his appetite when he got to thinkin' about all them guns circlin' in around us."

"Jace needs time to think where there's not a lot of useless yapping going on," I said.

Farrell and Harvey chuckled at my immature defense of Jason, and Hatcher grinned. Only Thumbs seemed oblivious to the tension in the room, and I wondered how much of Dr. Cook's cherry elixir he had left; I'd seen him out by the corral as we finished caring for the stock, slipping snorts on the sly. Refilling Jace's plate from the dwindling pot of stew, Farrell dug in with gusto. After a couple of bites, he looked at me and said, "What are you so glum about, boy?"

"I'm thinking, too."

"He's thinking he got himself into the wrong business, I'll bet," Hatcher supplied from the counter.

"If he is, he's smarter than he looks," Farrell replied.

"He'd have to be," Hatcher added with a taunting grin.

Ignoring them both, I went over to where Quintin Haus was propped against the wall, arms splayed limply to his sides. Hunkering down next to him, I said, "Quint, can you hear me?"

His head moved in a barely perceptible nod.

"I'm going to take off your bandage and look at your leg. It might hurt."

Quint nodded again and licked his lips like he wanted to say something, then decided against it. Sliding my Green River— the same knife I'd gotten from Billy, the night I first showed up at his place—I gently sliced through the ruby-glazed fabric and eased it away from the wound. Although I'd never liked the guy, Quint was a member of the Kid Jace gang, and I was determined to do what I could to help him.

The bandages' removal brought a fresh gout of blood from the bullet-torn flesh, and a low, hoarse cry from Quintin's throat. I quickly returned the crusted fabric to the injured limb and glanced over my shoulder to Billy. "I need some clean bandages."

Billy looked at Hatcher, who shrugged like he didn't care. Stepping behind the counter, Billy pulled a bolt of calico off a shelf and flipped it open. "We'll need to wash the wound, too," he told Hatcher, and received another noncommittal shrug. "Elizabeth, go get a pan of water from the kitchen," Billy said, although he continued to watch Hatcher to make sure the gunman didn't protest.

"Sure, let her go," Hatcher said. "Just so she understands that if she tries anything that might cause me upset, I'll kill every son of a bitch in here."

"She knows that," Billy replied, and Hatcher grinned and winked, reminding me in that instant of a cat toying with a mouse it wasn't quite ready to kill yet.

Billy came over with a yard or so of calico cloth; Elizabeth arrived a few minutes later with a pan of warm water that she'd likely already had on the stove for dirty dishes. She acted like she wanted to help, but Hatcher wouldn't allow it.

"Get back over here where I can keep an eye on you," he commanded, and after a helpless glance to her husband, Elizabeth rose and did as instructed.

Me and Billy bathed Quint's wound as best we could, but it was an ugly puncture going in and even worse where the bullet had come out. Billy's expression was peaked as we finished wrapping the mangled appendage. "You know he's going to lose that leg, don't you?" Billy said to me after Quint had passed out.

I nodded morosely. The bone had been shattered—the whole thing felt more like mush than limb—with splinters and larger fragments poking out of the meat like porcupine quills. After all that time in the saddle, it was a wonder he wasn't dead.

"I can't do it," I said.

"I doubt if either of us could, not without killing him. He needs a doctor."

I rocked back on the balls of my feet, elbows resting over my knees as I contemplated the calico bandage snugged around Quint's leg, already soaked through with new blood. It occurred to me that if we didn't do something pretty quick, he'd be as apt to bleed to death as die of infection.

"Is there a doctor nearby?"

"There's one in Tucker."

I shook my head. "Watson's men would be on us like a bear on honey if we took him there."

"Then the next nearest one that I know of would be in Ardmore."

I mumbled a curse. Ardmore was way the hell east of us, not to mention smack-dab in the middle of the area we'd just come from. Going back would likely put us directly into the path of those Lighthorse policemen Billy had warned us of.

"We could haul him there in the wagon," Billy suggested, noting my hesitation but misreading its cause. "Pile some hay in the bed and lay blankets over the top. He'd not make it in a saddle, but he might if we took our time and didn't jostle him too much."

I glanced to where Hatcher was standing at the counter. Harvey Judd and Farrell Crow had finished their meals and were standing with him, sharing a bottle of Old Overholt that Farrell had found in one of the back rooms. [Editor's Note: Old Overholt is a rye whiskey originally distilled in Overton, Pennsylvania; the company was founded in 1810. Old Overholt, one of the oldest continually distilled whiskeys in the United States, was a popular brand throughout the American West.]

"They wouldn't allow it, would they?" Billy said, his expression marked with defeat. "They'd rather see this boy die than find him some help."

"They mostly wouldn't want the law getting to him," I said. "They'd be afraid he'd spill too much information to make a deal for himself with the courts."

"I know every face here except this one." He tipped his head to Quint. "I imagine Watson's posse and the Lighthorse do, too."

"I wish you'd quit calling Watson's men a posse. They're no more lawmen than I am."

"Fair enough, but changing what we call them doesn't change what they are."

"Man-killers?" I said it to goad him, but Billy's expression never wavered.

"Every damn one of them, from what I've heard," he agreed. "Watson probably wouldn't have hired them if they weren't." Billy studied me intently for a moment, then said, "Have you shot anyone yet, Lige?"

"No, sir, I don't believe I have."

"They were talking about the Erda raid before you and Thumbs came in. They said there was a lot of shooting."

I nodded affirmatively. "There was, but I didn't shoot anyone."

"But you did shoot?"

"I didn't have much choice about that."

"There's always a choice, Lige. Remember that." He hesitated and I thought he was going to say something else, but instead he pushed to his feet, his knees popping like Papa's used to on wintery nights, and walked back to stand with his wife.

I went outside without eating, even though I was fairly famished. I looked for Jace but couldn't find him, so I got my bedroll from my saddle and took it over to the same tall stack of hay where I'd slept the last time I was there. It was a lot colder tonight, the chill made even worse by the ground's dampness from the past week's rains, but I decided I'd rather sleep there than inside with the others.

I wasn't too worried about the Goodwins or their friends, Little Tall Man and Seth Monroe and their wives, Betsy Tall Man and Sings Along Monroe—Chickasaws, all. Jace had given his word they wouldn't be harmed, and barring some kind of provocation from the captives, his decree would be honored. Despite a growing animosity toward Jace, I didn't believe anyone would dare to buck him. Not yet, anyway.

I fell asleep immediately, but woke up early the next morning with a niggling sense of unease. The sky was just starting to lighten up in the east but the birds weren't singing, and that seemed odd. I lay unmoving for several minutes, listening to the sounds of the night—the movement of the stock in the corral and the faint rustle of a mouse or some other small creature deep in the hay where I'd made my bed. Nothing seemed out of place except for the lack of birdsong, and the longer that continued, the more it bothered me. With clear skies and dawn so near, they should have been out in force after so many dreary days of rain.

I eased onto my side and pushed up on one elbow. Although nothing moved, an icy apprehension rippled across the back of my neck. It was the damnedest feeling, and a new one for me, although I realize now what it was—that sixth sense of the hunted, rather than the hunter, of prey instead of predator. Feeling a need to *move,* I slinked into my hat and coat, kept warm inside my bedroll along with my rifle and revolver, then pushed my blankets back and slipped on my boots. Rising cautiously, I stepped away from the clotted shadows of the haystack. As I did, I heard a distinct, metallic clatter from the direction of the creek, and instinctively ducked back behind the rick just as a shot fractured the icy, predawn stillness.

A distant yell of reprimand was followed by a spattering of more gunfire from the scrub along Cow Creek. Then, as the first ragged volley tapered off, I sprinted across the yard to Goodwin's front porch, leaping onto it from the side and racing down its length. Bullets smacked the trading post wall before and after me, but I made it to the front door without getting scratched and Bob Hatcher quickly threw it open and yanked me inside.

The rest of our bunch was there by then, breaking out windows and returning fire. Muzzles flashed like fiery stems from the creek bank, yellow centered but spitting hot red sparks in blossoms as the excess powder burned off. Peering past the edge of a window frame, I counted five such blooms sparking and fading, then sparking again.

Whoever was out there, they weren't nearly as shy about being shot at as those folks in Erda, who would duck out of sight and stay there for a good long time whenever a bullet came too close. These boys were returning our fire without hesitation, and they were good shots, especially considering the dim, predawn light.

With at least five shooters out front, it occurred to me that somebody ought to be checking the rear. Jace must have read my mind, because as soon as I caught his eye, he jerked his head toward the back rooms. I nodded and scrambled across the trading post's floor on my hands and knees, a crosshatch of hot lead stitching the air just inches above my scalp.

Thumbs was already in back with the Goodwins, keeping them covered with his Colt. He jumped and swung the revolver toward me as I scooted inside.

"Take it easy," I chided him, then thrust my chin toward a lamp sitting on a small, sofa-side table, its wick turned low to provide just enough illumination for him to guard his prisoners. "Blow that out," I said, and he immediately did.

With the room back in shadow, I elbowed the door shut and stood up. Expecting a storeroom, I found myself instead in a small parlor with a pale green sofa against one wall, a couple of rocking chairs across from it. A door to my left revealed what looked like a bedroom; the kitchen was to my right. Having been there on my last visit, I knew there was a set of narrow stairs against the inside wall that led to the second floor where the Goodwins' children had slept while still at home.

A pair of tall windows seemed to monopolize the parlor's north wall, with flowered chintz curtains—red blossoms against a whey-colored fabric—tied back on either side. I sidled up to one of them and peeked out. Even though the room was fairly dark, I guess the view from outside was sufficient for objects close to the glass, because as soon as I eased an eye past the sash a shot rang out from a coulee a couple of hundred yards away. The glass above me was blasted inward, flinging jagged shards across the room, and I cursed and flung myself to the side.

"What's happening?" Thumbs cried in a panicky voice. "Who's shooting at us?"

"Watson's men," I replied, although I truthfully had no idea who it might be.

"How many are there?" Billy asked, and he sounded a lot calmer than Thumbs. They were all—the Goodwins, the Monroes, and the Tall Mans—crouched behind the sofa that Billy had pulled away from the wall for them to hide behind. They looked concerned but not particularly frightened, and I admired them for that.

"I don't know," I said. "I counted five out front, and there's at least one back here."

"Six?" Billy nodded thoughtfully. "That sounds about right. If it is Watson's men, they've probably already sent someone to Tucker to wire for the train from Duncan's Store."

"How long will that take?"

"Figure twenty minutes to Tucker on a fast horse, another forty from Duncan to Tucker by train, then whatever it takes to get back here."

"A couple of hours?"

"No more than that."

Thumbs was whispering tersely under his breath, bringing a smile to Billy's lips. "What's the matter, Thumbs? Getting worried?"

"You just mind your words don't get you in more trouble than they can get you out of," Thumbs answered. He looked at me. "We gotta get outta here, Lige."

Well, I couldn't argue with that, but first we had to contend with the shooters who had us pinned down. "Watch this window," I said. "I'll go see what Jace wants to do."

Thumbs nodded and scurried over on bent knees while I

returned to the main room in a similar pose. The gunmen along
the creek had been hard at work destroying the interior of Goodwin's Store. There was broken glass and riddled tins everywhere,
and the floor behind the counter was slick with molasses—a
five-gallon keg of the stuff had been rived by several rounds—
and the spilled juices of canned peaches, tomatoes, peas,
kerosene, and Lord knew what else, all if it creeping languidly
across the floor.

Skirting the worst of it, I crabbed over to where Jace was
kneeling behind a heavy trunk filled with blankets that he'd
pushed up against the front door. [*Editor's Note:* An etching
from a photograph of the trunk Two-Buck mentions here was
published in several local newspapers shortly after the battle at
Goodwin's trading post, including the Erda *Eagle* on November
6th; although the trunk's current location is unknown, its size is
estimated at four feet by two feet in diameter and at least three
feet tall at the crest of its domed lid; a total of thirty-nine bullet
holes in the top and along one side are visible in the etching,
suggesting the trunk had been placed on end during the fighting.]

I risked a quick look, then ducked back when a bullet
whiskered past my jaw. "Careful," Jace cautioned.

"I reckon. What's going on?"

"Same thing as when you left. I heard shooting out back."

"Yeah, there's one guy back there. At least I only saw one
muzzle flash." I told him what Billy had said about the rest of
Watson's men being there possibly as early as sunup. I kept my
voice low so that the others couldn't overhear, although I'm not
sure anyone could have heard me anyway; after all that shooting, I know my ears felt like they'd been stuffed with cotton.

"We're going to have to make a run for it before they get
here," Jace said.

"How are we going to reach our horses?"

Jace wiggled around to put his back to the trunk and called for Farrell and Harvey to come over while he punched empty brass from his revolver. When they got there, he said, "I want you two to make a break for the saddle shed before it gets any lighter."

"The hell!" Farrell exclaimed.

"We have to get those horses saddled before the rest of Watson's men show up," Jace said firmly.

Farrell looked at me. "Let the runt do it."

"No, I'm tellin' you to do it." With his revolver loaded, Jace calmly racheted the hammer to full cock. Farrell's eyes narrowed, but Jace spoke before he could say anything. "Put a cork in whatever you're thinking, Crow. You and Harvey are going. Me and Bob and Lige'll cover your asses from here. When you get there, get the horses saddled and ready to ride, then wait for my signal."

"What kind of a signal?" Harvey asked.

"I don't know," Jace admitted, "but you will when you hear it." His gaze slid over to where Haus lay slumped again the wall, still breathing but with his eyes closed, unaware of the chaos erupting around him.

"I ain't worryin' about him," Farrell growled.

"I ain't asking you to. Just saddle horses, then we'll either make a run for you, or have you bring the horses here." He leveled his gaze on the two men. "We'll keep that Erda bank money here, too, in case either of you get an itch to take off on your own."

"Are you sayin' we'd run," Farrell challenged.

"I'm saying that if you do, it'll be without the cash." Jace paused as if waiting for a response. When none came, he said, "Wait 'til we start shootin', then jump out that side window and hoof it for the saddle shed as fast as you can."

Harvey and Farrell exchanged glances, then Harvey shrugged,

settling it between them. As the two men crept to the small side window, Jace looked at me. "You loaded, little brother?"

I nodded that I was. Although I had the Marlin with me, I intended to use my Colt when we started pumping rounds into the brush along Cow Creek. It would be faster, and would also require me to expose less of myself to our ambushers. With Farrell and Harvey in position, Jace took a deep breath and said, "Let 'em have it, boys!"

SESSION EIGHTEEN

Well, we gave 'em hell for a couple of minutes there. I shot the Colt dry and dumped it back in its holster, then shouldered the Marlin and began levering round after round into that creek-side scrub. The others were doing the same, a kind of rolling thunder that must have caught our ambushers by surprise, because I didn't see a single puff of gun smoke from their shelter as Farrell and Harvey made their sprint for the saddle shed.

I was about halfway through the Marlin's magazine when Jace yelled for us to stop shooting. For a second, I couldn't understand why we'd want to quit when we had them pinned down so solid they couldn't even raise their hopes without getting them blasted off by one of our bullets. Then it dawned on me that if we shot everything empty, we'd be sitting ducks if they decided to rush us.

I fell back with a kind of breathless cry of satisfaction and began reloading the Marlin with rounds from my coat pocket. My hands were actually trembling from the rage and excitement that was surging through my veins, and my ears hummed from the detonation of so many rounds fired within the enclosed room. As you might expect, the second we stopped shooting, those bastards along the creek opened up with a renewed vengeance of their own. Their bullets smashed into the store's walls, inside and out, busting what few panes of glass hadn't already been broken and shattering what merchandise still remained on the shelves.

"Lige," Jace hollered, and motioned toward the back of the store. I nodded and pushed away from my place under the front window, but he stopped me before I'd gotten halfway across the room. "Don't let anything happen to the hostages."

I remember that kind of hit me low in the gut, as I hadn't considered the Goodwins, the Monroes, or the Tall Mans in that light. "What do you mean?"

"I mean we're gonna need them when we make a break for the horses," he replied, already turning away.

I knelt there a moment as Jace's words flowed like ice through my veins, then numbly hurried on into the parlor and closed the door behind me. Thumbs was crouched next to the window, but looked around at my entry. "Did they make it?" he asked.

"You heard?"

"I came over to see what was happening," he confessed.

Chuckling, Billy said, "Thumbs was afraid you boys might leave without him."

"You just shut up," Thumbs returned.

Billy's grin widened, but he held his hands up in a sort of surrendering gesture and said no more. I asked Thumbs if he'd seen anyone outside and he allowed that he had.

"There's a bunch of 'em out there now," he stated glumly. "Down in that gulch."

He meant the coulee where the man who'd shot at me earlier had harbored. It ran across the rear of the Goodwins' summer pasture, but Billy had confided earlier that it seldom held any water. That was to our advantage, as it didn't encourage the growth of concealing scrub the way the creek out front did. I eased an eye past the window frame for a look. It was a lot lighter outside than it had been even fifteen minutes before, making it easier to see the bobbing movement of four or five men, although no solid targets. A sense of foreboding hung over me as I wondered how long they'd been there. Had they been there all along, or were they recent arrivals? It occurred to me that we could have been spotted last night, and that Watson's entire crew was even then creeping into position.

"Lige," Billy called quietly, and I crabbed over to where he was sitting slightly apart from the others. "What's Jace planning?"

"We're going to make a run for it."

"All of you?"

Thinking of Quint, I shook my head. "Probably not."

He eyed me thoughtfully for a minute. "Do you remember me saying the last time you were here that you had some enlightenment coming your way, at least as far as your brother was concerned?"

"Yeah, I remember."

"I was wondering what you thought of him now."

"He's my brother," I replied stubbornly. "Nothing's changed that, and I intend to stand with him to the end."

"Even if it means your own death?"

"Even that," I replied, although I'll admit the prospect was disconcerting. Just how far would I be willing to go? I wondered.

"I guess I can understand the way you feel," Billy allowed. "I'd probably do the same for my brother, although I can't envision him doing anything like this."

"He might if he was pushed hard enough."

"Meaning Watson?"

"That, and three years in Leavenworth for something he didn't do."

"Jace got a raw deal, there's no denying that."

"It was worse than raw, and it took something good out of him. He came home as bitter as a summer persimmon. We all saw it. It was like he hated the sun for shining and the wind for blowing."

Billy was silent a moment, staring at the far wall. Then he

said, "Have you ever asked yourself why Watson's done what he has to your family?"

"Every damn day," I said, my words harsh with emotion. I was staring at him, wondering. "Do you know?"

"Yes, I know."

"Tell me. Mama never would, and I don't think even Jason knows all of it."

"No, I doubt if he does." Billy hesitated, perhaps questioning whether he should have brought it up at all, but there was really nothing to lose at that point. Mama and Papa were both dead, along with my siblings. There was just me and Jace left, and it didn't seem likely we'd be around much longer.

Taking a deep breath, he said, "It started a long time ago, Lige, before your daddy and mama ever met. Did you know Kermit wanted to marry your ma? He wanted it so bad I swear he'd just about start panting every time he saw her. But your ma wouldn't have anything to do with him. I've always suspected she saw what kind of a man he was, or at least what he had the potential to become, even then.

"Your ma was teaching at the Bloomfield Girls Academy outside of Kemp at the time, and Watson had a small place nearby, along Sandy Creek. He'd go to the dances and other social functions at the academy on a regular basis and ask your ma to dance, but she always refused. That burned Watson's pride. He's not a man to accept public humiliation graciously, although I suppose not many are. But he kept trying and she kept putting him off, until one day your daddy showed up, and after that any chance Watson might have had with your ma was lost forever." Billy smiled fondly. "I believe those two fell in love almost the minute they laid eyes on one another. Everyone saw it, but Kermit wouldn't accept it. As far as he was concerned, your daddy was just a dirt-poor redskin who didn't even own his own horse at the time."

Billy stopped talking and just stared at me as if waiting for some kind of response. I had to try a couple of times to get some words out, my throat feeling as dry as dust on a windowsill. "Papa's dead," I finally managed. "Mama, too." Then, after another pause, "So, why?"

"I suppose because Watson's anger isn't dead. It's still alive, and it must gnaw at him to know he'll never have her now." There was sadness in his eyes. "He needs someone to blame, Lige. Someone to hang his anger on. Kind of like Jace does."

"So this is all because Kermit Watson wanted to make Mama pay for refusing him?"

"That's about the size of it."

"Why would he do that if he loved her?"

"I never said Kermit Watson loved your ma. I said he wanted to marry her, and there can be a big difference between those two things sometimes. When your ma and daddy got hitched, Kermit went after a Chickasaw woman named Pretty Horse and married her. She was the one who gave his territorial holdings a legality he hadn't had before, and wouldn't have had if he'd married your ma. It also allowed him to grow his business in the Nation, in your daddy's backyard, so to speak. I've always suspected it was his anger at your ma that spurred him to want to possess so much. Like that farm on the Washita, a couple of stores and a stage line, and then that bank in Erda. Kermit's worth more in money and property than just about anyone else in these parts, but it was never enough to make a dent in your ma's love for your daddy.

"Pretty Horse died last year. I've heard people speculate it was Watson who killed her because after all those years, she finally became pregnant, and he wouldn't abide a mixed-blood child as an heir. I've also heard people say it was because he knew he wasn't the father. Or maybe it was appendicitis, like the doc in Tishomingo claimed. All I know is that after her death, Watson already owned all he wanted and a whole lot more than any one man needs. Legally, he was set as far as the Chickasaw Council was concerned, so there wasn't anything to stop him from pursuing your ma." Billy paused and looked at me. "Do you understand what I'm saying, Lige?"

I nodded that I did. Hell, it wasn't all that hard to grasp, at least on a basic level. It was understanding how a man like that thought, how he could live with himself after all he'd done, that was beyond my comprehension, then as now.

"Are you all right?" Billy asked gently.

"Yeah, I'm fine."

"I've never told Jace any of this, and I'm not sure why. Maybe I didn't think he'd be able to understand it the way I hope you will."

"All right," I replied hollowly, and wondered if it was ever possible to grasp what another person *meant.* I mean, how the hell do you measure something like that?

"What are you going to do now?" Billy asked.

"I don't know," I replied, then stood and returned to where Thumbs was kneeling at the window. I could see Watson's men in the distant coulee, rifle barrels poking up like a row of broken twigs against the autumn-tanned landscape. There must have been a dozen out there now, and I had to believe at least an equal number were waiting in front for us to make our break. Then I spotted something that hit me like a fist buried wrist-deep in my stomach, and I croaked, "Thumbs?"

He looked to where I was staring, then fell back with a drawn-out moan. His eyes looked like two big saucers hanging off the deep ridge of his brow. "Oh, Lord," he breathed.

"What's going on?" Billy demanded.

"They've got a cannon," I told him, and knew at the very center of my being it was the same one they used to blow up Mama's house, back on Two-Buck Mountain.

Billy hurried to my side, although careful to stay low and out of sight; at that range, no one could count on Watson's gunmen telling the difference between friend or foe—or caring. "Where?"

"To the left, just coming into the coulee."

He saw it then, and swore sharply. "They'll use it, too." He looked at me, and for the first time I saw fear in his eyes. "You can't let them do this, Lige. They'll destroy everything I own, and this place is all I have. It's taken me a lifetime to build it."

"It ain't me doing it, Billy."

"You can stop it."

"How? By giving myself up?"

His lips moved wordlessly, as if searching for an answer that didn't include me and Jace and the others getting strung up or gunned down. Then he sank back against the wall, his eyes moist with tears. I couldn't blame him. I mean, I wasn't going to die for him, but I could understand the despair he must have been feeling. My gaze strayed to where Elizabeth and the others were seated. They were watching me, waiting for my decision; Thumbs, too, I noticed.

"All right," I said, giving in to what I knew was right, if not especially smart. "You're getting outta here. It's the best I can do."

Billy scowled uncertainly until I yanked at one of the curtains, pulling it and the rod down in one motion. I knotted the two together and thrust the bare end of the wooden rod into his, then motioned Elizabeth, the Monroes, and the Tall Mans over.

"Farrell ain't going to like this," Thumbs said, though softly, as if afraid of being overheard by those in the front room.

"Farrell can go to hell, and take what he likes and doesn't like with him."

"Jace ain't gonna like it, either."

I almost said Jace could go to hell, too, but bit it off at the last minute. I was betraying Jace's trust, yet I couldn't allow him to use innocent people as hostages. This war, or whatever you want to call it, was between us and Kermit Watson, and we had no right to pull in folks who didn't want any part of it. That applied to the citizens of Erda, as well. We'd done wrong robbing their bank. Kermit Watson would never reimburse his depositors, and that meant the harm done to those folks had been at the hands of the Kid Jace gang, no one else.

"I can't guarantee they won't start shooting as soon as they see you," I said to Billy.

"It doesn't matter. Our odds will be better out there than in here." He hesitated. "You and Thumbs could come with us, Lige. Leave your guns here and I'll—" He stopped at the adamant way I was shaking my head.

"I won't abandon Jace. I wish you the best, and I'm sorry about your store, but we're staying." I glanced at Thumbs, who nodded gamely that he was also staying.

"All right then." Billy thrust his hand forward. His grip was firm, his gaze penetrating but without condemnation. "Good luck, Elijah."

I thanked him, then stood back as the three couples crawled out the window and scurried across the back pasture with Billy in the lead, that pale white flag held high and fluttering. The last I saw of the Monroes, Betsy Tall Man, and Elizabeth Goodwin was when they dropped safely into that coulee like billiard balls into a deep side pocket. Of course I'd see Billy and Little Tall Man again, and if you've heard this story before, you already know that. But if you haven't, then sit back and listen, because we're closing in on the final days.

SESSION NINETEEN

As soon as Billy and the others were out of sight, I went into the front room and told Jace what I'd done. It surprised him, and it made Bob Hatcher mad enough to threaten to shoot me, which brought Jace back to my side of the enterprise.

"Try it and I'll spill your guts over the floor with the rest of this mess," Jace said, referring to the molasses and other juices that had spread across a good portion of the trade room floor.

"Those hostages were our shield," Hatcher countered—along with Harvey Judd, Bob was one of the few men I ever knew who never displayed any hesitation at another's threat of violence.

"Well, they ain't no more," Jace said. He looked at me. "Go on in back and keep an eye on Watson's man."

"There's more than one of them out there now," I said, and explained how others had been showing up all along; then I told him about the cannon, and Jace's expression fell hard. Hatcher uttered a curse that would have scared the hell out of me under different circumstances, although that day at Billy's I gave him barely a glance.

"What now, Kid?" Hatcher demanded.

"We're gonna make a run for it."

"Without hostages to shield us?"

"That's right." Jace caught my eye. "Go on in back and keep an eye on what they're up to, Lige, and send Thumbs out here. I want to talk to him."

I nodded and took off, circling wide around the maple-flavored pond to enter the Goodwins' parlor. I told Thumbs that Jace wanted him, then settled down beside the window where I could keep an eye on the coulee without exposing too much of myself. It was full daylight now, the sun not far from raising its head on a new day. Scanning the rim of the coulee, I counted no less than eight men, but I wasn't confident I'd seen everyone. I couldn't tell what they were up to, and didn't see the cannon, either, but I knew it had to be there. I felt our biggest hope lay with Billy being able to talk them out of cannoning the trading post, although I wasn't optimistic. Had it been federal marshals or the Lighthorse, they might have listened. Watson's men wouldn't give a hoot in hell what their destruction meant to Billy or Elizabeth.

Even though I was keeping my head back and not poking more than an ear and an eye past the window frame, they'd occasionally send a bullet my way. Time to time I'd throw some lead back at them, just to let them know we were paying attention. My bullets must have been coming close enough to earn their respect, because none of them were showing any more hide than was necessary. It continued on that way for some minutes, and had I not heard Jace and Hatcher arguing in the trade room I might have thought they'd already sloped for greener pastures. After about ten minutes of their muted bickering, Thumbs came back with a brace of revolvers in one hand and two others shoved in his belt. He gave me the two he was carrying.

"These are for you," he said, and handed them over. "When Jace gives the word, you're supposed to empty your rifle at that coulee yonder, then leave it behind and come out front with them pistols. Farrell and Harvey ought to be there with the horses by then, and we're all gonna jump in a saddle and light a shuck for the horizon. Jace says we're to take whatever horse is closest, and not worry if it ain't our own. He says we can switch 'em later, those of us that make it."

"I'm not leaving my rifle," I said, and there must have been some heat in my words, because Thumbs took a startled step backward.

"Hell, it don't matter to me. All I know is what Jace said to tell you, which is when we get in the saddle, we're supposed to shoot these pistols dry, then just toss 'em away."

I examined the revolvers. They were Smith and Wessons, both of them brand spanking new, fresh out of the box and still heavily oiled. They were fully loaded, too. Nodding reluctantly, I tucked the revolvers behind my belt. "All right, tell Jace I'm ready when he is."

"It ain't gonna be long now," he assured me, and went back into the main trade room.

I hefted the Marlin and ran one hand along its fore stock. That rifle had been in the Two-Buck family since before I was born. It was part of my heritage, a connection to both of my parents. Yet I knew that when the fat hit the flames, I'd have to leave it behind. Anything less could jeopardize everyone's chances.

Pressing my back to the outer wall, I rose to my full height and eared the Marlin's hammer to full cock. I was as ready as a man could be. Then I heard a distant boom, a trailing whistle that grew instantly louder, and felt a bone-crunching punch against my spine—and the world disappeared in a flash of brilliant white.

For a long moment there was nothing, neither sight nor sound nor knowledge, just a sense of confusion, of being lost and utterly alone in a place I didn't recognize. Then the pain showed up. It arrived in a molten wave that immediately attempted to pull me under. I fought back as best I could, struggling to draw air into my oxygen-starved lungs, to resist a creeping blackness crawling toward me like a thousand writhing serpents. I sucked in a gulp of air and choked and coughed from the grit that came with it. The pain seemed to constrict briefly in my chest, then surged outward with the erratic cadence of my pulse, until even my fingers and toes felt like they were on fire. Breathing was difficult, and I thought surely something massive had dropped on my chest from above, but when I was finally able to focus my eyes, to squint past the spiraling dust, I saw that there was indeed a chest of drawers—I assume from one of the rooms upstairs—lying across my legs, but nothing on my chest.

For a while everything seemed dull and distant, my senses scattered by the explosion of the cannon's shell fired into the trading post's back wall. It was Jace shouting my name that helped pull my thoughts together, but it was only when I tried to stand that I realized I was lying against the building's inner wall. I'd been blown clear across the parlor in the blast.

"Lige," Jace kept repeating, and I slowly brought my gaze around as I strived to understand what, "Can you hear me?" actually meant. It took a couple of minutes before I was able to nod that I did.

"How bad are you hurt?"

"I'm all right," I croaked, which brought a relieved smile to his face.

"Like hell you are," he said. "Can you stand?"

"I think so, if you'll get that chest off my legs."

He grabbed a corner and tipped it clear, then swiftly ran his hands down both my legs below the knee, watching my face for any indication of pain. "Nothing seems to be broken," he said, then reached down and grabbed my arms and pulled me to my feet.

Well, nothing may have been broken, but I'll guarantee my legs felt as wobbly as a couple of sprigs of wet grass. I'd have fallen flat on my nose if he hadn't kept a firm grip on me—one arm around my waist, the other on my wrist where I had it draped over his shoulders. He led me into the front room, and that, too, was a holy mess; the shell's concussion had emptied the shelves behind the counter, destroying what little Watson's men had missed with their rifles. [*Editor's Note:* In later testimony, it was revealed that the Goodwin trading post was struck by a single shell from Watson's field cannon, but with an explosive bomb inside that detonated upon impact with the store's outer wall; financial damages were estimated at $26,400.]

Hatcher and Thumbs were standing at the front door, barely discernable in a choking cloud of white. I'd find out later, from Billy, that he'd had nearly half a ton of flour stored at one end of the trade room, and that a couple of dozen twenty-pound sacks of the stuff had ruptured in the cannon's blast. Watching from the coulee, he said it had billowed out the store's windows like ghosts departing the bodies of the dead. In recollection, I'd have to say Bob and Thumbs looked the part; their faces and clothing were coated with flour, their eyes appearing unnaturally wide where their tears had washed the stuff off from under their eyes.

As soon as we appeared, Hatcher shouted, "Let's go, god-damnit! Crow and Judd are waiting."

Jace nodded and half dragged, half ran me across the room to what remained of the veranda. I caught a glimpse of Quintin Haus sitting against the far wall, watching stoically as the tattered remnants of the Kid Jace gang made its escape. He had to understand we were leaving him behind, but there was no plea for assistance. I don't know, maybe he was too far gone by then to ask for help, or to want it if it had been offered.

We exited the trading post with guns blazing. Not mine, but Thumbs and Hatcher and Crow and Judd were laying down a withering fire that kept the men along Cow Creek crouched below the bank while Jace half slung me into my saddle. I was happy to find myself riding Minko rather than someone else's horse. The others weren't so fortunate. Vaulting astride Hatcher's gray, Jace forced the horse up behind Minko to slap the pinto's rump with his hat. The others were mounted by then, and we took off from there like so many hornets fleeing a burning nest. Crow had the lead with Hatcher close behind on Jace's sorrel, then a gap between them and me and Jace and Thumbs; Farrell brought up the rear, yelling Chickasaw war cries like some Johnny Reb raiding a Yankee stronghold.

I guess I must have passed out at some point not long after leaving Goodwin's, because when I looked around again Bob Hatcher and Harvey Judd were gone. There was just me and Jace—who was back in the saddle of his own horse again—and Thumbs and Farrell Crow, all of us riding hard to the east. Toward the Arbuckle Mountains, and home.

SESSION TWENTY

The next few days were a blur for me. I know we were chased by those gunmen of Watson's, but they made a poor showing of it. It's possible they hadn't expected us to run, as Jace later told me it took them awhile to get up any kind of pursuit. Still, if they weren't entirely ready for us to bolt, they weren't too far behind in the chase, either. And they were a determined lot, I'll say that for them. It didn't seem like we ever stopped for more than a few minutes at a time, although I know that can't be true. Our horses had been exhausted even before we got to Billy's, and wouldn't have lasted if we'd run them the way my muddled thinking recalls. Our biggest advantage after that first harried day was that we could switch directions at night, when it became too dark for them to follow our trail. Even so, it was a long time before we were able to shake pursuit.

One thing I do remember clearly is how cold I felt, especially that first night. I couldn't seem to stop shaking. Even Farrell remarked on it, saying he thought a few times I was about to shimmy right out of my saddle. Jace said it was a fever that had me shivering so bad, addling my judgment and weakening my limbs until I staggered every time I climbed down.

I was still cold all the way through when we reached Thomas Red Corn's cabin a few days later, having taken a roundabout approach to get there. My teeth were chattering even as sweat rolled down my face to soak the collar of my shirt. We hauled up atop the same oak-covered knoll where we'd stopped the last time we were there. Back then the place had looked abandoned, with no hint of life save for that half-starved dun mule in the corral, unable to reach either grass or water. That day there was a column of smoke purling from the chimney, along with several head of livestock in the corral. I noticed a splotch of dun hide among them, and was glad Red Corn's mule had survived. He'd looked pretty rough the last time I saw him.

"What do you think?" Farrell asked, his breath streaming in the cold afternoon air. We were sitting our horses four-abreast, Thumbs with one arm tucked inside his coat in lieu of a sling after taking a bullet through the pad of flesh between his thumb and forefinger, while Farrell favored his left arm, his coat sleeve stained a lackluster red from lost blood—our flight from Goodwin's had been successful, although not without its price paid in flesh.

"I don't think we've got a choice," Jace replied hoarsely. He looked like he was ready to tumble from his saddle, he was so worn out; it was a condition we were all suffering from.

"Then let's get it done," Farrell said, and heeled his mount forward.

We rode up to the cabin single file, Farrell out front with his rifle across his saddlebows, then Jace leading Minko by the reins—which I still don't recall having surrendered—and Thumbs trailing along behind. We made no effort to conceal our approach, and had Watson's men beaten us to the place they could have easily picked us off as we waded our horses across the creek in front of the cabin.

The sun was down by then, hidden behind the tall hills to the west as we splashed our horses up out of the creek. We'd barely made it to shore when the cabin door was flung open and Sarah McFarland—Thomas Red Corn's daughter, if you recall—burst out toting a Winchester rifle like she was ready to start shooting.

"That's far enough," she commanded.

Farrell hauled up, but Jace didn't. He rode around Crow with his right hand raised palm forward, save for the forefinger, which was still gripping Minko's reins.

"Mrs. McFarland," he began, then stopped when a second figure appeared in the door behind her. It was another woman, dark-complexioned and attractive in a blue gingham dress with a lace-trimmed bodice, long black hair flowing down over her shoulders in a silken stream. For a second I didn't recognize her. Then I did, and did a double take. [*Editor's Note:* The expression "double take" has its roots in the film industry of the 1920s and '30s; its use here is likely a reflection of the year the Two-Buck ALC interview was recorded—1937.]

"Milly?" Jace said hesitantly.

I shared his bewilderment. It was the first I'd ever seen Milly Bolton in anything other than baggy male attire, usually with her hair tucked up under the dented crown of her badly used slouch hat. I have to admit the transformation was appealing; it also left me momentarily speechless. Then George showed up at the cabin's dark entrance with a grin stretching from one side of his face to the other. He still looked haggard from the bullet that Ardmore stagecoach messenger had punched through his chest, but he was acting a lot spunkier than the last time I'd seen him.

"Damnation, boys, fall off them broncs and come inside," George invited. He was looking at me—so was Milly—no doubt both of them noticing my slumped and shivering form, and the fact that Jace was holding Minko's reins.

We rode the rest of the way in and Sarah lowered her rifle, even though she didn't seem too happy about it. I guess she hadn't been all that thrilled when Milly and George showed up, but considering we'd been the ones who'd likely saved her father's life, there hadn't been much she could say about it. I noticed she wasn't saying much about us, either, although I couldn't blame her. We were demanding a lot for someone with an ill father to look after.

Jace helped me down from my saddle and Milly took over from there, guiding me inside to a table where supper had already been laid out. There was fried squirrel on a platter, along with cornbread and gravy and hot coffee, and some kind of thick soup on the stove, wafting its rich aroma throughout the cabin's interior. Thumbs came inside with me while Jace, Farrell, and George took care of the stock.

"Sit down," Milly instructed, propelling me toward a handmade chair held together with wooden pegs and straps of rawhide. "Do you want me to take your coat?"

"No," I replied, clutching it to my chest.

"I'll keep mine on, too," Thumbs said, which earned him barely a glance from Milly.

Although I'd been to the cabin before, this was the first I'd been inside. I took a moment to look around. It was solidly built, two rooms and heavy doors front and back, with good glass in the windows and a puncheon floor. Thomas Red Corn was lying abed in the front far corner, looking more like parchment stretched over a frame of dried sticks than anything human. A thin sheen of spittle glistened at the corners of his mouth, and the poor fellow's cheeks were badly sunken, as if he'd lost all his teeth. If not for the jerky rise and fall of his chest under a patchwork quilt, I might have figured him for dead.

Thumbs dug into that squirrel with enthusiasm, but even as hungry as I should have been, I managed only a rear leg and a few sips of coffee before I had to stop.

"What's wrong?" Milly demanded.

"I ain't hungry."

"You don't look like you've eaten in days."

"He ain't, not hardly," Thumbs confirmed.

I tried to recall my last meal—some cold venison eaten in the saddle shortly before we'd reached Goodwin's trading post, if I remembered right—but it didn't matter. As delicious as that meal looked, I flat had no appetite for it.

"He's dog-tired, that's his problem," Sarah announced from where she was standing in front of the stove, keeping an eye on whatever she had bubbling there in a cast-iron kettle.

"He needs to lie down," Milly said.

"There're plenty of places along the creek for him to lie down."

"He needs to be inside where it's warm. He can have my bunk."

"No," Sarah said sharply.

"I'm all right," I protested.

"No, you're not," Milly retorted. "You need rest."

"He's hurt, too," Jace said, coming through the front door with George and Farrell on his heels. "Maybe a cracked rib or something, the way he acts." He was staring at Sarah in a kind of challenging manner. "Can you take a look at him?"

Thrusting a wooden ladle toward him like a dagger, dripping broth over the floor in front of the stove, she said, "He's not my responsibility, Jason Two-Buck. I have enough to do taking care of my own family."

"Damnit, I'm fine," I said, but my voice was scratchy and weak, and no one paid me any heed.

"Ain't no reason we can't lay him down in the back room," George said, echoing Milly's opinion from earlier.

"No, I won't have it."

"They won't hurt her," George replied kindly.

"Won't hurt who?" Farrell asked.

"Her daughter," George said.

I remembered the daughter then, from the night me and

George had spent at the McFarland farm, after telling Sarah how we'd found her daddy lying half-dead outside his cabin. Emily, they'd called her, a pretty child just blossoming into womanhood as I recalled, and suddenly I understood Sarah's reluctance to have us stay, a bunch of scruffy bandits on the run from who knew what.

"It's okay, Ma," said a feminine voice from behind me.

I shifted around in my chair as Emily McFarland emerged from the back room. She was the spitting image of her mama, or how I imagined her mama must have looked like before age and bitterness began to dull the sparkle in her eyes and the smile on her lips. There was no doubt she would soon be breaking hearts all across the Nation, though. Hell, even as poorly as I was feeling, I noticed her appeal right off. I guess Milly noticed my noticing, too, because she eased half a step sideways to block my view.

Sarah's jaws looked like tiny millstones grinding wheat into flour, but she must have known she was beaten. Motioning toward the back room, she said, "Go light a lamp, then."

Milly put a hand on my shoulder. "Can you stand?"

"Sure," I replied, but made no effort to do so. I figured Jace might be right about my having cracked a few ribs when that exploding shell sent me flying across Billy Goodwin's parlor. Although the pain had been manageable while on the run, it seemed to be worsening as my muscles started to relax in the cabin's embracing warmth.

Jace helped me out of my chair and into the back room, which turned out to be a combination storage room and sleeping quarters. A winter's worth of food lined one wall—canned goods and garden truck alike—and a pair of cobbled-together bunks sat to either side of the door. Milly guided me to what I assumed was her bunk and she and Jace eased me down onto it, then pried the boots from my half-frozen feet—the first time in nearly a week they'd been free of their leather cells. Thumbs came in after me and showed Sarah the bloody rag he'd wrapped around his hand.

"I been shot, too," he announced, holding up his paw like it was some kind of prizewinning display from a county fair.

"Sit down over there," she told him, motioning to the other bunk. "And you," she said to Jace. "Get out of here and let us tend to our business."

Her words reminded me of something I'd heard Mama say a time or two over the years, usually to one of my sisters: *A woman's job is to care for her man, to doctor him when he's hurt, feed him when he's hungry, and build him up when he's down. It's the only time she's ever in charge.*

Jace must have remembered it, too, because he nodded obediently and backed out of the room. When there was just me and Thumbs and the women, Sarah instructed Emily to help Milly get my coat and shirt off while she examined Thumbs's injured hand. It was Milly who slipped my coat off my shoulders and dropped it on the floor next to my boots. Then Emily helped her tug my badly torn shirt up over my head. The effort brought a small, involuntary cry from my lips, and I fell back across the bunk afterward, embarrassed by my reaction, barely aware of Emily's startled cry.

"Ma!"

"Oh, Lord," Milly breathed.

Sarah left Thumbs with his hand half unwrapped and hurried over.

"Hey, what the . . ." Thumbs began, but Sarah shushed him with a sound and a backward wave of her hand. She leaned in for a better look, then told Milly to bring the lamp closer. I could tell from her expression that I wasn't going to like what she had to say.

"I reckon it's bad, huh?" I asked.

222

"It might be," she answered, studying my bare chest in the lamplight. "Does it hurt?"

"Some. Mostly I feel really weak, like I can barely lift my arms, and I'm always cold."

Sarah gave me a kindly look, which I swear scared me more than anything she'd said so far. "You have a nail in your chest," she explained. "There's a sliver of wood still attached at the head, so I can't tell if the shank went in straight or at a slant, but it's a long one, and the head is directly over your heart."

"Is that why he's so cold?" Milly asked.

"It's possible," Sarah said. "Emily, go ask Jason to come in here."

"Yes, ma'am."

"Can you pull it out?" I asked.

"We'll have to. If it's . . ." She stopped when Jace came in. I reckon he'd been waiting just outside the door, maybe even listening in on the women's conversation, judging from the worried look on his face. "Your brother has a nail in his chest," she told him matter-of-factly, then went on to detail what she knew—which wasn't much—and what she suspected—which made me want to crawl under the bed and hide.

"But you can't tell if it's actually in his heart?" Jace asked.

"No, but it appears to be a tenpenny nail, and your brother has a thin chest. Unless it went in at a sharp angle, I don't see how it could have missed puncturing something." [*Editor's Note:* A tenpenny nail measures three inches in length and has a width of .148 inches; a typical male of slim build has approximately two inches of tissue from the outer layer of flesh to the outer surface of his heart.]

"Then why ain't he dead?" Jace demanded.

"I don't know, other than that maybe it's God's will that he live."

"Hell, it's probably just 'cause it's a muscle," Thumbs opined, standing at the foot of my bunk where he'd come to observe the proceedings. "It's a tough one, too. Anyone who's ever butchered a cow or a hog knows that."

"That's possible, too," Sarah conceded. "My concern is what will happen when it's removed."

No one replied to that. My gaze traveled the room, noting Jace's fear, Emily's terror, Thumbs's morbid fascination, Sarah's grim determination, and, finally, a look on Milly's face I couldn't have explained in a month of Mondays, but which warmed me through nonetheless. I realized then that she didn't hate me. Lord, but I was a naïve clod in those days.

"Jason, what do you want me to do?" Sarah asked softly.

"I want you to save him."

"I'm not a physician. I can try to remove the nail, but I can't guarantee the result."

Weary of voice and with his shoulders slumped in resignation, Jace said, "Do the best you can, that's all I'll ask."

Me, I turned my eyes to the rough planks of the ceiling and tried to pretend it was someone else's life they were discussing. Someone else perched on a ledge above an abyss with no bottom.

"Would you like a moment alone with him?" Sarah asked, still in that frightfully gentle tone.

"No, just do what you've gotta do." Leaning down, Jace awkwardly patted my shoulder. "You remember the first time you forked that paint horse of yours?" he asked, meaning Minko. "He'd never been rode before, but you by God got the job done. You've likely got another hard ride comin' up here in a few minutes, little brother, but you just do what you did then. You grab that saddle horn and hang on and don't get throwed for no reason. You hear me?"

I nodded that I did and he started to walk away, motioning for Thumbs to come with him. Before he could reach the door,

I called him back. It took a moment to put my thoughts in order—hell, I hadn't intended to say anything—but I finally got out what I could.

"I've been proud to ride with you, brother."

Jace nodded and swallowed hard, and said, "I've been proud to have you." Then he spun on his heels and fled the room.

Well, you're sitting here listening to me jabber into this Dictaphone, so you know I didn't turn up my toes and croak, but I'll admit it was a wild ride there for a spell. A lot rougher than what Minko had put me through my first time on top of him. Sarah told me what she was going to do, which was grab that sliver of wood affixed to the nail with some pliers and give it a slow, hopefully steady upward pull until it popped out. "Milly and Emily are going to hold you down, but I need you to do everything you can to keep from moving, too. Do you understand?"

"Yes, ma'am."

She took a deep breath. "I wish you the best, Elijah."

I nodded solemnly. "I wish you even more," I replied.

She smiled faintly at that and took the pliers Emily had fetched off a nearby shelf. Then Milly and Emily positioned themselves at each shoulder and Sarah pressed a knee firmly into the muscle above my pelvic. "Hold on," she told me, then lifted that nail right out of there.

Sounds slick, doesn't it? Trust me, it wasn't. My body's reaction was immediate. I spasmed into a solid length of hardwood that sent Emily staggering and my heart bouncing around inside of my chest like a moth against a lamp's glass chimney. Pain lanced through me from toes to scalp, and my mouth stretched open in a scream that never really got all the way out of my throat. Then the world just went blank, like I'd been encased in a brilliant white sheet drawn so tight I couldn't breathe. After a bit I saw people off in the distance, and I'd swear one of them was Mama, smiling even as she waved me back, like she didn't want me coming any closer. Following that came darkness, kind of scary until I slipped all the way into it.

SESSION TWENTY-ONE

I didn't feel as bad as you might expect when I woke up. Just noodle-weak and used up through and through. I thought at first that I was alone, but when I turned my head there was Milly, leaning close with a hand dropping gently over my forehead as if searching for a fever.

"You're awake," she said quietly.

"Appears like," I acknowledged.

"You've been asleep."

"Feels like it." Real careful, I stretched my limbs under a heavy wool blanket that had been pulled up to my chin. "Feels like I'm alive, too."

She smiled and nodded, and for a moment I thought I noticed a moistness in her eyes. Then she pulled away real quick and went into the other room. When she came back, she was carrying a tin mug of fresh, cool water, and her eyes were dry, though they looked kind of red around the edges.

"Drink this," she said in a businesslike tone, and I obliged her, as I was feeling as dry as a September corn husk. I believe I could have swallowed a gallon of that sweet-tasting spring water, but she only offered me the one mug, and I didn't ask for another, figuring I'd already put folks out more than I should have.

"Where's Jace?" I asked.

"He and George rode out to have a look around. They'll be back later today."

"Today? You mean I slept all night?"

She smiled. "All night and all the next day, too. You woke up awhile last evening, but you weren't making much sense. Do you remember that? Something about a cat getting into the cream?"

"Lord, no," I said, and wondered where such a thought could have originated. We'd had cats on the farm, of course, but never had any trouble with them getting into the cream bucket.

"It doesn't matter, you seem clear-headed now. You're not as pale as you were, either. Sarah listened to your heart earlier and says it's fast but regular. When she pulled—" Her voice caught briefly, then she went on as if she'd only needed to clear her throat. "At first it was really abnormal. I could see it against your skin, it was beating so hard. For a long time, I wasn't sure it would ever slow down, or if you'd ever come back."

"I had to come back. I'd have to say goodbye to you before I could die, wouldn't I?"

I'd meant that to be lighthearted, but Milly acted like I'd slapped her face. She reared back and her lower lip trembled a bit, then she jumped up and took off like a streaking bobcat. I stared after her, puzzled by her reaction but too tired to call her back. I lay there staring at the ceiling for a couple of minutes, then closed my eyes thinking I'd just rest a minute, and promptly fell asleep.

When I next awoke the light was growing dim and I could hear voices in the front room. Taking a moment to gather my strength, I eased my legs out from under the blankets and sat up. I was still as weak as a newborn and kind of light-headed, but I was thinking clearer than I had since that shell exploded against the side of Goodwin's Store. Across the room, Thumbs was also sitting up on the side of his bunk. He was fully dressed save for his hat and coat, and his hand was heavily bandaged.

When he saw me looking at him, he held it up to catch my attention.

"She cut off my thumb," he said, sounding as woeful as a lost hound.

"Which one?"

"The little extry one."

"Is that a bad thing?"

"Yeah," he replied emphatically, looking at me like I was daft. "It's all I had."

Well, there you go. And I knew exactly what he meant, too. Even his names—Thumbs, or Three Thumbs Boy—alluded to that extra appendage. It was who he was, his identity so to speak, and in that hard land it had made him special. Without it he was just another shiftless drifter.

Standing in the door with her arms crossed under her breasts, Sarah said, "It had to come off. It was getting infected."

She sounded both angry and defensive, and I've wondered since if it had really needed amputation or if she'd sliced it off as something she deemed unnatural and offensive. Remembering how the bullet to Thumbs's hand had penetrated the fleshy part between his thumb and forefinger but missed that extra digit completely, my suspicion grew.

Jace slipped past her carrying a plate of what looked like flapjacks in one hand and a cup of coffee in the other. He was wearing a heavy mackinaw I'd never seen before, with gloves poking out of the side pockets.

"Hey, he's awake," he said, grinning. "You hungry, little brother?"

"Some, I reckon."

He brought it over—half a dozen 'jacks smothered in corn syrup and four big sausage links—along with a fork and knife. He set the coffee on the floor next to my stockinged feet. "Eat up," he said. "Then get ready to ride. We're pulling out as soon as it gets a little darker."

"If I'd known you intended to kill him, I wouldn't have bothered pulling that nail out of his chest," Sarah said. She was glowering in Jace's direction, but from her tone I could tell she wasn't surprised. This was something that they'd already discussed, and that she clearly didn't approve of.

"We don't have a choice, Mrs. McFarland," Jace replied with uncommon patience. "I've paid you for your time and the food we've—"

"It's not your money I want, Jason Two-Buck."

"I know, but that's all I have to offer."

"No, you have one other item I crave," she said bitterly. "After you leave here, I want you to never come back." She looked at Thumbs, then me. "All of you, just . . ." Her gaze slid past Jace to the front room where her papa lay in a bed he'd likely never leave. Not of his own accord, at any rate. "Just . . . go, all of you," she finished, and turned away.

Jace watched her leave, his countenance as flat as the brim of a spanking new Stetson. Then he looked at me. "I reckon it ought to be your decision, Lige. Do you want to stay here a spell, at least until you feel better?"

"No, I'm coming with you."

"What about me?" Thumbs asked.

"You're a free man. You can go where you please."

"Is Farrell still goin' his own way?"

"Farrell's already left," Jace replied, and Thumbs's jaw flopped toward his chest. He wagged his head sadly.

"It's all comin' apart, ain't it, Kid?"

"I don't know what you're talking about."

"Ever'thing. My thumb's gone, and now Farrell's gone, too. Why'd he leave without me? We'd been riding the same trails together near to five years."

"Sometimes a man just needs to go his own way, Thumbs.

Maybe it's time you did the same."

"I ain't got no place to go."

"I don't know what to tell you."

"Can I come with you'n Lige?"

After a pause, Jace shrugged. "For a ways, I reckon. At least until we get clear of the Nations."

I looked up.

"We're leaving?"

"Yeah, we're leaving."

"And George is coming with us?"

"No, he and Milly are staying here. George says he's tired of riding the owlhoot, and I ain't lettin' Milly follow along no more. It's time she went back to her family."

"George told me she doesn't have a family."

"Well, he's wrong. Milly's Creek, and has kin up in that Nation."

"Creek," I murmured, momentarily thrown. Here I'd thought all along that she was Kiowa or Comanche. Or else Choctaw, Jace and George having found her in that country. Studying Jace's face in the dim light, puzzled by its lack of animation, I said, "What's George gonna do?"

"He ain't said, which is just as well. That way we can't none of us ever slip up and let the law know where he went."

"The law?" Thumbs echoed worriedly.

"I ain't planning on us getting caught, but it's something we gotta think about. You can bet Watson's men are still out there looking for us."

I mulled that over as I took another bite of flapjack. Upon reflection, it did seem kind of odd that Watson's crew hadn't already tracked us down. Then I decided Jace had probably taken more pains to hide our trail than I realized. Whether that was the reason or not, I was as certain as he was that they hadn't given up.

I won't lie and say George's decision to leave us didn't give me a hollow feeling in the pit of my stomach; I can't say the same about Farrell, though. I guess it was as Thumbs had remarked; it was all coming apart, although faster than I'd anticipated.

Jace told me to finish eating, and he and Thumbs went into the front room. I sat on the edge of the bed wearing my long-handles with a blanket pulled over my lap for modesty's sake. The rest of my clothes had been stacked on the floor next to me, everything recently washed and nicely folded, my boots freshly oiled. The Colt lay on top of my vest, but the Marlin wasn't there; it took a moment to recall my leaving it at Billy's after being knocked catawampus across the room from the cannon's blast. Oddly enough, with everything that seemed to be busting apart at the seams—the gang disbanding and George going his own way—it was the loss of Papa's rifle that brought an unexpected lump to my throat.

I made short work of those 'jacks and sausage links, and the coffee was tasty, too, strong but flavorful. Finished, I quick-like skinned into my clothes. The shirt fit snug when pulled down over the heavy bandages around my chest, but everything else seemed looser, like I'd lost weight. When I stood up, I had to wait out a spell of dizziness, then strapped on my revolver and went into the front room where the others were gathered. Jace and Thumbs and Emily were at the table; George stood just inside the front door wearing his coat and hat and pulling off a pair of wool mittens as if he'd just come inside. Sarah was perched on a short, three-legged milking stool next to her father's bed, whispering something into his ear. Only Milly was absent, and I feared not seeing her before we pulled out.

Smiling at my appearance, George said, "There he is, upright and looking pert as a newborn colt." I made some kind of small greeting in return, but my gaze was probing the corners for

Milly. Cocking a brow toward Jace, George added, "I'm mighty glad to see him on his feet again. I expect you know I didn't figure he'd make it."

"Ol' Lige is as tough as a hickory burl," Jace replied. "If anybody could do it, it'd be him."

"Well, you called it right." Then his tone changed. "Your horses are saddled and waiting out front."

Jace stood and pulled his gloves out of his pocket. "Let's ride, you two," he said to me and Thumbs, and we all walked outside. Even Sarah and Emily tagged along to see us off.

We paused in the yard to allow our eyes to adjust to the gloaming. I was happy to see we'd be riding our own stock. Minko still looked thin, but he was rested and had been well cared for—thank George for that, I thought—and I reckoned he'd get me out of Indian Territory easy enough if we didn't run into any Lighthorse Police or some of Watson's men bent on giving us a hard chase. I didn't know where we were headed, but I was hoping it'd be far away from Kermit Watson. I hadn't forgiven the man for what he'd done, but I had no urge to seek further vengeance. At that point all I wanted was to find a place where I wasn't always having to look over my shoulder for fear of pursuit.

I asked George about Milly but he said he didn't know where she'd gotten to. "She lit outta here some time ago," he confided, "but I'll tell her you said goodbye."

We shook hands, and I said, "Aw, hell, I wish you were coming with us."

"I expect we'll run into one another somewhere down the trail," he replied, but I don't think either of us believed it.

I led Minko to the side, as I was still feeling pretty wobbly and didn't want to make a clumsy spectacle of myself trying to mount. In that regard, I failed miserably. I grabbed the horn and got a foot in the stirrup easy enough, but when I gave a pull to haul myself into the seat, I felt something give on the inside. The pain was quick and piercing, and I fell back with a raspy cry, my legs giving out and dumping me on the ground. I lay there while the stars whirled overhead; faces now and again poked in from the sides, along with distant voices; Sarah's was the first to form a coherent sentence, her words as harsh as lye soap in your eyes.

"You'll kill him if you put him on that horse."

The stars slowed and I became aware of Jace kneeling opposite her. He had a hand resting lightly on my shoulder. "Maybe she's right," he said. "Maybe you ought to wait here awhile."

"No, I'm coming with you," I insisted, and after a pause he nodded and helped me to my feet. It took him and George both to get me in my saddle. My chest burned and my pulse was like a drunk navigating a steep incline. Looking to where Sarah stood nearby, I tried to tell her how I appreciated all she'd done for me, but I guess she wasn't in a mood to hear it. She called me a damn fool before I got halfway through and stomped back into the cabin. Emily went with her. After that it was just me and Jace and Thumbs, with George standing at Minko's shoulder.

"You take care of yourself, Elijah Two-Buck," he said kindly.

"I plan to."

He smiled and gave my knee a friendly pat, then stepped back and Jace gave the command to ride. I nodded a final goodbye to George and reined away, and damned if my eyes didn't turn damp, my vision blurry for a hundred yards or so. When I finally looked back, it was so dark I couldn't tell whether George was still there or not, although I kind of figured he was.

Excerpts from:
Those Notorious Badmen of the Chickasaw Nation:
A Collection of Brief, Biographical Sketches of Some
of the West's More Renown Outlaws
by
Malcomb Combs
Six Falls Press, 1922

Farrell Crow

. . . following his departure from the Kid Jace gang in 1893, [Farrell] Crow returned to his roots along the Canadian River, where he alternated between a career of farming and stealing horses from Kansas ranchers, selling the horses throughout the Indian Nations. In 1896, Crow married a woman of the Choctaw Nation whose name has been variously given as Henrietta or Harriet; the couple may have had children, or else those on the 1900 Census—two boys and a girl, no ages or names supplied—were Henrietta/Harriet's from a previous marriage.

Farrell Crow was indicted in the murder of Johnson Walks High in 1905 and sentenced to ten years in the Chickasaw National Jail. During his incarceration, he was charged with an additional murder when the body of his cellmate, Adam Shaw, was found strangled in his bunk. Crow died in the National Jail in 1908 from stab wounds sustained in an altercation with inmates unknown.

Quintin Haus

[Quintin] Haus had a long and varied criminal history within the Indian Nations. Beginning in 1886, he was arrested by Indian Police in Pawhuska (capital of the Osage Nation) for public intoxication and assault. Although he was turned over to

235

federal authorities, because of his age he was never charged in that case. [*Editor's Note:* Quintin Christopher Haus was born in Lexington County, Kentucky, in 1872; he would have been fourteen years old in 1886.]

Osage officials later filed a complaint with the U.S. marshal's office in Fort Smith, claiming Haus, who was white, was an active member of a band of whiskey peddlers known to be trafficking in illegal spirits in the Rock Creek area. No known follow-up to these charges could be found.

. . . was briefly a member of Bill Doolin's Wild Bunch, operating throughout Kansas and Indian Territory in the early 1890s. He [Haus] was wounded when the Bunch robbed the bank in Spearville [Kansas] on November 1, 1892, and left the Doolin outfit to recover at an associate's cabin in the Chickasaw Nation. [*Editor's Note:* Despite Combs's allegations that Haus was a member of Doolin's Wild Bunch, solid confirmation is lacking, and many historians dispute the claim.]

Haus was later associated with the Bernard "Pit" Middleton gang, which merged with the Jason "Kid Jace" Two-Buck gang sometime in the summer or autumn of 1893. Haus perished in the assault on the William Goodwin trading post in November of that year, in a battle instigated by members of Kermit Watson's Regulatory Posse. [*Editor's Note:* Although the term "Regulatory Posse" occasionally shows up in reference to Watson's hired men, its first appearance in writing wasn't noted until 1918; it seems unlikely the phrase was used during Watson's time.]

Bob Hatcher

Robert Timothy Hatcher began his criminal career in New Mexico Territory in 1876, when he became an active member of the Seven Rivers Warriors. [See: Combs, *Those Notorious Badmen of the Lincoln County War: A Collection of Brief, Biographi-*

cal Sketches of Some of the West's More Renown Outlaws (Six Falls Press, 1919).]

[Hatcher] arrived in Chickasaw country possibly as early as 1887 according to . . . sources; he was positively identified by informants as a whiskey trader in September of 1888, and was indicted by federal authorities for theft in December of that year when he was accused of stealing a wagonload of "unshelled corn, destined for the manufacture of alcohol."

. . . sentenced to six months in the Fort Smith City Jail.

Hatcher was considered a member of the Kid Jace gang when that party robbed a Chickasaw Express stagecoach outside of Caddo, then murdered a man in Tishomingo . . . also a participant in the robbery of the First Bank of Erda.

. . . (after) leaving the Kid Jace gang following the raid on the Goodwin trading post . . . [he] continued his life of crime through Indian Territory and into Northern Texas.

Hatcher was killed in 1897 while attempting to rob the Rock Island Railroad outside of Kingfisher, Oklahoma, in the company of Otis Josephs and Frederick Turner. Josephs and Turner were later arrested . . .

Hatcher was credited with killing nine men during his career; he claimed thirteen and "some Indians," but that figure could not be confirmed.

Harvey Judd

[*Editor's Note:* Although Harvey Judd was not listed in Combs's *Badmen of the Chickasaw Nation,* he is briefly mentioned in the author's *Badmen of the Big Piney* collection (Six Falls Press, 1927), covering outlaws and gunfighters commonly associated with Eastern Texas and Western Louisiana. According to Combs, Harvey Judd was charged in Pierce, Louisiana, in 1899, for the robbery and murders of Franklin and Almira Barringer. Found guilty on all counts, he was sentenced to twenty-five years in the Louisiana State Penitentiary, but was taken from his jail cell in Pierce and lynched by persons unknown before he could begin his official sentence.]

Enoch Anderson

[*Editor's Note:* Although no mention is made of Enoch Anderson in Combs's *Badmen of the Chickasaw Nation,* Anderson's governance of the narrow Arbuckle Mountain valley called the "Notch" seems sufficient for inclusion here. Despite Anderson's long association with the outlaw retreat, there is no official record of him having ever been charged with any crime; unofficially, he was said to have dealt regularly in stolen property, and to sell whiskey with indifference.

Regarding the Notch, there is ample evidence to suggest the location was well known at least as early as 1846, three years prior to Anderson's birth in 1849; this contradicts Two-Buck's assertion in these transcripts that the location was originally discovered by Anderson.

Notwithstanding its notoriety among lawmen, as well as its popularity with the lawless, no raid was ever conducted on the Notch. After Anderson's death of kidney failure in 1902, the outlaw element gradually dissipated. In 1913 the valley was claimed by the Alvin Sumner family, of Davis, Oklahoma, and in 1938 a road was carved into the side of the canyon, which allowed motor vehicles to access the area. Several cabins were subsequently built along what became known as Sumner Creek, and the site was used as a family retreat until it was sold by Alvin's descendants in 1961, when it was briefly turned into a private campground. Today the former hideaway is home to a youth leadership camp with an emphasis on outdoor activities such as horseback riding, rock climbing, and survival skills.]

SESSION TWENTY-TWO

We hadn't gotten too far along before I began to realize my mistake in wanting to stay with Jace. Although the pain leveled off after a bit, my heart continued its irregular solo against my rib cage. From time to time, it got so bad I'd have to lean forward over Minko's withers, hanging on and praying I wouldn't pass out.

It was a clear, cold night, stars glittering and my breath curling around my cheeks in a moist fog, but there was a different kind of cold chiseling into my fingers and toes, and I worried my blood wasn't getting pumped out far enough to warm those extremities. I asked a doctor about that once, not all that many years ago, but he dismissed the question, telling me that if my heart had actually been punctured by a tenpenny nail I'd have died almost instantly. I don't know how smart he was or how much training he had, but I never went back. Any sawbones who'll dismiss something out of hand like that isn't worth spending money on, is my opinion.

It didn't seem like dawn would ever get there, but of course it eventually did. As the light strengthened, I began to take note of my surroundings. I guess I'd assumed we'd head south for Texas before angling toward Mexico, so I was more than a little surprised, not to mention disappointed, when I saw the sun coming up directly in front of us. I called to Jace and he reined back to my side looking concerned. Thumbs pulled up a few feet away but didn't speak; his hand, I noticed, was still tucked between the buttons of his coat in lieu of a sling.

"What is it?"

"Where are we? I thought we were leaving the Chickasaw Nation."

"We are, but we're gonna swing past the Notch first. McNeil promised me he'd save us some fresh horses, and we'll likely need 'em before we get to Mexico."

Jace was talking about J.R. McNeil, that Chickasaw horse thief I'd met briefly in the Notch, the one who promised us first pick of some ponies he intended to lift out of some unsuspecting stockman's pasture. I don't know how Jace was so sure J.R. would be there waiting for us, and the way I was feeling, it didn't seem worth pursuing. Besides, as glad as I was to be riding Minko, I knew we needed fresh stock. I was just hoping that no matter which direction we went in after leaving the Notch, I'd be able to keep the pinto with me.

I started to say something to that effect but noticed Jace was no longer paying me any mind. He was staring back the way we'd come, and soon began grating out a steady string of curses. Well, I knew what that meant even before I craned my chin over my shoulder and saw Milly Bolton sitting her little bay gelding a couple of hundred yards down the trail. And damned if she didn't have that pack mule with her, just like old times. Jace lifted his reins as if to go after her, but I said, "Leave her be."

"Since when have you started giving orders?"

"It's not an order, I'm just saying leave her be. If she wants to ride with us, she's earned the right."

"Your brain's gone mushy," Jace grumbled, but Thumbs chuckled.

"It ain't his brain, Kid, and it ain't gone mushy, either."

Oh, we knew what he was talking about, but we both chose to ignore it. Pulling his sorrel around, Jace drove his heels into the animal's ribs and took off at a lope. I held Minko in place.

"Wave her up here, Thumbs."

"What's the matter, can't you wave her up?"

"Just do it," I snapped, but the truth is, I wasn't sure if I could. I wasn't hunched all the way over my saddle horn anymore, but I was curved in that direction and afraid to let go for fear of tumbling out of my seat.

Making a big production of it, Thumbs eased his injured hand from inside his coat and gently waved her forward. After a long hesitation, she headed our way. No one was smiling when she got there—least of all Milly, who was watching us as you might a snarling cur on a frayed rope—but I couldn't hold back my grin when I saw she was still wearing her blue gingham dress, the skirt pulled down somehow to cover both ankles.

She looked at me and her brows furrowed. "What's wrong with you now?"

"He's bleeding again," Thumbs said, and when I glanced down the front of my coat, I saw that it was indeed shaded red. Had I been braver I might have opened it up to peek inside, but I decided to wait until we reached the Notch to do that. Too much knowledge when there's not a damn thing you can do about it ain't necessarily a good thing was my thinking at the time.

"Lead out, Thumbs," I said, and nodded down the pike to where Jace had slowed his mount back to a walk.

Thumbs gigged his horse into motion; Milly guided hers up alongside of Minko. "Is your heart beating crazy again?"

"Some," I hedged.

"You should go back to Red Corn's. I'll take you."

"It's too late to go back. Besides, we're closer to the Notch than we are to Red Corn's."

I recognized the narrow road we were following. We were well east of Henry McFarland's place, apparently having passed it in the dark, although I'm damned if I know how I could have missed it. The agricultural smells alone—cows, hogs, chickens, and horses, not to mention recently harvested grains—should have alerted me to its proximity.

We pushed on after Jace and Thumbs, keeping our horses to a walk until the sun broke its ties with the horizon. We stopped then, and Jace told Milly to rustle up a quick breakfast. After shooting him a dirty look, she slid off her horse and began rummaging around in one of the mule's panniers. I dismounted on my own, but Jace was there to grab me when my knees started to buckle.

"I figured as much," he said, helping me over to a young oak tree where I could sit with my back to the trunk. He started to reach for the top button of my coat, but I waved his hand away.

"I don't want to see it."

"Ignoring it ain't gonna make it better."

"Let's wait until we get to the Notch."

Jace shrugged and stood when Milly came over with a couple of chunks of bread wrapped around some thinly sliced strips of venison. She acted mad when I declined her offer.

"You have to eat."

"I had a good meal last night, flapjacks and sausage. I'm not hungry now."

She looked at Jace, who shook his head. "It's Lige's call," he said evasively. "Best we can do is get him to the Notch where he can rest."

"What's Enoch gonna say about us comin' in with a posse on our asses?" Thumbs asked.

"We don't have a posse on our asses, and we need those horses McNeil is saving for us. Besides, someone there'll likely have fresh news about Watson's hired guns. It'll make it easier for us to slip past them if we know where they are."

I think Thumbs said something after that, but I didn't catch it. I must have dozed off, because when I next lifted my head and looked around, the sun was approaching midmorning. I spotted Jace thirty yards or so down the trail, squatting in a piece of sunlight with his rifle across his knees. Thumbs was an equal distance in the opposite direction, standing and lazily smoking a cigarette. Milly sat cross-legged nearby, watching intently until my gaze settled on her.

"Where are we?" I asked in a croaky voice.

"Where we stopped just after sunup. How do you feel?"

"Not very good."

"Can you ride?"

"Get me on my horse and I'll stick like a cocklebur."

Although she looked doubtful, she stood and waved the others in. Then she came over and helped me to my feet. By the time Jace and Thumbs got there I was in my saddle, although not as confident as I'd been a few minutes earlier that I wouldn't fall off before we got too far along. The pain in my chest was throbbing with a peculiar rhythm, quick little bursts that made my nose run and my eyes water, and there was a coppery taste deep in my throat that no amount of swallowing could scare off. Sitting there trying not to puke or pass out, the concept of death—something I'd really not paid much mind to, being just sixteen and largely invincible—suddenly became a deep-dread reality. It dawned on me that I wasn't just badly wounded, but that I could well be *fatally* wounded, and the thought of that just about took my breath away. Noticing Jace's expression when he rode up did nothing to shore up my listing morale.

"You gonna make it, little brother?"

"Yeah, I'm gonna make it," was my raspy reply.

Thumbs was less tactful. "You gonna puke, Lige?"

Good ol' Thumbs, I thought, and said, "No, I ain't gonna puke."

"You look like you're gonna puke."

"Let it go, Thumbs," Jace said, and reined his sorrel into the woods.

Like last time, we didn't follow any kind of trail. I suppose that was a big part of what kept the Notch's location a secret for so long—limited access and its patrons' commitment to never coming in the same way twice. Taking a roundabout course, we were nearly an hour reaching the little creek that would guide us to the Notch. We splashed our horses into its purling waters and turned upstream. Me, I was fading in and out by then, but still hanging onto the reins while Minko instinctively followed Jace and Thumbs. Eventually a trail did appear and we left the creek to follow it. I recalled that on our last ride this way the oaks had been a canopy of flaming scarlet; that day the limbs looked bare and spidery, our path buried under a sodden carpet.

Free of the rock-strewn creek, we began making better time. My thoughts continued to drift, though, so that it took a moment to realize we'd stopped. Lifting my head, I saw Jace hauled up in front of me with his right hand raised above his shoulder. He was talking to someone standing in the middle of the trail, blocking our way. Focusing on their words, I heard Jace say, "He's hurt, he can't hear you."

"What?" I pushed myself up in the saddle, not all the way up, but closer to straight than the question mark I'd been slumped in. No one appeared to hear my query, but it no longer mattered. I realized the man standing in the trail had a rifle pointed at Jace's belly, and that others, guns drawn, were already gliding out of the deep oak and hickory forest surrounding us like demons in a nightmare.

There must have been seven or eight of them, all on foot. Then the man Jace had been talking to gave a holler and two others showed up on horseback. A couple of the ones on foot stepped forward to tie our hands behind our backs, and I'm ashamed to admit I cried out as the muscles across my chest were stretched tight. Jace voiced a protest, but the man with the rifle told him to shut up.

My gaze settled on the mounted men. I wondered if one of them was Kermit Watson. It had been so long since I'd last seen the man, and then only from a distance, that I wasn't sure who these two were until they were almost on top of us. Neither was Watson, but they were both white men, as were several of those on the ground. One of the men on horseback was wearing fairly new-looking range clothes and sat his mount with the unfamiliar stiffness of someone more accustomed to desks and fountain pens than saddles and handguns. The other guy looked just the opposite, a hard-bitten man somewhere in his thirties, with a short beard, rough clothing, and a revolver sporting carved ivory grips. He was the one who rode his horse up closest, forcing the guy with the rifle to move aside.

"I told you they'd be along sooner or later, Mr. Patrick," the bearded guy said.

"Yes, you did," the store-bought rider agreed. "I still think it would have been wiser to arrest them at the Indian's cabin."

"No, sir, you're wrong there. If we'd taken them at Red

Corn's, we'd've given the Lighthorse a reason to raise a stink with the federals. This way, they're all ours." He grinned when he said that last part, revealing a row of crooked teeth the color of ripe corn.

"It was your decision, Ambrose," Patrick acceded. "I'm here only to monitor the capture and be certain any claims made for the reward are justified."

Ambrose!

Even in my fuzzy state of mind the name was like a mule's kick to the gut. Ambrose was the man Watson had sent up to the cabin to talk to Mama, right before the shooting started. Which meant he'd been there, had maybe even helped when they'd fired that grasshopper cannon into the house and killed my family.

Ambrose glanced at that rifle-toter and winked. "What he means is, he's here to make sure we don't lie about running down this half-breed horse thief and stringing him up in a tall tree."

"Ain't no doubt who we got as far as I'm concerned," the rifleman replied.

"Me, neither," said Ambrose, and turned to the other horseman. "What about it, Mr. Patrick? You satisfied?"

"Yes, I'm satisfied. Barring the man's escape, you'll receive your reward as promised."

Ambrose looked at Jace. "You ready to meet your maker, Kid?"

"I'm ready, but these others weren't a part of it." He jerked his head toward me and Thumbs and Milly.

"The hell they weren't. That's that three-thumbed freak behind you, and I reckon the youngster is Farrell Crow."

"No, sir," the rifleman interjected. "That's Three Thumbs, all right, but the kid ain't Crow. I know both of 'em from up around Purcell."

246

Ambrose scowled in my direction. Then he glared at Milly as if she'd said something insulting. "Who's that?"

The rifleman shook his head. "I ain't never seen her before. The boy, neither."

"Well, the hell with 'em. They're riding with Kid Jace, so they can damn well hang with him."

"No!" said a voice from the trees to our right, and we all turned as Billy Goodwin and Little Tall Man rode their horses out of the trees.

"I told you to stay back out of sight, Goodwin," Ambrose growled.

"I know what you told me, and you know what I said about the boy."

Ambrose's gaze narrowed in my direction. "So he's the one cut you loose, huh? Well, he's still a cattle rustler and a bank robber, and as far as I'm—"

"No," Billy repeated, staring at Ambrose as if daring him to argue. It surprised me some, Billy's quick command of the situation. It surprised me even more when Ambrose seemed to back down, his face flushing the same shade of red as the soggy leaves under our horses' feet. "You'll not hang the girl, either," Billy continued. "Neither deserve a part in your connivance."

"The kid was there, damnit, in your store."

"I know where he was, you damn fool. I was there, too, and if Elijah hadn't set us free, I'd still be there, mangled and dead after you and your men blew my place to hell."

"I already told you that couldn't be helped," Ambrose returned, but I saw his eyes flicker slyly, and knew he was lying.

Billy placed a hand over the revolver holstered at his waist, one of those heavy Smith and Wesson American models that I knew would pack a hell of a punch if he ever tripped its hammer. "Cut him loose, Ambrose. The girl, too."

Ambrose glanced at Patrick, but the desk jockey merely

shrugged. "There has been no mention of a woman in any of this," he said. "My suggestion is that you release her."

I suppose it was kind of funny the way they all glanced at Milly and nodded their heads in agreement. What made it even more humorous was that, while she hadn't been at Erda when we robbed the bank there, she'd sure as heck been in on the Ardmore robbery. The thing is, she'd been wearing a man's clothing then—trousers, shirt and vest, brogan shoes, and a floppy-brimmed hat—and with all the yelling and shooting going on, I reckon no one had picked up on the fact that one of the bunch was female. They wouldn't make that mistake a second time, I knew. Not with her wearing that blue gingham dress with its lacy trim, her blue-black hair spilling down over her shoulders to glisten in the sunlight—beautiful enough to take your breath away, I thought.

"What about the boy?" Ambrose asked Patrick in words smoldering with a barely contained rage. It would be some weeks later before I found out that, in addition to the salary he was paying his gunmen, Watson had put a $100 reward on the heads of "all known associates" of the Two-Buck gang, along with the $500 he was offering for Jace. It wasn't my participation in robbing the Ardmore stagecoach or the Erda bank that was bolstering Ambrose's indignation, it was the money he'd lose by setting me free.

After a moment's consideration, Patrick replied, "He'll have to hang, too."

My muscles kind of drew up at that, but I kept my mouth shut. If I was going to die, then I intended to do it with as much dignity as I could muster. But Billy wasn't giving up just yet. His grip tightened on the Smith and Wesson and his gaze hardened. We all saw it, and I don't think anyone there doubted his determination to brace Ambrose and his men if he had to. Even Little Tall Man had moved his hand back along the stock of a single-barreled shotgun—more to back Billy's play than save my hide, I reckoned, although the results would be the same if it came to a shooting match.

"No," Billy said in a low, terse voice. "Lige put his neck way out there to save my hide. The least I can do is save his."

One of the men behind Ambrose—in line with Little Tall Man's scattergun, I noticed—nervously cleared his throat. "Don't you reckon it'd be enough to hang Kid Jace and the freak?" he suggested.

"Mr. Watson wants 'em all hanged," Ambrose replied. "He wants this scourge on the land wiped clean once and for all."

Taking note of the effect his weapon was having on the man behind Ambrose, Little Tall Man shifted the muzzle toward Patrick, and the desk-puncher's eyes grew noticeably wider. "I believe, upon contemplation," he pronounced loudly, "that the boy and the woman should both be removed from responsibility for the crimes committed by others."

"Huh? What the hell does that mean?" Ambrose said.

"You have my decision, Mr. Ambrose." Patrick's gaze shifted briefly to Little Tall Man, then darted away. "The, uh, the other two will have to be held accountable." He was looking at Goodwin then, his eyes pleading.

"You do what you have to with them," Billy said. "It's Lige and the girl that I want."

I looked at Jace and Thumbs, sitting their horses close together, hands bound behind their backs. So far neither of them had spoken a word in their own defense. I suspect they both understood that any kind of protest would not only be futile, but also humiliating. I know Jace would have considered it akin to begging, and would rather cut his own throat than be perceived as a coward or weakling.

Little Tall Man cleared his throat, and Patrick snapped, "Cut him loose, Ambrose. Right this instant."

"Chickenshit bastard," Ambrose muttered, though loud enough for all of us to hear. Then he gigged his horse alongside mine and drew a knife that must have been razor sharp, because he sliced through the ropes binding my wrists without any noticeable effort. My arms fell limply forward and I damn near followed them, over the horn and to the ground; it took quite a bit of effort to keep my seat, even more to raise my hands to the saddle horn where Minko's reins were looped.

"Lige," Billy said quietly, his hand still tight on that Smith and Wesson. "Come over here."

"He can't," Milly said.

"No, I can do it," I replied—but I didn't. Instead I was looking at Jace with a helplessness that shamed me then, and still does today. But there was nothing I could do, not in the weakened state I was in. Hell, there wouldn't have been anything I could have done no matter what kind of shape I was in.

Jace must have sensed my anguish. "It's all right, little brother. I'll be fine. To tell you the truth, I'm kind of glad it's done with."

"If I could . . ." I began, and he nodded when my voice choked and failed.

"I know, but you can't. Neither of us can, so go on back with Billy and stay out of trouble." He smiled crookedly. "Aw, hell, Lige, you was never cut out to ride the owlhoot. We all knew that, every one of us."

I swallowed hard and bobbed my head, and I offer no apology for the tears that blurred my vision. I wanted so badly to speak, but I couldn't get the words out, couldn't tell Jace how I'd always looked up to him, how I'd always admired him. I guess what I wanted to say, and knew I never would, was that I loved him. But I think he knew that.

I hope to God he did.

SESSION TWENTY-FOUR

. . . sorry, I'll speak up.

What I was saying, what I was *going* to say, is that folks will tell you today that Jace's mistake was in not taking our fight directly to Kermit Watson. A few have even claimed we could have gunned Watson down on the main street in Tishomingo and no one would have come after us, neither Lighthorse nor the federal authorities out of Fort Smith.

I don't believe that, not for one minute, but even if it were true, it wouldn't have changed the way Jace was thinking at the time. After years of putting up with Watson's harassment, then learning what he and his gunmen had done on Two-Buck Mountain, killing Mama and the others and burning it all to the ground, Jace wasn't in a mood to listen to what anyone thought. Right or wrong, the fact is he didn't want to kill Watson outright. Jace was convinced a bullet would have been too easy an end for him. He wanted Watson to suffer, and he truly believed the way to do that was to bleed the man from his heart—which for Kermit Watson, meant his wallet. Drive him into poverty and let him see what it was like to have nowhere to turn, no resources to fall back on, and no friends to shelter you.

I understand why Jace thought the way he did, but I also know, now, that we were wrong. We should have done what others have said and hunted the son of a bitch down and shot him, then let the law do what it had to do. Instead we tried to grab the devil by his horns, and we got our hind ends gored by the ol' boy in the process.

Sometimes life's lessons come with a horrible price.

But you were asking about the rest of the story, about what happened after we left that creek-side trail, abandoning Jace and Thumbs to their fate.

I was all the way out of it on our ride back to Red Corn's cabin. Part of that might have been the weight of knowing what was going to happen to Jace, and the guilt I felt even then that I'd not come to his defense. Logically, I know there wasn't anything I could have done to stop it, but logic doesn't soothe the soul when you're lying awake nights recalling those days, seeing in your mind Jace's last smile, hearing his assurances that it was all right.

A lot of what happened that day had to do with the puncture wound to my chest, too. I suspect it had started to close at Thomas Red Corn's place, but I'd surely torn something loose when I attempted to pull myself into Minko's saddle the evening we left there. And finally, when that man of Ambrose's pulled my arms behind my back to bind my wrists, something really gave away then. I *felt* it.

By the time we got back to Red Corn's the front of my shirt was slick with blood that had seeped through the heavy bandage around my torso. I was delirious with fever and so weak of limb I could barely cling to my saddle. The least little exertion left me winded. But what I mostly remember is being cold, like I'd been laid out naked on a slab of ice in the middle of a blizzard and left to freeze. Milly said later my lips were a pale shade of blue and I was trembling all over by the time Billy and George pried me from my seat and carried me inside.

At first Sarah McFarland didn't want anything to do with me. She said it was my own fault for traipsing off after Jace like some sickly kid sneaking off to see the circus. But, like it or not, there I was, and nothing she could do about it short of running us all off with her Winchester.

I lay abed for nearly two weeks after my return, drifting in and out of consciousness with what felt like an anvil strapped to my chest and ice webbing my fingers and toes. I was black and blue from my neck to my belly button, and various shades of purple elsewhere. I ached everywhere—muscles, joints, even my lungs when I took too deep of a breath. Sarah said I probably had some light internal bleeding that caused most of that—excessive fluids pressing against my organs—and speculated that was why I couldn't seem to catch my breath. I know a time or two I thought I'd drown for lack of oxygen.

It was George who suggested they sit me upright with a willow backrest he and Milly had woven, and that seemed to help as much as anything. Still, it was another week before I was able to crawl out of my bunk and hobble into the kitchen with George's help. He sat me down in a chair at the table, and after I got my second wind, I had a look around. I was surprised to find the bed in the front room empty.

"He passed away nearly two weeks ago," George explained.

"Where was I?"

He laughed at that, with good reason, I suppose. "Where do you think you were, Elijah Two-Buck?"

Still out of it, I supposed, although it was a little disconcerting to realize such a thing could have come to pass without my having been at least peripherally aware of it. George told me they'd buried Thomas Red Corn under a hickory tree close to the creek, and Billy, who had stayed on several days after escorting me and Milly back to the cabin, had promised Sarah he'd purchase a granite headstone for the old man and have it shipped to her.

"He's going to send one out for Jace, too," George said.

That brought a different kind of tightness to my chest. Jace's absence had been like a big ol' bear asleep in the corner, something I was aware of but didn't mention for fear of awakening the creature. I stared at the tabletop for a long moment, wondering what I was supposed to say, before George thankfully continued.

"Billy and Little Tall Man went back a couple days later. They buried Thumbs where they found him, but brought Jace here. He's down under that hickory next to Red Corn."

"I appreciate that. Is . . . is Billy still around?"

"No, he and Little Tall Man left about a week ago. Billy says he's going to rebuild his store, but closer to the Rock Island line this time. Says he's gonna try to siphon off some of the trade that's been going to Tucker. I expect you ought to know Billy stayed on here for quite a while because of you."

"What do you mean?"

"He was worried Ambrose might slip back and try to hang you, add another feather to his war bonnet, so to speak. Then J.R. McNeil showed up here awhile back and said the reward for the Two-Buck gang has been rescinded."

"Then I'm safe?"

"Not yet. The Lighthorse sent word, too. They want you to come in and stand trial for all the trouble you and Jace stirred up." George chuckled. "Figures the law'd wait until the shooting was done before they poked their nose into the gut pile."

"What do you think they'll do to me?"

"Couldn't say, Elijah Two-Buck, although I expect they wouldn't do anything if you was to shinny outta the country. Maybe go down to Mexico, like Jace talked about doing."

I thought about that over the next few days and weeks as I slowly recovered, but I think I always knew I wouldn't do it. Not without Jace. The Chickasaw Nation was my home, and that meant something to me, something deep inside that I couldn't have explained then, and probably couldn't now. So when I was finally well enough to travel, me and George and

Milly saddled our horses and rode into Tishomingo. It was the middle of January and there was six inches of fresh-fallen snow on the ground when we got there. The first thing I did was surrender my revolver to the captain of the Lighthorse. He seemed both surprised and annoyed that I'd come in of my own accord. I suspect he was hoping I'd slope like George had hinted at, and make everyone's life easier. But like I said, this is home.

Afterward, George fronted me the money for a room at a boardinghouse and a new suit of clothes. He said it was money he'd owed Jace for some time, and that he wouldn't feel right unless I took it. He might've been lying, but I didn't push it. I could make it right with him somewhere down the road—assuming they didn't hang me—and there's no doubt I was in need of a new outfit. My old duds were not only worn practically thin enough to poke a finger through, but they were also outgrown by several inches.

I remember standing in front of the department store's mirror in my new clothes that day, staring at myself and wondering who the hell it was returning my gaze. It hadn't even been three months since I'd ridden up to Billy's and noticed my reflection in the trading post's big front window. The image then had been that of a green youth; the one looking back at me that day in Tishomingo was of a hardened young man. Although still only sixteen years of age, there was nothing of the guileless farm boy left that I could see.

George didn't stay, nor did Milly. Tishomingo being the capitol of the Chickasaw Nation, it was a costly place to visit. Meals ran fifty cents a plate for just basic fare like meat and potatoes and a little corn or green beans on the side, and my room was a dollar a day, although that did include boarding—hay and grain—for Minko in a small stable out back, along with biscuits, grits, and gravy every morning for my breakfast.

Since I'd already turned my Colt in to the law, George loaned

me a spare revolver he normally kept in his saddlebags, a little
.36 pocket pistol that I could carry hidden in my clothing. For
protection, he said. "You ought to be safe here, but you never
know," was his reasoning, and I understood what he meant. The
word floating around town was that Watson had fired his hired
guns and the Lighthorse had chased them out of the Nation,
but you never knew what to believe in those days.

Another big concern dogging my stay in Tishomingo was
Kermit Watson. Being a white man, he could have easily filed a
complaint with the U.S. marshal's office in Fort Smith and
insisted they send someone out to arrest me. He could have
also hired witnesses and bribed juries and newspaper reporters
until folks everywhere came to the conclusion I was the worst
menace to the territory since Satan invented corn liquor. Had
he done so there was a damn good chance I'd have ended up in
the same Kansas penitentiary as where Jace had done his time.
But Billy Goodwin's influence, which I figured—incorrectly, as
it turned out—was an invisible shield that continued to protect
me even then, and Watson stayed out of it altogether. He didn't
even show up for my trial, which was held on January 22nd in
that year of 1894.

It was a clear, blustery day, with a wind that seemed to cut
effortlessly through my clothing as I walked the five long blocks
from my lodgings to the Chickasaw Council House where my
trial was to be held. I went alone, as neither George nor Milly
had returned for the proceedings. I was curious about their
absences. George was fairly well-healed by then, and with old
Thomas Red Corn passed on there wasn't any excuse I could
fathom for him or Milly to stay on at the cabin, but I wasn't
overly alarmed, either. It was a big territory, and even a source
as reliable as the moccasin telegraph needed a little time to
reach some of the more remote locations.

The council house was on Fisher Street, an impressive two-

story brick structure with creaky wooden floors and frost mut-
ing the view through the windows. A stove inside the courtroom
was throwing off shimmying waves of heat, but I still felt half
frozen as I shook hands with my attorney.

I was to have what's called a bench trial, meaning there
wouldn't be any jury. The judge was a silver-haired old fireball
named Jacob Moss. My attorney was Alfred Elktooth, short,
middle-aged, balding—always an indignity to an Indian—but as
it turned out, even more of a dynamo than Moss. In arguing my
case, Elktooth leaned heavily on all that had preceded my
crimes—my *alleged* crimes, as he would point out more than
once during the hearing. Papa's death at the hands of a couple
of Lighthorse policemen who had mysteriously disappeared
shortly after he was killed; Jace's widely-believed false conviction for the theft of Watson's thoroughbred—an accusation of
innocence even the prosecution didn't object to; and finally the
shelling by cannon fire of our home on Two-Buck Mountain
that left Mama and my siblings deceased—all were chronicled
in detail.

The trial lasted barely three hours. In his closing remarks the
prosecutor, a heavyset Indian named Iron Fox, sporting three to
four chins depending on whether he was looking up or down,
made much of the deaths of the Erda wagonsmith, Big Jack
Edgerton, and the stable hand in Tishomingo named Walter
Piegan. The temerity of our raids was likened to the wild days
of an earlier frontier, when the Kiowa and Comanche regularly
invaded the Nations bent on murder and mayhem.

"Do we invalidate the culpability of the boy who holds the
mounts of the savage intruder?" Iron Fox inquired. "Or do we,
rightly I would suggest, hold all accountable under the same
umbrella?"

It was an impressive speech, delivered with zest and authority, and I was feeling pretty discouraged by the time Fox rested

his case. But then it was the defense's turn to close, and Alfred Elktooth didn't hold his punches.

"What I want to know," Elktooth demanded, "is why in Hades is this young man being tried in the first place? Why isn't the real culprit here, charged with murder and felonious accusation?" [*Editor's Note:* Although the murders of Constance Two-Buck (Elijah's Mama) and her children were investigated jointly by the Chickasaw Lighthorse Police and federal officers out of Fort Smith, no charges were ever filed against Kermit Watson after numerous witnesses produced sworn affidavits stating he was nowhere near Two-Buck Mountain at the time of the bombing; nor were authorities ever able to comprise a conclusive list of participants in the incident.]

In nearly thirty minutes of summation, I noticed Elktooth was real careful not to mention Kermit Watson by name, but I think everyone there knew who he was referring to. Nor did the defense bring up the subject of our multiple attacks on Watson's property, although he did point out that the identity of the killers, Quintin Haus and Bob Hatcher—both of whom were white men, he was quick to add—was well established. "Who is to say?" he asked, "if my client even raised a firearm during this altercation?"

Well, I figure there were plenty of folks out there, and especially from Erda, who could have confirmed my involvement, but none were brought forth as witnesses. I also found it enlightening that Iron Fox kept his eyes on a small notepad in front of him the whole time, and never once uttered a word of protest. There was still a lot of green on my horns back then, but even I knew there was more going on behind the scenes of that trial than I was privy to.

When Elktooth finally wrapped up his summation, Judge Moss sat quietly for several minutes staring into space. I guess he normally he would have called a recess while he went off to contemplate the evidence and arguments, but he didn't do that with me, and I'll confess to quite a bit of pessimism as I awaited his verdict. I reckon it's safe to say that had I been in the judge's shoes I'd have likely found myself guilty as sin, but Moss must have been looking at a bigger picture than I was seeing that day, because after a time he motioned to the bailiff, who told me to rise and approach the bench. Elktooth went with me, but didn't speak.

"Under precedence, Mr. Two-Buck," the judge began, "I would have transferred this case to the federal court in Fort Smith. But the Council recognizes the extenuating circumstances in this matter, which behooves me to consider the charges against you in a different light than I might under more ordinary circumstances."

Moss glanced at the scattering of documents spread across the tabletop in front of him, while I speculated on the meaning of "behooved." That was a wordy bunch right there, tossing around terms I'd never heard before nor since—culpability and felonious being a couple that stood out—and whose meanings I could only guess at.

Exhaling loudly, Moss raised his head. "But, since the prosecution has made no objection thus far, and doesn't appear inclined to do so at any point in the near future, I am going to render judgement according to my own assessment of the crimes.

"Life was lost, Mr. Two-Buck, and while there is ample evidence to convince me you had no direct participation in the taking of those lives, your presence during the commission of these crimes cannot be ignored. Therefore, I am going to find you guilty of the charges presented against you, and sentence you to eight year's banishment from the Chickasaw Nation, effective as of the first day of February, 1894, and notwithstanding a grace period for travel." He looked me square in the eye.

"Do you understand what this means, Mr. Two-Buck?"

Well, I guess I did! I stood there a long moment feeling numb all over. I suppose a lot of people will think I was lucky not to be hung, or at the very least confined behind bars for a number of years, but those are mostly white people who don't understand the full impact of tribal banishment; among Indians, it was a pretty harsh sentence. The Chickasaw Nation, its people, laws, and culture, was all I knew. Being forced to give it up, to be thrust, alone, into a foreign land among a strange people—and to me the white race was that, at least in those years—just about sucked all the juice right out of me.

For a few seconds I swayed like I was going to pass out, until Alfred Elktooth leaned close and urged me to accept my punishment with the proud demeanor of any self-respecting Chickasaw. Glumly—as close as I could get to self-respect at that moment—I nodded my acceptance and swore under oath to comply with the judge's full ruling. With my word given and recorded, Moss banged his gavel and I walked out of there a free man some might say, although in my mind I was as shackled as if bound by ball and chain—an outcast for the next eight years.

SESSION TWENTY-FIVE

After thanking Alfred Elktooth for keeping me out of prison—leaving that Tishomingo council house and smelling the wild smells blowing in from the north, seeing those high clouds scudding overhead in a stiffening wind, reminded me that as lonely as banishment might seem, it was a hell of a lot better than spending the same amount of time in a dank prison cell—I went back to the boardinghouse and packed my few belongings. I suppose I could have stayed another night, but I was anxious to leave. City life had been smothering, and I still wasn't convinced Watson had pulled all his dogs off the hunt.

I camped at the edge of a fallow cornfield west of town that night, and rode on into Davis the next day. From there I followed Lick Creek west to the base of Two-Buck Mountain. Although I'd intended to go up and see what remained of the home place, as well as visit the graves of my family, in the end I weaseled out. Some might deem that callous, but I think it was just too soon yet. Instead I went to see Sam and Alice Harper, the older couple who had overseen Mama's burial, along with my brother Noah and sisters Rachel, Sally, and Rebecca.

They invited me in and Alice set out a fine meal of roast coon and fried squash, along with buttermilk and cornbread. Neither spoke much. I guess they hadn't heard yet that I'd already had my trial and was on my way out of Indian Territory to begin serving my sentence. I ate mostly in silence myself, with only an occasional comment about Alice's cooking or

Sam's trapping—he ran a line or two every winter, and sold some of the better pelts taken in that country. But the main reason I stayed quiet was I was trying to sort out a decision I needed to make before beginning my exile. My original plan after leaving Tishomingo had been to sell the Two-Buck homestead to the Harpers if they wanted it, but I'd had a change of heart while sitting my pony there along Lick Creek, staring up to where our house used to stand. By the time I sopped up the last of the juice from that roast, I'd made up my mind.

"I thought about selling the place," I confided to them later that evening, the three of us sitting before a roaring blaze in the fireplace while a light snow fell outside, "but I've decided to keep it." By this time, I'd already explained my situation with the court and my impending banishment, so they were taken aback when I said I needed someone to look after the place until I returned. "Would you be interested?"

Well, the quick answer was "yes," although it took another hour to work out the details. They'd get whatever crops they could harvest from Mama's big garden, and keep our three Guernseys for boot. I'd come back after my expatriation and reclaim the place. I also asked them to keep tabs on my family's graves. I didn't have the money for headstones then, but hoped to when I got back, and I'd want to know which grave was whose.

Sam bobbed his head affirmatively, and Alice said, "We would have kept up those graves no matter what, Elijah, you know that."

Indeed I did. Those Harpers were good people. Still, it was only polite to ask.

I stayed on a few more days to help Sam cut enough firewood to see them through the winter, then saddled Minko and put Lick Creek and all its memories behind me, at least for a while. And even though I was still broke—less than two dollars to my name by then—my saddlebags were near to bursting with all the extra food Alice Harper had sent along.

It was another two days to the Red Corn cabin. Smoke curling from the chimney assured me the place was occupied, but I didn't know by whom until I rode in and found George and Sarah sitting at the kitchen table playing a game of rummy. I was welcomed with open arms, even by Sarah, who seemed happier than I'd ever seen her before. It wouldn't be until later that afternoon when me and George went out to feed the stock that he told me how Sarah had packed her and Emily's belongings to go back home after her father's death. When they arrived, Sarah discovered their cook and housekeeper, that pretty Negro woman named Clarissa who I mentioned a few sessions back, had moved in with Sarah's husband, Henry.

"Sarah got her dander all the way up over that," George said, chuckling as he recalled her return to the cabin the next day. " 'Rissa wouldn't even allow her inside the house, so Sarah dragged her Winchester out of the runabout and took a few potshots at her and Henry. She said she missed a'purpose, but I expect it was more likely her temper that wrecked her aim. Sarah's a proud woman, too proud to beg for damn sure, so she came back here. Emily stayed with her daddy. I think being here with strangers comin' and goin' all the time might've scared her."

"I noticed Thomas's bed has been moved into the back room, too," I said, and George grinned sheepishly.

"Well, we get along," he allowed, but then wouldn't say any more on the subject. It was a strange land, those Indian Territories, and I've mentioned before how black and white and red could get all swirled together like some kind of fancy saloon concoction. Nobody thought much about it, either, not back then, before Jim Crow reared its ugly head and ruined the whole shebang.

Milly wasn't there, and George said he didn't know where she'd gotten off to. "I asked her if she was going back to her family in the Creek Nation, but she said no," he told me. "She said she wasn't welcome there no more, but never said why, and I never asked."

"Where else could she have gone?"

"I don't rightly know, Elijah Two-Buck, but she sure ain't around here no more."

"Which direction did she take when she left?"

"South, due south."

Back over that knoll where we'd stopped so many times before to look over the Red Corn place before riding down. From the other side of that hill she could have gone . . . hell, in a thousand different directions. I'll admit it bothered me, her moving on like that without telling anyone her destination, but George said that was just the way Milly was.

"That's the way a lot of women are, in my experience," he added. His expression was sympathetic, but sympathy was no help and I was out of time. I reckoned I was already well past any deadline for leaving the Nation that Judge Moss would have considered reasonable.

There ain't much point in my telling you about the next eight years—you'd likely run out of disks before I got halfway through—but I will say I spent them down in El Paso, Texas, where it was mostly either warm or hot, both of which I appreciated. Most of that time I worked for the Top Eagle Brewing Company as a shipping agent, making sure the correct orders were sent to the right locations. And just to say I'd done it, I'd cross the Rio Grande into Ciudad Juárez every so often to visit some of the cantinas there. Jace hadn't made it to Mexico, but I did, and I always had at least one drink in his memory before I hiked back across the bridge to my little rented two-room house on Montgomery Avenue. Time to time on a

Sunday, I'd saddle Minko and take a ride out into the desert east of town, although I never learned to love that land the way so many do.

But you want to know what happened after my return to the Chickasaw Nation, back in the spring of 1901, which is why I'm still talking, and why that machine of yours is still recording. You want to know about me and Kermit Watson, and if there's any truth to the rumors that have floated around over the years since then. Well, I'll tell you this, some of them are true, but most of them ain't. So maybe it's time to set that record straight, too, and tell you what really happened that day in Erda when I came back.

My first stop on my return to the Nation had been to the Red Corn place, although by then folks were already calling it the Holly farm. George had cleared maybe ten acres along the creek, half of which he'd put into garden truck for winter eating and the other half in tobacco for his cash crop. Sarah was there, along with a trio of bantlings from their union—I don't know if they were married by then or not, and I never inquired. It just wasn't important in those days.

That first night following supper, after the two oldest kids had been sent to bed and Sarah had finished nursing Julia, she brought out a rhubarb pie she'd hidden from the youngsters and told George to slice it while she burped the baby. I put my hand on my stomach in protest, but George just laughed and said, "You'd best get what you can, 'fore them kids wake up tomorrow and mow through anything that's left."

Well, you can't argue with that kind of logic and expect to be taken seriously, so I eased back a mite and loosened the two top buttons on my britches while George slid generous slices of pie onto three saucers and Sarah refilled our coffee cups one-handed while bouncing the baby on her hip with the other. It was about in there that I finally asked what had been on my mind ever since I'd left the Chickasaw Nation for West Texas.

"You ever hear from Milly Bolton?"

I tried to ask it casual-like, but George's head came up like he'd been punched under the chin. He quick-shot Sarah a warning glance, and my grip tightened on my fork.

"She ain't around no more," he said evasively.

I placed my fork gently beside my saucer. "What does that mean?"

"It means it ain't something we need to discuss, Elijah Two-Buck. I reckon that's what it means."

"No, tell him," Sarah said. She was standing next to the counter, eating one-handed while Julia drooled on a towel draped over one shoulder.

"No, ma'am," George replied emphatically. "It wouldn't do no one no good, and cause a whole bunch of hurt if I do."

"He has a right to know."

"George," I said, real soft, and the look in his eyes when he met my gaze reflected the worst kind of misery.

"She's around," he finally conceded.

"Here, in the Chickasaw Nation?"

"She's married, Elijah."

My heart sank a little at that, although I'm damned if I knew what I'd expected from her. For her to wait all those years, while I never sent even a letter back this way? Hell, she'd have been a fool if she hadn't gone ahead with her life. Still, my appetite seemed to evaporate with the news, and I pushed my plate toward the center of the table. I thought I was feeling about as low as a man could get, then Sarah sat down across the table from me, the little one fast asleep in her arms.

"There's more to it than that." She was looking at George, but he shook his head. "I'll tell him if you don't," she threatened, and he heaved a large sigh.

"All right, but before you go flying off the handle, Elijah

Two-Buck, you have to understand that what she did was for you, and that we didn't know about it until well after you'd left."

My fingers turned ice cold on my coffee cup. "What did she do?"

"She married Kermit Watson."

Well, I sat there for the longest time while George's words sank in with molasses-like slowness. I felt numb, crushed under the weight of my anger and her betrayal . . . and yet, something wasn't tracking straight. "Why?" I finally managed.

"That day when you came past here on your way out of the territory, you asked about her and I said she'd gone south. I reckon once she got over that knoll yonder she turned her pony east, to Watson's farm. I heard when she got there Watson was already getting into his buggy, intending to go into town to testify against you. Milly told him she'd been Jace's gal for a while and that now she was yours, but that if he'd stay away and not meddle in your trial, she'd be his wife. I guess—" His voice faltered. "I expect the thought of taking Jace's and your woman must've satisfied something in him, although I'm damned if I know what it might've been."

"It satisfied the wickedness of that evil man's soul," Sarah said, her feelings toward Kermit Watson like acid dripping off her tongue.

I stood and stepped clear of the table. Sarah gave me a puzzled look, but George knew what I intended to do. I reckon he'd known even before he told me, which was why he hadn't wanted to.

"Killing him won't change a thing, Elijah Two-Buck."

I walked over to where I'd left my saddlebags and bedroll and picked them up in my right hand, along with my rifle—I was carrying a Model '95 Winchester by then, something I'd purchased in El Paso—in my left, and headed for the door.

"Elijah," Sarah called in alarm.

George rose and followed me to the door.

"Don't go," Sarah pleaded. "We can talk again in the morning, when you've had time to think this over."

"I appreciate your kindness, Sarah," I replied, and I meant it, too. Her personality had flipped clean over from what it had been when I first met her, and I wished her only the best. But it didn't change what I had to do.

"Please . . . ," but I shook my head. There was no turning back then; I think we all knew that.

I went outside and down to the barn that George had built next to Thomas's old corral. George came along with a lantern. My tack was set up on a rack with the blanket turned upside down on top of the saddle, the bridle hanging off the horn. I went to the rear gate and whistled low and Minko came up in that moseying kind of way he had now. He was probably eleven or twelve by then, which isn't all that old for a horse, but it was enough that he'd lost a lot of his coltish foolishness, which was fine by me.

I saddled up in the barn's entryway with George standing to one side holding the lantern high enough for its light to reach whatever strap I was working with. He was brooding and silent until I lowered the near-side stirrup, then said, "Why don't you let me go—"

"No," I said, cutting him off. "This is mine to do and yours to stay out of." I looked around at him, at his dark eyes swimming with worry, and smiled to ease the pangs of guilt I knew he was feeling. I think that was the first time I truly understood what Jace was trying to say when he told me his capture by Watson's gunmen was for the best. George lowered the lantern, and the light went out of his eyes. Letting my gaze move on, I said, "It seems like you came out of this real good, George."

"I've been lucky," he acknowledged. "For some reason, no

one ever seemed to figure out I was one of the men helping Jace rustle them cows of Watson's, or that I was there when we robbed that Ardmore stagecoach."

"That's because with that coach, you got shot right off and was lying in the dirt like a turtle on its back before anyone got a good look at you."

A crooked grin tilted one side of his mouth. "I expect if a man can ever call himself lucky to take a bullet in his chest, it was me that day." He rolled the shoulder experimentally. "It doesn't hurt in this kind of weather, but it'll ache some next winter when it gets cold."

"Small price to pay for avoiding a noose."

"You notice I ain't complaining."

"Then stay here and take care of your family."

He nodded glumly. "I'd come and not take no for an answer if it wasn't for Sarah and our kids."

"I know you would, and that means everything right there. It's also another reason I don't want you coming along." I loosened Minko's halter rope and led him outside. It was a clear night and there was going to be a nearly full moon before I got too far down the trail; I could see its pale glow on the horizon even then. Pausing, careful to keep my face averted, I said, "Why'd she do it, George?"

"I expect it was to save your hide from the gallows. Either that or from getting a bullet in the back of your head. The Lighthorse said they'd chased all of Watson's hired guns out of the territory, but I know there were at least three of 'em on the man's payroll at the time. One of them still is."

"Who?"

"Hugh Ambrose. Remember him?"

I nodded, recalling the man clearly even after all those years— the scruffy beard and yellow teeth, a Colt revolver with carved ivory grips—a mean-eyed son of a bitch if there ever was one.

That was the first I'd heard him called Hugh, though.

"They say he ain't changed much," George continued softly. "They say he's even added a few notches to that fancy pistol of his since those days. I couldn't say personally, as I mostly steer clear of Erda and do my trading at Goodwin's."

"I'll watch for him," I said, straightening my reins along Minko's neck before swinging a leg over the cantle. From that high seat, I reached down to shake George's hand. "I'll be back if I can."

"I'll be watching for you if you do."

I hesitated, thinking there should have been more to say, the odds against me being what they were, but nothing came to mind, so after a couple of seconds I nodded a final goodbye and heeled my pony toward Erda.

SESSION TWENTY-SIX

I rode that night until the moon went down, and was back in the saddle again at first light. I pushed Minko harder than I probably should have, but I was in a hurry and he didn't seem to mind. Even so, it was late afternoon the following day—a Saturday, as it turned out—before I reached Erda. It being market day, there were a lot of folks in town, buying supplies or peddling their wares. Farm wagons and buggies were parked along both sides of the main thoroughfare, and the boardwalks were crowded.

I was kind of surprised at how the town hadn't changed much. I guess because I had, I'd expected the rest of the world to move along just as swiftly, but Erda looked much the same as it had when the Two-Buck gang robbed its bank in '93. Oh, there were a few changes. Edgerton's Wagon Works was now Kelly's Wagon Repair, and Charlie Plummer had replaced the old wooden barber's pole outside his shop with a newer one made of glass, a lot brighter and twice as tall as his earlier version, although the place itself still looked the same—right down to the bullet holes scattered around the door, where I'd shot high and wide to avoid hitting him.

The bank was still there, too, sitting prominently in the middle of the central block like some kind of decaying monument to some forgotten prosperity. It looked smaller than I recalled, its red brick walls duller, the windows grimier. As a matter of fact, the whole town seemed somehow dingier than

271

memory served, despite a few new buildings here and there and
more traffic on the street. Spring blanketed the Chickasaw Nation with fresh green grasses, budding trees, and blooming
wildflowers, but Erda seemed suspended in a lingering winter's
gloom.

Across the street from the bank sat what had been a hardware
store on my last visit. The structure had been expanded since
then, with a covered veranda added and a sign jutting from the
tall façade reading: *General Merchandise and Groceries.*

My gaze dropped to a buggy parked in front of the store and
a jolt of recognition damn near swept me from my saddle. The
woman sitting under the vehicle's fringed awning spied me in
that same instant, and her lips parted in what I assumed was
surprise. I stopped right there in the middle of the street and
returned her stare. A sense of euphoria surged through my veins,
and the view to either side of me, of us, seemed to haze over
and grow smaller, as if retreating into the distance. I was about
to tap Minko's ribs and cross the street to her side when a man
came out of the store. I didn't recognize him at first. He was of
middling height but gray haired and distinguished looking in a
brown herringbone suit and dark brown homburg leveled above
his brows. A waxed handlebar mustache under a too-slim nose
clung to his upper lip like a greasy worm, and laced shoes
sported a rare luster in that land of country roads and muddy
streets.

Pausing on the boardwalk, he surveyed his surroundings in
much the same manner I imagined a cattle baron might view
his herd, or a mine owner his slag heaps and tailings. When he
glanced at Milly and saw her looking at me his eyes at first narrowed in irritation, then widened in alarm. I knew then who he
was. It was pretty obvious he knew who I was, as well.

His expression twisting into a hard grimace, Kermit Watson
called sharply into the store. Milly started to climb down from

the buggy but he stopped her with a harsh reprimand, his voice echoing along the street. "Keep your ass where it is," he barked, and she fell back with a look of hopelessness I never would have expected from her.

She looked good, Milly did. A little plumper than when I'd last seen her, but strong and healthy. Her hair was pinned up under a modest bonnet, and she wore a drab gray dress that might have tried to mute her aura, but did nothing to hide the fullness of her figure. Despite her beaten expression, I thought she looked beautiful—beautiful and terrified.

Riding over, I stepped down in front of the store and dropped Minko's reins over the railing. Watson stood immobile on the boardwalk, looking kind of uncertain until a couple of men came out of the store to flank him. I recognized both of them immediately. One was the bookish Patrick, carrying a satchel tucked under one arm; the other was that hard-edged son of a bitch who'd wanted to hang me and Milly alongside of Jace and Thumbs.

Hugh Ambrose's deep scowl smoothed out with recognition. "Well, I'll be damned," he said. "You got gall, boy. Either that or you're jackass stupid."

Ignoring him, I walked around to the street side of the buggy where I could talk to Milly and still keep an eye on the store's covered boardwalk. Although Milly refused to look at me, she did say, out of the corner of her mouth, "Go away, Lige. Please."

"The lady's giving you good advice, *Lige,*" Ambrose said, stretching my name out like he was dragging it through a mudhole, and Watson added, "You should have stayed in El Paso, Two-Buck."

It didn't surprise me that Watson knew where I'd spent the last eight years. Money has its advantages, and Watson had apparently used some of his to keep tabs on my whereabouts. Once again, I ignored their words. Looking at Milly, I said, "I want you to come with me."

She finally met my eyes, and her lips parted in . . . what? Appreciation? Regret? Then they closed and she returned her gaze to the croup of her buggy horse. "I can't go with you, Elijah. I'm married."

"Divorce him," I said, as if such a thing would be as easy as cutting the price tag off a new shirt. I suppose I was thinking of George and Sarah and the happiness they'd found together, so I knew it could be done. I figured Alfred Elktooth could help us if he was still practicing law in Tishomingo, but Milly stubbornly shook her head.

A small crowd had gathered on the boardwalk to either side of Watson and his men. Although I didn't recognize any of them, it was as if they knew who I was and were waiting to see what would happen. Laughing, Ambrose said, "Looks like it's stupidity, after all." He glanced at his employer. "You want me to shoot him, or just run him out of town?"

"Neither will be necessary," Watson replied. Taking the satchel from Patrick, he came down the steps and slipped it under the buggy's seat. Speaking loudly enough for his audience to hear, he said, "He'll wander off soon enough, like a cur with its tail tucked between its legs." He gave me a dismissive smirk, before lifting a buggy whip from its footboard socket. "She is my wife, Two-Buck. As such, she is also my property." Then, stepping back far enough to have some leverage, he brought that whip down hard across the tops of Milly's thighs.

Milly gasped and stiffened, and her face turned pale, but she didn't cry out. As much as it had to have hurt, she didn't utter a word of protest or pain. Instead she stared straight ahead, her fists knotted and pale-knuckled in her lap, humiliation a hot blaze in her eyes. I knew then that this wasn't the first time she'd felt the whip's lash.

Watson's words seared: *My property.*

Like a horse, or a dog.

A cardinal mist blurred my vision as I stepped away from the buggy.

From the far side of the vehicle, Watson said, "And there's not a damned thing you can do about it, Two-Buck. So I'd suggest you crawl back on top of that nag you rode into town on and—" He stopped, his smile dissolving as he watched me walk around the rear of the buggy. He flashed a panicky look to Ambrose, who hurried down the steps to intercept me.

Putting a hand on his revolver, half drawing it in anticipation, Ambrose said, "You heard what the man said, Two-Buck. Fork that pinto and ride outta here while you can."

There was a grin there, I'd swear it, a grin and an invitation, but no expectation of what I'd do next. I don't guess anyone expected it, least of all me. The only thing I know, then as now, is that I wasn't going to stand there and allow that kind of abuse to go unchallenged. Nor would I let some two-bit assassin stand in my way. Slipping the .45 from its holster without slowing, I put a bullet square between Hugh Ambrose's eyes, and he went over backward like a felled tree.

Watson squawked and jumped, and his eyes grew wider than I would have thought physically possible as I raised the Colt in his direction. Our spectators had scattered before Ambrose hit the ground; Patrick was right behind them, fleeing into the store without even waiting for me to tell him to *git*.

I moved the Colt to Watson's chest. There was no doubt I wanted to shoot the son of a bitch, to see him lying in the dirt bleeding out like a gutted hog at butchering time. I wanted it so bad my hand was trembling. But it wasn't to be. Even as Ambrose fell and Watson disappeared with his coattails flapping, my finger hesitated on the trigger. Had I pulled it, I reckon I would have been labeled a coward and a murderer. Worse, I would have viewed myself in that same light. What I did instead was reach forward with my left hand and brush the lapels of Watson's jacket aside. I was looking for a shoulder rig, but he was unarmed.

Lifting the buggy whip from his sudden slack fingers, I holstered my Colt and switched the long crop to my strong side. What I did then . . . well, I ain't proud of it. I don't regret it, mind you, but I'll not boast of it, either. It's a sorry thing to lose your temper the way I did, to damn near pummel a man into his grave. I must have cut Watson in a hundred places, from boot tops to scalp. He didn't put up much as a struggle, either, not like I would have expected from a man of his cruel nature. I guess there's a difference between hiring something low-down done and doing it yourself.

When I finished, I found myself standing in the middle of the street without any recollection of how we'd gotten there. Watson lay on the ground before me, bleeding and whimpering and bubbling snot. My chest was heaving, my lips peeled back in a frozen snarl. Slowly, distantly, I became aware of hands on my shoulders, gently pulling me back. Looking around, I saw Milly standing there, her voice like something you'd use to calm a frightened horse—telling me he'd had enough, promising she'd go away with me if I only stopped beating an already beaten man. I straightened and turned, staring into the deep loveliness of her eyes, and the buggy whip slid through my fingers and fell across Watson's legs.

"Come," she said softly.

"I can't." The words sounded unfamiliar to my ears, a stranger's refusal to let go of his rage.

"Please don't kill him, Elijah. Don't place that memory between us, that you had to murder a man to have me. I'll divorce him, I'll go with you."

I stared back numbly, a thousand questions ricocheting through my mind. She answered all of them without my uttering a sound.

"Because I love you." She placed both of her hands against my cheeks, and they were warm, and they said more than words ever could. "I've loved you ever since that day in the Notch when Jason tried to beat me. It was you who came to my defense, who made him stop. Do you remember that?"

"Yeah," I replied raggedly. "Yeah, I remember."

"I love you," she said quietly. "Isn't that enough?"

I said, "Yes."

And by God, it was.

End Transcript

★ ★ ★ ★ ★

ADDENDUMS TO THE
TWO-BUCK TRANSCRIPT

★ ★ ★ ★ ★

Entry One
Letter from Alfred Elktooth Files to [Redactions by Request]
July 1912
Elktooth Family Archives (Private)

My Dear [Redacted],

I will tell you only what I know personally of the Two-Buck affair, and allow you to draw what conclusions you may. Regarding the lawlessness of the elder Bro. [*Editor's Note:* Jason Two-Buck], sufficient documentation already exists to satisfy your curiosity in that matter.

On the subject of the younger Bro., it is true I acted as defense for Elijah Two-Buck on his original charges before the court in Tishomingo. There was never any doubt in my mind of his participation in the crimes, nor did he deny them to me, but neither was there any doubt of Kermit Watson's provocation on the Two-Buck clan. Had Elijah's partnership with his Bro. been based on greed alone, I am confident he would have been sentenced accordingly, *i.e.* a trial in the Federal Courts in Fort Smith, with probable prison time the result. It was Watson's continual harassment of the family over a period of years which so significantly influenced the trial of the surviving member of the Two-Buck family.

Regarding the 1901 altercation in Erda, it is true I was once again retained by Elijah Two-Buck as his defender. Following the Saturday flogging given Watson in the street outside the General Store in Erda, Two-Buck and Milly Watson *née* Bolton, appeared at my office in Tishomingo on the Monday following. After hearing details of the encounter and anticipating charges to be filed by Watson for the attack and the Nation for the killing of Hugh Ambrose, I agreed to represent the young man's interests. A two-day trial was held in April of that year, with the result being acquittals on all charges. I personally feel that by this time the citizens of Erda, as well as those within the Chickasaw courts and police agencies familiar with the parties involved, had grown weary of the entire affair.

Citing spousal abuse of the most horrid kind, Milly Watson was granted a divorce in May, and she and Elijah were married in June, the 7th, if I recall correctly. The wedding was held in the town of Davis. Being unable to travel due to conflicting engagements, I sent a small gift and a bottle of champagne, a Perrier-Jouët, if memory serves, to the happy couple, along with my sincerest wishes for a long life together. To date, they seem to have fulfilled that challenge.

Kermit Watson's life deteriorated drastically following these numerous defeats. Rumors arose almost overnight to reignite Watson's alleged involvement in the death of his first wife, Pretty Horse Watson. It was reported that the investigation into the circumstances surrounding her demise were to be reopened by federal officers out of Fort Smith, and I have it on good authority that although the case was reviewed by impartial investigators in Arkansas, there was insufficient evidence to warrant a more in-depth investigation. In your most recent correspondence, you asked if I had an opinion on the inquiry. In a word, Yes, and that is all I will divulge on the matter.

Although Watson fully recovered from the physical injuries sustained by Two-Buck's very public flogging—some permanent scarring notwithstanding—information from sources within the community of Erda continued to trickle into my office throughout the remainder of 1901 and into the early months of 1902. They detail a moral, spiritual, and, quite likely, mental deterioration of the man's constitution. Alcohol was widely acknowledged as a contributing factor in Watson's "slide toward Hell," as it was described to me by one confidant. Rumors of morphine addiction were "floated" across the Nation as well, although without substantiation, as far as I have been able to ascertain.

What is well recorded is Watson's claim that on April 15th of that year, Elijah Two-Buck was spied "lurking in the bushes" along the lane adjacent to Watson's property on the Washita River, and that the younger man fired several rounds in his direction with the intention of committing murder. Had Elijah not had credible witnesses to his presence in Davis, coinciding with the birth of his and Milly's first child, it is possible an indictment could have been brought before the courts. As it stood, no charges were filed. Nor were allegations made against him by Patrick two weeks later, when Kermit Watson was discovered hanged from a rafter in his tobacco barn. [*Editor's Note:* Brendan Patrick was Kermit Watson's longtime confidant and accountant, the same Patrick in attendance at the capture of Jason Two-Buck and Three Thumbs Boy in the fall of 1893, and in Erda on the day of Elijah's return to that community in 1901.]

Regarding Watson's accepted suicide and the events following in the deposition of his estate, there is sufficient accessible documentation for your perusal. I will add only that, despite rumors, neither Milly, nor Elijah in her agency, ever made any claim for assets.

I now close the matter of my involvement in the Watson and Two-Buck franchise, and wish to receive no further correspondence on the subject from you.

I remain, Sir, Your Most Obedient Servant,

[Signed] Alfred C. Elktooth, esq.

Entry Two
Editor's Note
June 2, 2020

According to records kept in the Tishomingo public archives, George and Sarah Holly were officially married in 1897. They raised five children—all daughters—and remained lifelong friends of the Elijah and Milly Two-Buck family. George died of pneumonia in 1952; Sarah died the following year of natural causes. Both are buried in the Holly Cemetery, along with Thomas Red Corn and Jason Two-Buck. Their descendants still live in Chickasaw country.

Entry Three
Excerpt from Erda *Eagle*
December 8, 1944
Digital Archives, Oklahoma State Historical Assn., Tulsa

News reached here yesterday of the death, two days previous, of one Elijah James Twobuck [*sic*], 68, most recently of Pauls Valley, formerly of near Davis. Older residents of our burg will recall the name with an understandable sense of trepidation, and word of his passing with equally deserving sighs of relief. While TwoBuck [*sic*] lived out his final days in relative (and presumably law-abiding) obscurity, those of us of a certain age still vividly recollect the terror inflicted upon our community by the notorious Kid Jace gang, of which Elijah Twobuck [*sic*] was a senior member.

It was the Kid Jace gang which robbed our fair burg in the waning days of outlawry for which the Indian Nations was once so famous, and from which the lead scarring of their rascality can still be viewed in the brickwork of our bank and the Sinclair Gas Station, which formerly housed a wagon manufacturing plant, and from whence our first fatality from criminal activity occurred. [*Editor's Note:* This is hardly a fair statement, as there were six recorded murders, plus numerous assaults, recorded in the *Eagle*'s weekly editions in the previous thirteen years of the newspaper's existence.]

While some may mark Twobuck's [*sic*] efforts at redemption during the latter years of his time on earth as admirable, others among us will find it harder to forgive, and wonder if his passage from this mortal plain has led him to more fiery accommodations farther "South," if our inference is recognized.

From the *Pauls Valley Ledger*, we learn that Twobuck [*sic*] was born on June 25th, 1876, and left this life on December 6th, 1944. He was preceded in death by his wife, the former Milly Watson, a one-time resident in our vicinity, and is survived by several children and grandchildren. [*Editor's Note:* The *Pauls Valley Ledger* was a weekly publication from its founding in 1919 to the electrical fire that destroyed its archives in 1949; the Erda *Eagle* likewise ceased publication in 1957, presumably due to declining subscriptions and advertising.]

Entry Four
Excerpt from Erda *Eagle*
Letters to the Editor
December 15, 1944

It has come to my attention that the *Eagle,* as it has been wont to do since its inception, has once again abandoned fact in favor of "color" in its depiction of Elijah Two-Buck (editor, please note the correct spelling of the man's name) as evil incarnate. Truth paints a less sinister portrait by taking into account the murders of young Two-Buck's—he was only sixteen at the time—parents and siblings by a far more villainess force.

As Elijah Two-Buck's defense counsel in his trial for participation in the Erda bank robbery of 1893, I feel I enjoy a certain intimacy with the subject, and the circumstances predetermining his involvement. While far more pages can be devoted to this story than I am certain the *Eagle* would ever allow, I will urge those seeking the truth to peruse less biased sources for their information.

[Signed] Alfred C. Elktooth
Attorney at Law (*Retired*)

Postscript:
R.I.P., Old Friend

ABOUT THE AUTHOR

Michael Zimmer is the author of twenty novels, including *The Poacher's Daughter,* winner of the prestigious Wrangler Award from the National Cowboy and Western Heritage Museum. His work has been praised by *Booklist, Publishers Weekly, Library Journal,* and the Historical Novel Society. He is the winner of the Spur Award from the Western Writers of America for his short story, *The Medicine Robe.* His novel *City of Rocks* was chosen by Booklist as a Top Ten Western for 2012, and both *City of Rocks* and *The Poacher's Daughter* were finalists for the Spur Award. Born in Indiana, and raised there and in Colorado, Zimmer now resides in Utah with his wife, Vanessa, and their two dogs. His website is www.michael-zimmer.com.

The employees of Five Star Publishing hope you have enjoyed this book.

Our Five Star novels explore little-known chapters from America's history, stories told from unique perspectives that will entertain a broad range of readers.

Other Five Star books are available at your local library, bookstore, all major book distributors, and directly from Five Star/Gale.

Connect with Five Star Publishing

Visit us on Facebook:
  https://www.facebook.com/FiveStarCengage

Email:
  FiveStar@cengage.com

For information about titles and placing orders:
  (800) 223-1244
  gale.orders@cengage.com

To share your comments, write to us:
  Five Star Publishing
  Attn: Publisher
  10 Water St., Suite 310
  Waterville, ME 04901